INSURGENT

KEN LOZITO

Published by Acoustical Books, LLC

KenLozito.com

Cover design by Jeff Brown

If you would like to be notified when my next book is released visit

www.kenlozito.com

ISBN: 978-1-945223-35-8

1

Connor entered the command center where soldiers were actively working at their stations, their holoscreens gleaming with an amber outline in the dim light. They were comlinked to the teams out in the field, and the energy had ratcheted up with all the anticipation of a major operation about to go off the rails. He strode past the phalanx of workstations and headed directly for the holotank.

Captain O'Brien saluted him. "General Gates."

"Sitrep."

"The 7th Ranger Company has taken up support positions near the planetary arch," O'Brien said.

In the center of the holotank, an image of a Krake arch was displayed deep in the jungles of Kuret. The New Earth candidate planet, or NEC in this alternate universe, orbited closer to the star, which made for much higher planetary temperatures. The planet was nearly bursting with life—what Connor liked to think of as extreme vegetation. Almost every land surface was covered in some kind of jungle. It was sweltering and humid, and there was no shortage of rainfall. There was also no shortage of concealment on this planet, and the Colonial Defense Force would use every advantage it had.

"Good," Connor said. "The briefing said that Monin was impatient to begin."

"Yes, General, that is correct. The Gesora are anxious to take control of the Krake arch to eliminate the chance that reinforcements can be called."

Connor didn't doubt it. The CDF had been conducting clandestine operations on this planet for four months. They'd chosen it because the Ovarrow in this universe were prime candidates to rebel against the Krake.

The Krake had hidden their presence here as best they could, choosing to manipulate the Ovarrow by controlling the higher levels of government. It was a tactic that had been reported from other worlds they'd observed. However, one of the things that made moving forward with this partial coup d'état a priority was the lack of a space gate in the star system. Uncharacteristically, the Krake had restricted their activities to the planetary surface. Intelligence analysts theorized that perhaps there were limits to how many simultaneous operations the Krake could conduct across the multiple universes in which they had a presence. Regardless of the Krake reasoning for such a limited presence on this particular planet, Connor planned to exploit it and hopefully gain another ally to fight against the Krake.

The CDF wasn't limited to the single arch that was displayed in the holotank. They had multiple arches and space gates to traverse between universes, and they'd deployed a stealth satellite system that had been actively monitoring the planet for the past ninety days. The system currently had its minimum of three satellites in use, which was enough to cover the NEC. The satellites were equipped with subspace communication systems, which allowed for transmissions among them, and although line of sight was still a factor in observing the enemy, it no longer impacted their communications capabilities. For some reason, the Krake had chosen to ignore the high ground, and the war doctrine of any human military confirmed that he who controlled the high ground controlled the war.

"What is the status of the Qompiry?"

Captain O'Brien used the holotank controls to switch the view to an Ovarrow city. Dark, towering obelisks, shimmering like obsidian, were sheathed in a bronze metallic alloy at the tips. In the middle of the city were domed edifices similar in architectural design to those built by the Ovarrow they'd encountered on New Earth.

"The Qompiry's position at the capital is here," O'Brien said, and a waypoint flashed. These were the insurgency that had been rebelling against the Krake for years, which was an arduous undertaking since the Krake hid their presence on the planet. "Lieutenant Wade's platoon," he continued, "is on the north side of the city, and the Warlord's First has a platoon of Mekaal soldiers with Yerid's rebels."

The Mekaal was the military unit of the Ovarrow from New Earth. They'd been partnering with the CDF over the past year, participating in off-world operations in alternate universes.

Connor nodded. "Cerot should be able to keep Yerid in line."

The Qompiry was a rebellious group of thieves that had resisted the Krake social order almost since the beginning.

They were hotheaded and immature but had conducted multiple operations, thwarting the Krake as often as they could. Connor wondered why the Krake had chosen to conceal their identity here while working out in the open on other worlds. He thought it must have something to do with the experiment they'd sanctioned for this world.

The Krake had done an excellent job of dividing the dominant nations of Ovarrow on this planet. They'd utilized virus outbreaks to cripple the Gesora's economy, and they preyed upon their religious beliefs in a way that had shaped almost all public discourse into shouting matches, fostering a culture of contempt. This had been easy to manipulate and exploit, and had later given rise to skirmish wars.

The CDF had managed to convince critical Gesora leaders from multiple provinces that the major events in their recent history were the result of Krake manipulation. These select few leaders were privy to the knowledge that the Krake were an entirely different species, but their operation today would make this knowledge open to the general public. It was an all-or-nothing effort. They had to take control of the arch, as well as the capital, where the Krake had the most influence. Hopefully, this operation would be the catalyst to free the Gesora from a Krake experiment that had been ongoing for nearly seventy years.

"Captain O'Brien," Corporal Taylor said, "I have a comlink request from Yerid."

"Engage encryption protocols and vocalizers," O'Brien said.

The Ovarrow in this universe weren't aware of humans, and it was the CDF's top priority to keep their involvement a secret. To this end, they'd used Ovarrow from New Earth to help convince others of their cause. Connor knew the Krake were hunting for humans, and if they were going to operate in alternate universes, they needed to keep their presence there a secret. As far as the Krake were concerned, this was just another rebellious Ovarrow group operating under the Krake's radar but causing trouble just the same.

O'Brien glanced at Connor, who bobbed his head once.

"Mekaal COMCENT, this is Yerid. The Qompiry are in position. How long do the Gesora intend for us to wait before they reach their target?"

"Confirm Qompiry are in position, Yerid. Hold tight. We are waiting for confirmation from the Gesora," O'Brien said.

"We can't stay here," Yerid said. "My teams will be compromised if we do. We have to go. Tell the Gesora that we're beginning our assault on the capital."

Connor heard both the commitment and the urgency in the Ovarrow's voice, even though it was coming through a translator. He could hardly blame them, but at the same time, he needed them to wait.

"Yerid," Connor said, "the only way this operation is going to work is if both you and the Gesora attack at the same time. If the Krake at the capital figure out what's going on, they'll alert the soldiers at the arch. If that happens, they'll bring the defenses online and possibly call in reinforcements."

There were a few moments of silence before Yerid replied. "Warlord Gates, I know you are aware of what the Krake have done here. Today is a day of reckoning. Today, we take back what's ours. The Qompiry will attack now. Yerid out."

The comlink severed, and O'Brien shook his head.

"Sir," Corporal Taylor said, "Lieutenant Wade has confirmed that the Qompiry are advancing on the capital. Stealth recon drone surveillance shows thousands of

Qompiry soldiers infiltrating the tunnel network under the capital."

O'Brien's lips pressed into a grim twist, and he looked at Connor. "What are your orders, General?"

Connor stared at the aerial view of the capital city in the holotank. It showed the positions of the CDF platoon, as well as the Qompiry taskforces that were moving into the capital. "Tell Lieutenant Wade that his orders are to observe and advise Yerid and the Qompiry soldiers. They'll need to assist them by disrupting all communications from the capital."

The original plan had called for Lieutenant Wade and his platoon to keep their position outside of the capital city, but in order to disable communications from the capital, they'd need to move in.

"Tell him we're sending air support," Connor said. So much for sitting this one out.

O'Brien gave Connor a sidelong glance.

"What is it, Captain?" Connor asked.

"Captain Samson said you'd find a way to see some action, General."

"He did, did he?" Connor replied. Samson had been part of the original Ghost Platoon that Connor had led before being shanghaied onto the colony ship that ended up at New Earth. "What else did he say?"

"He told us not to get too comfortable, sir. We have two Hellcats on standby. I'll see to it that they're ready to go," O'Brien said.

The young captain stepped away from the holotank and began giving orders to several soldiers nearby.

Connor opened a comlink to Samson, and the Spec Ops

captain answered almost immediately. "I hear you're spreading lies about me."

Samson grinned a little. "What happened?"

"Yerid couldn't suppress his need to get his gun off, so the Qompiry have started their assault on the capital. I've ordered Wade to move in and disable communications from the capital, but it's going to be a close thing."

"Understood, General. I'll let Monin know. To be honest, I'm surprised they've worked together as long as they have. They don't trust each other at all," Samson said.

Connor took control of the holotank and switched the aerial view back to the arch. "It's not all their fault. This is what happens when you foster a culture of contempt. It's hard to trust anyone when you've been taught all your life that someone else's ideas aren't to even be considered, and anyone who thinks differently is branded a traitor."

"If you say so, sir."

"Can you reach the arch in time?"

"We can if I can get your permission to showcase some of our capabilities," Samson replied.

The CDF soldiers were all in the latest Nexstar combat suits but had slowed down to keep pace with the Gesora soldiers. The Gesora were at home in the jungle and could traverse its terrain with ease, but the Nexstar combat suit leveled the playing field considerably. The onboard combat AI assisted the wearer to efficiently handle any terrain, be it terrestrial or low-gravity situations. What Samson was requesting was permission to remove the restrictions that were in place to help them blend in.

"Understood, and permission granted, but don't get too far

ahead of them. You still need the Gesora. You can't fight this war without them."

"Acknowledged, General," Samson said, and the comlink went dark.

Over the past year, they'd conducted clandestine operations, but this was the biggest. They needed a mission success for this effort; otherwise, the Colonial Security Council would order them to stop. They'd never find the Krake home world if they stopped exploring the alternate universes. And a successful mission would also mean that they didn't have to fight the Krake alone if they could find allies along the way.

Connor glanced at the holotank and rested his hands on the edge. He heard the high-pitched whine of the Hellcat's engines powering up and felt a surge of adrenaline course through him in anticipation. Breathing in deeply, he sighed and turned to O'Brien. "Captain, you're to support Lieutenant Wade with disabling communications in the capital. You're cleared for weapons-free."

For half a second, O'Brien's gaze widened. The CDF captain had expected Connor to join them. They'd all expected it, but Connor had made a promise that he wouldn't always be the one to take all the risks. The CDF soldiers were the best-trained military he'd ever seen. Connor had made them that way.

"Understood, General."

"Good hunting, Captain," Connor said.

2

LIEUTENANT THOMAS WADE of the 7th Ranger Company, 3rd Platoon Leader, alerted his unit that they'd be moving out. Yerid, the leader of the Qompiry, was moving forward with the attack. Given what the Krake had done to these Ovarrow, Wade couldn't blame them. He'd want revenge too. The Qompiry had been hunted by the very Ovarrow they hoped to save from the Krake. The group of Ovarrow that had become the Qompiry was composed of multiple factions who were considered noncompliant. They were the outliers and the rebellious few who'd chosen not to bury their heads in the sand. They'd chosen to resist, and Wade had come to respect that. He'd conducted multiple operations in alternate universes over the past year, and the one thing he'd learned about the Krake was that they were ruthlessly efficient in the way they carried out their experiments.

The fifty soldiers in his platoon were outfitted with Nexstar combat suits, with four of them configured for heavy weapons.

Wade gestured for Sergeant Mason to come over to him. "Yerid is pressing on with the attack, and we can't allow the Krake to send a warning to their base. Looks like the Gesora are running late."

"Getting into the capital won't be a problem. It's getting out that will be," Mason said.

"We've got air support, so they'll be our evacuation as well," Wade replied.

Mason grunted. "We'll need to look for a couple of alternatives in case our air support gets held up."

"Oh, ye of little faith."

"Negative, sir. I just have an aversion to getting caught with my pants down."

Wade agreed.

Gesora regulars operated security checkpoints throughout the city, and there were strongholds with a significant troop presence at each. They were strategically placed within close proximity to the capitol building, which had its own direct-action force that maintained a presence there. Across many Ovarrow cities, insurgent activity in response to the Gesora's militaristic regime had prompted the buildup of military forces.

Wade knew they'd be engaging Gesora soldiers who either were unaware or simply didn't believe their political leaders were Krake infiltrators or were being controlled by the Krake. The Ovarrow in this universe were being manipulated into fighting a civil war. The goal for the CDF was to prevent the civil war by initiating surgical strikes to change regimes and expose the Krake. Presumably, these actions would incur less loss of life than an all-out war. Wade hoped that was true. On New Earth, they'd seen the remnants of the devastation from countless wars the Ovarrow had fought among each other and eventually with the Krake. They had to stop the same from occurring here, as well as possibly gaining a powerful ally to fight the Krake.

The Ovarrow had been on a heightened state of alert for years. Skirmish wars had become the norm, and they were prepared for a frontal assault. Meanwhile, the Qompiry rebels had created a path by linking various tunnels under the city that would bring them close to the capitol building.

"We need a better vantage point," Mason said. "From there, we can put some sharpshooters up to take out whatever the Krake have on the roof."

"Agreed," Wade replied and peered at the city, looking for a good location for his snipers. "Send Dixon and his squad. I've marked a few waypoints for them."

Mason opened a comlink and relayed Wade's orders. Then he looked at Wade and nodded.

"Let's move out," Wade said.

The 3rd Platoon was stationed to the north of the capitol on the outskirts of the city. They couldn't just waltz down the street, so they'd commandeered a couple of Ovarrow ground transport vehicles, which they loaded up and set off in. They wouldn't reach the capitol, especially once the Qompiry began their assault, but at least they could penetrate some of the perimeter before they had to stop and fight.

Wade rode in the front, and Mason had control of the vehicle.

"Do we know how many Krake are in there?" Mason asked, jutting his chin up a little.

"Not exactly. Best guess is about forty of them, but they're not soldiers. They're administrators, politicians. They probably have some security details, but we need to keep them from warning their base."

"Understood," Mason said.

They headed to the interior of the city, making it through one of the security checkpoints. Wade had several reconnaissance drones patrolling and saw where the Qompiry had engaged the Gesora military that was defending the capitol. Those soldiers didn't know they were fighting for the wrong side. The Qompiry leveraged smaller squads to distract the defenders, and then their main fighting force engaged.

The Gesora regulars reacted quickly.

"We've been made," one of the CDF soldiers said from the back of the vehicle. Wade turned around and saw that the Gesora regulars manning the security checkpoint were emphatically pointing in their direction.

"We've got incoming," Mason said.

Ovarrow howler missiles launched from the capitol and sped off in multiple directions, with several heading right for the CDF soldiers. The howlers' promise of death and destruction screeched across the sky, and the CDF soldiers abandoned their vehicles only moments before the missiles slammed into them. The platoon of armored CDF soldiers was engulfed in flame for a few moments before the explosion cleared, but they'd gotten far enough away that the Nexstar combat suits had withstood the force of the explosion.

"We've got eyes on us," Mason said.

"Stick close to the buildings," Wade said.

"It was that damn checkpoint. We should have taken them out."

Wade accessed the stealth recon drone feeds and saw that the Qompiry soldiers were emerging from the underground sewer access points. They were closer to the capitol than his platoon was.

They made their way closer to the capitol and stopped at a complex of domed buildings. Wade ordered his snipers to the tops of the buildings to survey the area. The Qompiry were now leading the ground assault on a direct path toward the capitol.

"Lieutenant, I have a target. Krake tech on the west side of the roof," Sergeant Dixon said.

Wade accessed the targeting coordinates and peered at the video feed. A metallic cylinder had emerged from one of the air conditioning units on the roof. There was a flash of purple light as something spun inside.

"Take it out, Sergeant."

The two sharpshooters opened fire with explosive rounds, and more of the metallic cylinders emerged onto the roof.

"I need heavy ordnance. We need to fire on that capitol now," Wade said. He knew the Krake would notice this attack because he was using weaponry that wasn't available to the Ovarrow.

The reconnaissance drone shrieked an alert, which appeared on Wade's internal heads-up display. He cursed, and Mason looked at him questioningly. "Krake comm signal detected. We need to move, *now*."

SAMSON INFORMED MONIN, a warlord of the Gesora, that the Qompiry were beginning their assault on the capitol. Monin began to bellow orders to his Ovarrow soldiers, and they hastened their approach to the arch complex.

Samson had deployed multiple combat drones. It was easy

for them to keep out of sight with so much vegetation in this godforsaken jungle. He couldn't wait to get back to New Earth. He never thought he'd have a thought like that, given how much he hated humanity's current home. He missed Earth, and that would never change. He was resigned to the fact that no matter how much time passed, he would always miss the home he'd lost and the people he'd never see again. They were always in the back of his mind. It had been fifteen years since he'd come out of the stasis pod aboard the *Ark—the* day everything changed—but Samson banished those thoughts. It was ancient history. He had a job to do, and there were Krake to kill.

The Krake didn't have a large operation on this planet, but they were always well fortified. The arch gateway was only fifty meters from end to end—medium-sized, which was good for transporting small vehicles and as many Krake soldiers as required. The Krake relied on automated defenses that could kill humans and Ovarrow alike. As tough as the Nexstar combat suits were, they couldn't withstand the high-powered particle beams from heavy defense turrets. Krake soldiers used particle beam rifles, which were precise and lethal. They could penetrate CDF combat suits in seconds; however, Krake armor was actually inferior to the CDF's, which gave them a bit of an advantage. The CDF employed a combination of kinetic weaponry, but they'd also included plasma rifles that had been reverse engineered from the Vemus weapons.

Lieutenant Layton opened a comlink to Samson. "Their defenses are coming online. I think the jig is up. They know we're coming, Captain."

"That's it," Samson said. "No more sneaking around. I want you to take out your first-priority targets, then move on to the second. We'll meet up in the middle."

He opened a comlink to Monin. "The Krake know we're here. We need to attack now."

"We are almost in position," Monin said.

Samson cut off the comlink, and Cerot came to his side. The young Ovarrow was eager to fight. Samson had been working with Mekaal soldiers in a joint task force to engage the Krake for the past year.

"The Mekaal are ready, Captain," Cerot said.

The CDF had enhanced the Mekaal's weapons and armor, which had been over two hundred years old. Even now, they weren't on the same level as the CDF, but it was much better than what they'd been using. They needed every advantage they could get.

There were several squads of Krake soldiers near the arch, which was coming online. CDF combat drones opened fire, and the Krake soldiers scattered for cover. Krake defensive turrets began firing at them, mainly targeting the Gesora. No doubt the Krake sensors were better at detecting the Ovarrow. They'd detect the CDF soldiers once they were closer.

Over one hundred and forty heavily armed CDF special forces soldiers closed in on the Krake installation from multiple directions. The Krake had chosen this location because of its isolation from the Ovarrow. That meant Samson could fight this battle using all the weapons in his arsenal, and the Krake wouldn't know what had hit 'em.

Connor stood in front of the holotank, monitoring the attack on the capitol. A secondary section showed the Krake arch installation where the battle had begun in earnest. The

Qompiry had successfully breached the defenses of the capitol, and the attack was proceeding just as he expected. The Hellcats were providing air support, and they were almost inside the capitol. There was a lot of confusion as the Qompiry engaged the Gesora strongholds for the purpose of keeping them distracted and out of the main battle. The CDF had sustained some losses, but so far, they'd accounted for their dead. There would be nothing left for the Ovarrow to find or the Krake to make use of. The Krake couldn't learn that humans had had a hand in this rebellion.

Connor brought up the drone video feeds of the attack on the arch gateway complex. Krake defensive towers were mainly targeting the Gesora, and Samson had abandoned any pretext of concealing their attack method. They could've destroyed the arch, but Connor had given orders that it was to be taken intact. It wasn't enough to keep the Krake from this planet. They needed the Ovarrow to be able to control that arch so it could be used in the future.

The Krake soldiers adapted quickly, considering that they'd been taken by surprise despite the warning they'd received, and they'd managed to get their defenses online. The Krake had been operating on this planet for nearly seventy years, and they'd had no indication that anyone knew the location of their base. They also hadn't expected that someone else could open a gateway to this planet. This gave Connor and the CDF a much-needed advantage, and they'd seized the opportunity to oust the Krake from power with minimal loss of life, but Connor knew this was only the beginning. They'd basically sparked civil war among the Gesora and the Qompiry. The fighting in the capital was still going on, but soon they'd call for a cease-fire. Monin had survived, and Samson had his combat engineers disabling the archway. They'd learned a lot about the arch, particularly how to disable it without destroying it. This meant the arch could be used at the behest of the Ovarrow on this planet, which was what Connor wanted. It was also what they needed to accomplish when they found the Krake home world.

3

A CDF Hellcat touched down on an elevated landing platform at the Krake base of operations. The deactivated arch gateway was no more than a hundred meters away, and the dark metal glistened with moisture from a recent rainfall.

Connor and Captain O'Brien walked down the loading ramp and were greeted by Sergeant Foster, who snapped a salute at Connor. "General Gates, if you'll follow me, I'll take you to Captain Samson."

Connor returned the salute. "Lead on, Sergeant."

Troop carrier transports were landing in the area, and CDF soldiers were climbing aboard. The battle for the arch had been won, and it would now be turned over to the Gesora.

Foster led Connor and O'Brien to the Gesora encampment just outside the Krake base. Connor glanced up at the arch. The data on his helmet's heads-up display showed that the arch was sixteen meters tall. He'd seen much larger arches, as well as massive space gates. Despite the significant Krake presence on this planet, Connor believed that this was a minor effort on the Krake's part. But it was a start. They had liberated other minor systems like these in alternate universes, but Connor had to wonder how many they could free before the Krake finally caught on to what they were doing.

Gesora soldiers watched them as they walked past various staging areas where wounded soldiers were being cared for. A short distance away, the Gesora soldiers gathered their dead in preparation to return home. This battle had cost them, but it was one they'd needed to fight. At least these Ovarrow now had a chance at a future free of the Krake.

Foster led them to a command tent where Samson and Cerot were speaking with Monin. There were several Gesora soldiers nearby, listening intently. The Gesora warlord looked at Connor and noticed the deference given to him by the CDF soldiers in the area.

"Warlord Monin," Connor said, "congratulations on your victory."

The warlord from the jungle world regarded Connor with cinnamon-colored eyes. He had vertical pupils that looked more feline than reptilian, but his brown, pebbled skin was akin to that of a reptile. Pointy protrusions stemmed from his shoulders and elbows. The Ovarrow were bipedal, lean and strong, but they had a bit of a stoop that made their heads bob when they walked.

"This victory wouldn't have been possible without you and your soldiers," Monin said. "In fact, if we hadn't listened to you all those months ago, we wouldn't be here today," he said and looked at the dead soldiers being gathered before turning back to Connor. "Their sacrifice will be honored."

"Don't forget the Qompiry," Connor said.

Monin's features tightened. "Yes, of course. There's still some fighting going on at the capitol. I've sent a data burst to the Gesora regulars requesting a cease-fire. We'll be journeying there soon, and I'd like it if you'd join us there."

They'd managed to capture some of the Krake at the capitol. The CDF soldiers had already turned control of the building over to the Qompiry and the Gesora regulars they'd convinced to help them. However, there were still militant groups fighting in the city. Connor thought they were Krake sympathizers who'd been activated when the capital fell, and they couldn't rule out that some of the Krake might have escaped, but their options would be limited without access to their arch gateway. Connor expected there'd be more urban fighting the Gesora would have to contend with in the coming months before the dust settled and they could start rebuilding.

"You have all the evidence you need to convince the rest of the Gesora of what the Krake have been doing here," Connor said.

The Krake had conducted many experiments over the years, including facilitating the "discovery" of certain technology and biological weapons to manipulate powerful nations against each other. They'd also had significant control and influence over the Ovarrow economy, which seemed to the Gesora as being wielded at random, but with the help of the CDF, the Gesora had been able to identify the artificial nature of key events that the Krake were directly responsible for.

"We can't stay here any longer," Connor said. "We need to move on. There are other universes out there that need our help, and we should continue searching for the Krake home universe. You'll be able to help with that once things stabilize here," Connor said.

Monin looked at Cerot for a few seconds, considering, and the Mekaal soldier returned his gaze in kind. Then Monin looked at Connor. "He is Ovarrow, although not from this world," Monin said, gesturing toward Cerot. "But I think you are something different, despite the Warlord First's insistence that you are the same."

The CDF soldiers wore their Nexstar combat suits with the helmets fully engaged. There was no way for Monin or any other Gesora soldier to see their faces, and suspicion didn't mean confirmation as far as Connor was concerned.

"What would you like to know?" he asked.

"I want to see the faces of my allies."

"I can't do that," Connor said. "It's as much for our protection as it is for yours. We have restrictions on what we can share with you. Just accept that we're hunting for the Krake home world, and when we find it, I hope you'll remember what we've done here today. We'll need your help in the future."

Monin looked up at the arch and the equipment the CDF had installed so they could control it. "That equipment—the controller— will render the arch useless."

"It will give you control of when to use it," Connor said.

"But it won't stop the Krake from coming here."

Connor shook his head. "They could use a different arch from an alternate universe to open another gateway to this world, and you're right to be concerned about that. We have the same risk on our home world. You'll have to try to monitor for this as best you can, but you control this arch now. You'll be able to contact us through it, and eventually other Ovarrow."

Monin regarded Connor for a few moments. "What if it's decided that the arch is to be destroyed? Ever since we learned about the Krake, there are some who believe that isolation is the best defense against them. Does knowing this affect your perception of us?"

"We won't regret helping you if you decide to destroy the arch, but don't make any rash decisions. Destroying this arch would only remove your ability to engage the real enemy. As I said before, we'll need your help when it comes time to deal with the Krake where they live. That's the only way this cycle ends and all of us can be free of them. I hope you can convey that to your leaders."

Connor was silent for a few seconds. Monin was conflicted about them and Connor couldn't blame him, but they couldn't reveal themselves at this time. "And don't forget what the Qompiry have sacrificed for this. You must overcome your biases against them if you're to have a future."

Monin looked unconvinced and then seemed to reconsider. "To contact you, we must use the arch, but this gateway won't be to your home world. Is this correct?"

"Yes, that's right. The risk to our world would be too great if the information fell into the wrong hands. However, we do maintain a presence on a world you can contact through the arch. The communication protocols you've been given work both ways—for us to confirm your identity and for you to confirm ours. If we fail to meet any of the challenge protocols, it means this world has been compromised by the Krake, and I'd advise you to sever all communications from it. Eventually, we'd reestablish contact with you ourselves or through one of our other allies. I assure you that you are not alone in this fight with the Krake. Try to remember this," Connor said.

"You have given me no reason to doubt you. You've gone above and beyond what any ally to the Gesora and the Qompiry have done in the past. Our fight is not yet over. There are factions sympathetic to the Krake that need to be rooted out, but I'll do my very best to make sure all Ovarrow know we had help—*your* help," Monin said and paused for a few moments. "You said you had other allies from alternate universes. Will we be able to contact them?"

"Yes, you will, but for their protection we're not sharing their information with you today. They've faced the challenges that are ahead of you. As time goes on, we'll bring you further into our operations against the Krake, and this includes sharing other Ovarrow who have proven they will fight," Connor said. He could tell that Monin didn't appreciate being kept in the dark, but it was for the best. The Gesora had to prove themselves first.

"Perhaps we'll search for alternate universes to explore ourselves," Monin said.

"The arch belongs to all of you. I would strongly advise you to use caution if you start exploring other universes, and remember that the gateway works both ways," Connor replied.

They left the Gesora command tent and headed back toward the troop carriers. After they climbed aboard and were heading to their own egress point, Connor looked at Samson.

"You're unusually quiet."

Samson bobbed his head to the side. "The Krake had a few surprises for us, and I think there might be more. I'm just wondering if they'll still be here with Monin in command when we check in with them a month or two from now."

"It's not a perfect system, but it's what we have to work with."

Cerot nodded. The Ovarrow had been listening nearby and had adopted the human custom of nodding their heads in acknowledgment. It had become much more natural for the Ovarrow as time went on.

"Now they have a fighting chance. It was worse for us back home, especially at the end. At least the factions here are still willing to communicate with one another," Cerot said.

For as young as Cerot appeared to be, he had witnessed many horrors before going into stasis. He had seen the collapse of his civilization and the measures they'd used to survive. It was easy for some people to forget, but not Connor. He had helped study Ovarrow ruins on New Earth and was familiar with just how bad things had gotten before they'd gone into stasis. However, unearthing the archaeological record and living through it were two different things.

4

Sadoon stepped off the transit platform, and the arch gateway towered above him. It had been many months since he'd been allowed to return to Quadiri. The demands on his time as sector chief were such that didn't allow for traveling beyond once a year. He glanced at the night sky overhead and saw Quadiri's sister planet Ovren. Ovren had once been a living world, but thousands of years ago, in the first wars, the Quadiri military had vanquished the Ovren invaders. Even without enhanced eyes, he could see the pale green of Ovren's poisonous atmosphere. Many Krake looked at Ovren's demise with dignified pride. And why shouldn't they? The Krake had not been the aggressor, but they had learned early on the need to be the victors.

Sadoon walked over to a waiting transport vehicle where the automated systems captured his credentials and payment. The metallic door opened with a quiet hiss, and he climbed aboard. It was empty inside. The automated systems controlled the vehicle and would take him to his destination. The transport vehicle's engines activated, and it lifted into the air, swung around, and sped in the direction of the sprawling metropolis. After many months of waiting, the overseers had finally deigned to meet with him to discuss a new research project with a primary focus on the Humans and their Colonial Defense Force. As sector chief of an R&D installation on an Ovarrow world, he had proposed to end the project he'd been working on early so he could pursue something he believed was far more important. The Humans had powerful weapons, and he later learned that their warships had engaged the Krake Space Navy on multiple occasions. Given how much destruction these Humans had caused, Sadoon thought he would've been granted a great deal of leeway when it came to finding them. The Krake were a vast empire that spanned multiple universes, and until recently, they'd encountered only Ovarrow on other planets.

Sadoon knew he wasn't the only Krake interested in being granted the rights to a research project focused on the Humans. There were multiple military leaders interested as well, particularly those of the Krake Space Navy. For months, he'd waited for a summons from the overseers in response to his numerous petitions to run the project.

Quadiri was home to vast cities that took up precisely forty percent of the continents. Any further expansion would impact the planet's climate and was therefore forbidden. Expansion onto other worlds was limited, and breeding was tightly controlled. Only Ovarrow bred uncontrolled, which was characteristic of such a juvenile species.

The transport vehicle flew over the city, and its azure glow seemed to invigorate him. Krake architecture was built not only for the purpose it was designed but also for aesthetics. Nothing Sadoon had ever seen had come close to Quadiri's splendor.

The transport vehicle landed on a designated platform, and Sadoon climbed out. He stepped onto a moving walkway, which ushered him inside the administration building where there was no shortage of Krake. The fact that the overseers had been willing to meet with him did convey a level of acknowledgment few Krake achieved.

Sadoon had studied every scrap of evidence he could find about the Humans since his own encounter with them. He remembered their remarkably resilient mechanical armor and the Ovarrow they traveled with. Sadoon hadn't been able to identify the universe they'd come from. His scientists had been able to extract useful data from DNA samples from the Ovarrow but not the Humans. The Humans' mechanical armor self-destructed when they died, destroying all evidence of them down to the microscopic level. They were clever, worthy of the Krake's attention, and Sadoon wanted to be the Krake to win this contract.

Once he was inside the building, a message was sent to his comlink, acknowledging his arrival with instructions directing him where he needed to go. He had expected to meet with the overseers in their primary audience chamber, but that wasn't what his orders contained. He was directed to a solitary room used for secure communications. This was little more than a capsule with room enough for only him. Sadoon stepped inside as the door shut behind him. His identification was confirmed, and the room darkened. A few seconds later, the walls of the room became transparent, and he found himself standing in the middle of the audience chamber of the overseers. Sadoon knew that in the actual chamber, he appeared as a holographic image.

In front of him was a high table where seven ancient Krake overseers sat. They were many hundreds of years old. The overseers lived the longest among the Krake.

"Sector Chief Sadoon," said the Krake from the center of the table.

Their identification appeared on Sadoon's internal heads-up display, and he nearly betrayed his shock when he realized he was being addressed by Prime Overseer Ersevin. "Prime Overseer, I have come here, as you requested."

"We are here because of your request—repeated requests, I might add."

"There is sufficient evidence to support that persistence is often rewarded, Prime Overseer," Sadoon replied.

Ersevin regarded him with ancient eyes. They were piercing, and Sadoon felt his resolve being tested under their weight. "Persistence is often confused with arrogance."

Sadoon felt something cold stir inside him. He was afraid, and rightly so. With a single word, Ersevin could end Sadoon's career. His next words could forever influence the path he walked.

"In this case, my persistence is for the benefit of all Krake."

Ersevin held his gaze for a few moments. "As is every effort that comes before us," he said and gestured toward the other overseers sitting at the high table.

Sadoon's gaze swept across them. They were all old and powerful, with hundreds of years of authority and knowledge at their disposal. He bowed his head in respect.

"We are here to review your request for a new research project."

Sadoon looked back at Ersevin. "I am at your disposal, Prime Overseer."

"We have reviewed the evidence you've put together and have concluded that the Humans are a limited threat. We acknowledge that their weapons are impressive, but all predictive models indicate that the Humans are vastly outmatched by our capabilities," Ersevin said.

"Prime Overseer, are you saying we shouldn't study them?"

"I'm not saying that at all. We are in agreement that the Humans are worthy of study once we've identified which fringe universe they reside in. However, no additional resources will be allocated to that project."

"I urge you all to reconsider," Sadoon said and looked at the other overseers. "This project should have alpha resource allocation."

Ersevin's pale blue skin wrinkled along his brow ridges. "Alpha resource allocation?" he repeated. "Tell me, Sector Chief Sadoon, do you have a new predictive model we should review that supports your position?"

"Negative, Prime Overseer," Sadoon replied.

"We understand that you've had direct contact with these Humans and are intrigued by them. We commend your enthusiasm. However, we do not have infinite resources to indulge in every research priority that comes to us for our review. We have protocols in place to help us prioritize our resource allocation, as well as those for cataloging fringe universes."

Anger and frustration flooded through Sadoon's mind, but he couldn't let it show. He must appear calm, even though with one simple sentence, the Prime Overseer had dismissed his request for additional resources.

"Will you grant me clearance to pursue the Humans on my own? I'm willing to segregate my own resource allocation," Sadoon asked.

"You have a research project you're in charge of, and our records indicate that this project is not complete. Do you wish to nominate another Krake to take over your work?"

This simple question was as dangerous as an active warship combat drone. If he nominated another Krake, they could take everything he'd built and increase their own standing among the Krake hierarchy. But his research project was years from completion. Sadoon doubted he'd learn anything else that couldn't already be predicted, but if anything, the Krake were thorough in their research endeavors. He couldn't abandon years of work, not even to study the Humans.

"I do not wish to nominate another Krake. However, I would like to be granted a second research fellowship that would allow me to further gather evidence about the Humans and their Ovarrow allies," Sadoon said.

Ersevin considered it for a few moments. As the seconds went by, Sadoon suspected that the overseers were communicating with each other, although he couldn't detect any means of it. Perhaps it was being filtered out. If he'd been granted a live audience with them, he might have been able to detect additional comlink signals.

"We will consider your request at our next review of the project for which you are responsible. However, you are free to request information from the data repository to further develop a predictive model that justifies a review of resource allocation to your proposed project. I must caution you that this is secondary to your primary research project. We will not tolerate any neglect in that endeavor. Is this understood?"

"I will not neglect my current efforts in the least bit," Sadoon said.

The overseers' chambers faded, and Sadoon found himself standing inside the comlink room. The door behind him opened, indicating that his session with the overseers was over. He stood there for a few moments, reviewing the conversation in his mind. If he had gotten the overseers to escalate the priority of the Human research project, he could've changed projects without losing any standing among the oligarchy. But they wouldn't let him.

A warning appeared on the wallscreen, indicating he should leave. The room was reserved for the next occupant. Sadoon stepped out and allowed the next Krake to go inside. He was heading back to the automated walkway when he received a comlink request. He'd been so focused on reviewing his session with the overseers that he acknowledged the comlink before he realized he could not identify the sender.

"Your request was denied. Do not attempt to trace this comlink. We have been following your repeated inquiries to the overseers' office, but you had to know this was going to fail."

"You are remarkably well-informed. Why hide yourself?"

"Others may pretend we don't exist, but that doesn't change the facts."

"You are the fifth column. I will report this session immediately."

"If you'd like to wait twenty-five years to find the universe where the Humans are, then, by all means, do so. That estimate is based upon current allocated resources."

Sadoon stopped walking and frowned. He'd been about to forward the comlink session to the authorities but decided to wait. "What do I call you?"

"You can call me Aurang. You're not the only one who has intimate knowledge of the Humans and their CDF. I've been aboard one of their most powerful warships. I've seen them face-to-face, and I'm willing to share this information with you."

Sadoon couldn't be sure if Aurang was lying to him. "And what would you want in return?"

"Cooperation and help when I need it. What if I told you I could cut the timeline to find the universe where the Humans live to one to three years?"

"How?" Sadoon asked. He didn't believe it was possible.

"You've tried to go through official channels to get what you want. Have you ever considered using unofficial channels? I happen to agree with your assessment of the Human threat. They *are* a threat to us. The overseers are blinded by their own arrogance. There is much that will change."

"What exactly are you offering?"

"I'm offering a way for you to study the Humans up close and personal," Aurang said.

"These feeble acts of persuasion are not compelling."

"I believe they are. You see, we've been conducting our own research for many years. There are things many Krake realize but don't talk about."

"Such as?" Sadoon asked.

"Our biggest enemy."

"I think you might overestimate what the Humans are capable of. They are a threat, but they are not our biggest enemy. Not even close."

"You mistake me, Sector Chief. Stagnation is our biggest enemy."

Sadoon paused for a few moments, going over what Aurang

was saying. One to three years was much better than languishing for the time it would ordinarily take. However, it meant working with the scourge of their society. The fifth column worked toward anarchy. They were rebels, but could they give him what he wanted? He knew the overseers wouldn't grant him another audience for at least a year, but they could delay it even longer.

He recalled the image of the CDF soldier in mechanized armor fighting his Krake soldiers. The Human was defiant, even in the face of overwhelming odds. Sadoon had seen similar behavioral traits in the Ovarrow they had studied. He wondered what else he could learn about the Humans. What were they capable of? Could he come up with a predictive model for the Humans as well?

"I'd like to hear more," Sadoon said.

"I thought you'd like to. I'm going to transfer a set of coordinates. Do not come to them from Quadiri. You'll need to use one of the tertiary worlds and a secondary arch gateway. From there, you'll receive further instructions."

He received a data packet through the comlink. Sadoon opened it up and examined it. It contained everything Aurang had said. It wasn't just a simple journey through an arch gateway; it was a complex set of instructions. All this to meet with the fifth column.

"I should also warn you," Aurang continued, "that if you attempt to involve any authority, you will never hear from us again. You'll be cut off, and instead of studying the Humans, you'll learn about them from someone else. You're not the only interested party. Is this clear to you?"

Sadoon's first thought was that Aurang had worked with other Krake before. He wasn't the first Krake Aurang had tried to win to his cause, and that was telling in and of itself. "I understand."

"Excellent. I look forward to meeting with you. And when we do meet, I'll share all the knowledge I've gathered about the Humans. I'm sure you'll find it quite insightful. And you've scratched only the surface. I look forward to working with you, Sector Chief Sadoon."

The comlink severed, and Sadoon resumed walking toward the automated walkway. He would return to his research world, gather a few things, and then meet Aurang and the fifth column. The Krake had been so confident of what he had that Sadoon didn't even doubt it. That kind of authority came with the certainty of knowledge at his disposal. Sadoon had used it himself and knew enough to recognize it in another Krake. Perhaps this trip hadn't been a waste after all.

5

CONNOR WALKED into the administration wing of the governor's offices at the capitol building in Sierra. He passed the brightness of the wide corridors displaying cycled images of colonial accomplishments with little notice. He was already running late to the meeting. He gave a slight nod to people around him, those he recognized but didn't have time to talk to. Eyes forward, he walked as though he was on a dogged march toward the next objective. There was a grim set to the line of his mouth that wasn't quite a scowl, but most people got the hint and stayed away. He wasn't in the mood for talking. This day had been taxing enough already.

When Connor walked in, the strategy session was already in full swing. Twelve colonial leaders and members of their respective support staffs sat at the elongated conference table. He headed for the open seat next to Nathan, and Governor Wolf gave Connor a small nod, her aged features warming slightly.

Bob Mullins glanced in his direction with a pinched expression, then looked back at the young man who was speaking. He had a snobbish voice that sought to keep the attention of the attendees but wasn't succeeding. There was a presentation on the holodisplay showing a dashboard for various colonial project statuses. Connor looked at the young man, and a name appeared on his internal heads-up display. Brian Ramsey. His pale-skinned face had rounded cheeks that made him look more like a child than a man, and the minuscule patches of hair on his chin and jaw only contributed to the baby face he probably hoped to hide.

"General Gates," Ramsey said, making a show of looking at the clock. "I'm sorry, but you've missed the first part of the strategy session for civilian defense protocols in our cities."

"You can continue, Mr. Ramsey. General Hayes will fill me in on what I need to know," Connor replied.

"Of course, General, but with Governor Wolf in attendance, don't you think she's owed some kind of explanation for your late arrival?" Ramsey said.

Connor's gaze hardened, and Ramsey's face flushed a little bit. Assertiveness born of insecurity never quite worked, and yet so many young men and women became victims of the folly. Connor thought Ramsey was probably a smart young man, but right then, he was being foolish. And Connor didn't care.

Governor Wolf leaned forward. "That's not necessary."

Ramsey's gaze darted toward her, and he blinked rapidly. "Of course, Governor," he said meekly.

Connor glanced at the others around the table, and he could tell their curiosity was piqued. He drew himself up and leaned forward, cutting Ramsey off as he was about to speak. "If you really want to know why I was late, I was informing the families of the CDF soldiers who died in the line of duty. It's the least I can do when a soldier makes the ultimate sacrifice for the rest of the colony."

Grim, stone-faced silence lowered the atmosphere of the room by several degrees. Ramsey swallowed hard as he looked at Mullins, his gaze pleading. Bob gestured for him to sit down, and the young man beat a hasty retreat.

Mullins looked at Connor solemnly. "I think I can speak for everyone here when I express my sincerest condolences for the loss of our colonists, and we acknowledge the sacrifice of the soldiers in the Colonial Defense Force."

Connor nodded his head once. Throughout his military career, he'd seen many soldiers die. They'd lost thousands of them in their war with the Vemus alone. He didn't think he'd ever get to the point where the death of a fellow soldier was simply a number or a cost to be paid for the price of their survival. Lives mattered. They mattered to him, and they mattered to the families of the fallen. He couldn't visit every family of the soldiers who died. It wasn't practical, so the burden was spread among senior officers. He could have delegated the task, but he wouldn't. He owed his soldiers that much at least. It was a necessary duty that was never easy, but it kept him grounded, and reminding a room full of civilians—his fellow colonists—of the CDF's sacrifice helped ease the burden. It made them aware that there was a price to be paid for their survival and that it *did* affect him. He'd never be friends with Bob Mullins, but Connor had no doubt that Mullins worked on the colony's behalf. They didn't agree on a lot of things, but when it came to the importance of colonial lives, they were aligned.

"General Hayes has provided us with a briefing of the

mission involving the Gesora," Governor Wolf said. "Do you have anything you'd like to add?"

Mullins had killed the slide on the holoscreen, so they were clearly going off topic from the original presentation.

"The Gesora have a long uphill battle on their hands, but this was always going to be reality for them," Connor said and paused for a moment. "Nothing the Krake do could be considered by us as minor, but on the scale of a Krake research endeavor, much of what was happening to the Gesora has been seen in various configurations before—government and economic manipulation. But in this case, they added touching upon beliefs held sacred to the Gesora."

"Religious in nature? What sort of . . ." Mullins began to say but then stopped. "I don't want to . . . Please continue."

Discussions about the Krake sometimes led down a few rabbit holes. While it was interesting to do sometimes, more often than not it ate through their meeting time.

"Not overtly religious in nature," Connor said, "but just certain beliefs or ideas that divide a society, for example. They seemed to have explored multiple ideas along these lines. They combined these efforts with what we would call biological warfare, but those closely resembled prophetic references to their ancient history."

"Biological warfare can mean a lot of different things," Nathan said. "What the Krake have been doing on some worlds is introducing certain mutations and ideas to influence the Ovarrow's reaction to them. We've been working to isolate these efforts in order to try to understand what the Krake are studying."

Governor Wolf nodded. "Natalia informed me about this."

Natalia Vassar was a trusted CDF intelligence analyst

Connor had trained. Governor Wolf was looking to find a new head for the Colonial Intelligence Bureau, and Connor had recommended Major Vassar. He knew Mullins wanted to limit the influence of the Colonial Defense Force and that he likely viewed Natalia's candidacy as increasing that influence, so Mullins had put forth his own candidate.

"Not all the Krake intelligence operations are so complex," Connor said. "Some of them are pretty straightforward, but the typical trial for a Krake research project can last for years or, in some instances, hundreds of years."

"It's difficult to gauge how long the Krake conduct experiments or operations," Mullins replied. "I read the reports from Darius Cohen, and the Ovarrow history here on New Earth is spotty at best. The Ovarrow who went into stasis remember a world that had already fallen. In essence, they don't know exactly how long the Krake had maintained a presence here."

"We've been making significant gains in understanding Krake operations," Nathan said, "but of the hundreds of universes documented by the Krake, we've visited only a small percentage." He paused for a moment and added, "About fifteen percent of the total number."

Governor Wolf nodded. "Believe me, the number of universes that have been documented by the Krake has been subject to a lot of debate. The theory of a multiverse isn't new, and we've had limited proof of its existence until now. But our theories always indicated that there could be an infinite number of universes, and that's just not what we're finding, at least according to the Krake."

"And they've been at it for a lot longer than we have," Connor said.

"Does anyone have any idea how long?" Mullins asked.

"It's pure speculation," Dr. Curry said, "but based on the data we have here on New Earth and the intelligence gathered by CDF operations, it's easy to estimate that the Krake have been at this for hundreds of years. Five hundred years would be a conservative estimate, but it could also be as much as a thousand years." She paused for a few seconds before continuing. "There have been a lot of theories discussed about it in R&D, but I wouldn't say there's a consensus. What's been gaining traction among our ranks is that perhaps we're dealing with certain laws of the universe we haven't even conceptualized yet."

"What do you mean?" Mullins asked.

"Nothing is static. There is absolutely nothing here," Dr. Curry said, gesturing with her hands toward the table, "that's absolutely still. We're always in motion. And not just here. Everything is in motion—the planets, stars, and galaxies—so why not universes?"

Connor frowned in thought for a moment. "So, universes, as we know them, are in motion and . . ." He paused, and Dr. Curry smiled and nodded for him to continue. "The question becomes, What keeps them in motion?"

"That is the big question," Dr. Curry said. "The gateways we're able to open, thanks to the space gates and the arches, bend the laws of physics. At least the laws as *we* understand them. For example, we all know we can't go faster than the speed of light. We perceive that as a universal constant—gravity and mass, and that whole thing—but we've managed to bend those laws on our own. Otherwise, we wouldn't have artificial gravity. However, this is something else. So, if you can accept that multiple universes are out there and are in motion, then perhaps there's something that prevents us from accessing an infinite number of universes."

The room was silent for a few moments as everyone considered Dr. Curry's words.

Connor felt the hint of a smile tug at the edges of his lips. "You make it sound like it's a neighborhood."

Dr. Curry nodded. "You're not too far off with a simple explanation like that. Yet it means that even with a space gate, we can access only certain universes for what might be a limited amount of time, but keep in mind that 'limited' is a relative term here. In terms of space travel, the word 'limited' has a much different meaning than it does in terms of our lifespans."

"Let me see if I get this straight," Mullins said. "Are you saying that we will have access to certain universes for only a few years and then possibly never again?"

"That's just it, Mr. Mullins. We don't know. If it's relative in certain terms, it could be for as little as a few years like you said, but it could also mean thousands of years. And we think that the Krake must be aware of this theoretical universal constant we're talking about here. It would explain their reference to what they call a fringe universe. Since they have it in their terminology, the indication is that they must have knowledge that they can't always access a universe they've been to before."

Mullins's eyes widened, and Connor noticed that his weren't the only ones. Mullins looked at Governor Wolf. "So, we could wait out the Krake, in theory, and possibly they would never get to us?"

"You don't really think we'll get that lucky, do you?" Connor asked.

Mullins shrugged. "It's still something we could consider.

It's an option or a scenario we should *seriously* consider. What if the threat of the Krake is something we can just endure, and it might actually just pass us by? The point I'm trying to make is that we just don't know."

Connor took a sip of his water. "It *is* interesting, and we should try to find more data to support the theory."

"That's exactly my next point," Dr. Curry said. "And again, I must emphasize that these are just theories we're considering ourselves. I don't want to inundate the CDF with requests for acquiring data that just may not be out there. I mean, what if we're wrong?"

Governor Wolf smiled. "It's discussions like these that are the reason we have these strategy sessions. It's a way for *all* of us to come together and deal with the Krake. It shouldn't fall entirely upon the shoulders of the CDF."

"I agree," Mullins said. "But given this discussion, how are we ever going to answer the question of how much time we really have before the Krake find us?"

Nathan cleared his throat. "If I could give you a definitive answer, then I would. They're looking for us. We've clashed with them enough to know that they're aware of us. The measures that the Krake have gone to in dealing with Trident Battle Group is certainly testament enough for that."

"We need to find the Krake home universe before they find us," Connor said. "If they find us first, we'll be fighting them here and looking for the Krake home universe at the same time. And that's assuming they don't bring an overwhelming fighting force here."

"And what is the strategy if we do find the Krake home universe?" Mullins asked.

"We recon the system," replied Connor. "There's no reason

for us to attack as soon as we find it. But as for a strategy, it's similar to any other kind of enemy we've faced throughout history. We remove their ability to make war."

"Some of these things will have to be defined as we learn more," Nathan said. "We know the Krake have operations outside their own universe that support their industrial complex. We don't know how extensive they are, but the more we find, the better we might be able to cripple their industrial complex."

Governor Wolf nodded. "I understand the enormity of the task that the CDF is being called upon to deal with," she said. "I think what Bob is asking for, and what I think we need, is something a little bit more specific, even if it's a theoretical scenario. A 'what if,' if you will. If we find X, Y, and Z, then we do these things." Her gaze slipped to the table for a few moments as if she was lost in thought. Then she quickly shook it off.

"We'll make sure you have what you need," Nathan said.

"Thank you," she replied. "I think that wraps up this session; however, I need to keep the senior staff here for a few minutes. Everyone else can go."

The people around the conference table rose and started exiting the room. Connor stood up and walked toward Governor Wolf. "What did you think of Natalia?"

"She's everything you said she was—cunningly brilliant—and I think she'd make a fine director of the Colonial Intelligence Bureau," Wolf said.

Mullins joined them but remained quiet.

Connor arched an eyebrow. "I feel like there's a 'but' coming."

"We want to avoid what happened with Meredith Cain. Bob

has made a proposal of not quite a co-leadership position but a strong second-in-command like your XOs serving on CDF warships—someone to help Natalia with the job I'm going to offer her." Connor nodded. "But there's something else I need to tell you. She'll need to resign from the CDF to take this position. Do you think she'll do that?"

Connor considered this for a few moments before replying. "I can't speak for Major Vassar. I've worked closely with her, and I think she'll be a perfect fit for the role. I assure you we'll do whatever we can to help," he said and looked at Mullins. "Who's your candidate, Bob?"

"He'll be her second if she takes the job. His name is Jerry Sherman. He's worked a lot of logistics-type projects that deal specifically with resource allocation. He's a good fit for the job too. He has a highly analytical mind," Mullins replied.

Connor glanced at Governor Wolf and thought about asking her a follow-up question but decided against it. There was something on the edge of his thoughts that he couldn't quite put into words. "I'll leave you to it," he said.

"Connor," Wolf said, "is there anything we can do for the families of the CDF soldiers?"

He looked away for a moment. "There isn't much we can do that isn't already happening. I wish there was more, but if I really had a choice, it would be that we didn't have to deal with the Krake at all."

"I understand. If there's anything you need, let me know."

Connor left the meeting and joined Nathan. "They're not going to like it," he said.

"They need to understand what we'll have to do when we find the Krake home world. They need to be prepared," replied Nathan.

"I know, but I just think they might balk at some of our ideas."

"Then it'll be our job to convince them of what's necessary. Come on, let's hammer out some of these details."

"Right," Connor said. "You be conservative, and I'll be extreme."

Nathan chuckled. "You always get to be extreme."

"Just lucky, I guess."

6

WHILE LIVING at Sanctuary over the years, Connor had discovered that he had to travel ever farther from the growing city to reach the New Earth countryside, and he'd found that he did his best thinking when he was moving around. The trail he currently walked smelled of decaying wood, wildflowers, and moss-covered boulders. An army of croakers contested for the loudest calls over by the marshland that became part of the nearby river during the rainy season.

He'd spent a lifetime moving around from place to place, and living at Sanctuary with Lenora had been the longest he'd ever spent in a single home. Despite the extensive travel he'd done in recent years, he still had the itch to explore. He enjoyed going where no one had ever been before. There was a certain amount of satisfaction in that—a sentiment shared by most colonists. Connor may not have started out as the ideal colonist, but he'd certainly grown into one at heart.

He walked along a hiking path, easily navigating across the uneven ground, and emerged from the forested area onto a dry patch. Puffs of dirt kicked up as he strode quickly along. Connor rarely walked at a leisurely pace, except when he had Lauren with him. At those times, his two-year-old daughter set the pace.

The marked trail was easily fifteen kilometers long. It was essentially a giant loop that led to another part of Sanctuary. He remembered first exploring New Earth when people were rightly cautious about venturing beyond the fenced compounds they'd built. They'd known so little about the planet back then—a great mystery, a new world, but not the one they'd thought they were going to. Regardless, New Earth had become their home.

Connor glanced at the exotic plant life that had become the norm to him. To his right was a dazzling display of the broad multicolored leaves his wife often referred to as an artist's palette. He thought about the other worlds he'd seen through the gateway—worlds with poisonous atmospheres or frozen over because of some catastrophe—lifeless, deserted places he hoped never to see again. Things could have been much worse here on New Earth. Had the *Ark* arrived a hundred years earlier, for instance, things would have been much different. New Earth had been a frozen world because of an artificially induced Ice Age that hadn't relented until almost fifty years before their arrival.

The population of the colony had more than doubled in size and continued along a steep growing curve. Sometime within the next ten years, they'd probably have over a million colonists. Given the Vemus Wars and just the general challenges they'd faced in colonizing this planet, it was a huge accomplishment for humanity to thrive here.

Connor's memory of Old Earth was something of a dream. The people and places they'd left behind were no less important to him, but it was another life in every sense of the word. He had grown beyond the NA Alliance military officer he'd been. His enduring ache for the people he missed had become a permanent part of his existence here—friends and family, his son who'd died fighting the Vemus as part of a last-ditch effort to update the *Ark*'s destination and give the colonists a chance to survive. Connor carried so much guilt that he didn't think he'd ever be entirely free of it. There'd always be a longing for those events to have turned out differently. He wished he could have been there for his son, especially for the dark times he must have faced during the Vemus Wars of Old Earth. But an old friend had once told him that collecting a few regrets was part of living life.

Connor had purposefully taken this trail because of where it entered Sanctuary. He owed a visit to an old friend, and before too long he'd reached the edges of the city. Sanctuary wasn't the sprawling metropolis that Sierra was, but it was a city in its own right. They had room to breathe out here.

He looked at the sign above the large restaurant and smiled. It showed a cartoon rendition of a CDF soldier with furrowed brow and intense gaze. Beneath the picture was written "*I dare you not to love the food here!*"

The Salty Soldier had grown in size and popularity over the years. Connor remembered when Diaz had designed the sign that hung over the wide entrance. He remembered telling Diaz that he thought it was a little on the nose, to which Diaz had replied that this was the point. He didn't want a wishy-washy clientele coming to his restaurant.

Diaz had decided to take a page out of the history books and use hardwoods for the restaurant's construction. He'd claimed it was more inviting, and Connor agreed. The dark hardwood smelled of longevity and good times, as if the restaurant had always been there. As Connor walked toward the main doors, he caught a healthy whiff of the delicious food, and his mouth started to water. The early afternoon staff was preparing for what promised to be a busy dinner.

Connor walked through the main doors, and Victoria smiled a greeting at him. She came from around the bar to give Connor a big hug.

"You didn't bring the little peach today," Victoria said.

Connor smiled and gave her a peck on the cheek. "Not today. She's with her mother."

"Oh, I just can't get enough of her. Pretty soon, she'll have another little playmate," Victoria said and smiled with a twinkle in her eyes.

Connor frowned for a moment, and Victoria rubbed her stomach gently.

"Well, that's cause for celebration!" he said, lifting her into the air and swinging her around a few times before softly placing her back on her feet. She squealed in delight.

He heard a hearty laugh from across the room and saw Diaz walking toward him, bellowing a mock warning to stay away from his wife. He held his arms out wide and had a broad grin across his face. Diaz had a stocky build with a bit of a barrel chest. Connor noticed there was less worry around his eyes.

"Hey, hey, she must have told you about lucky number six," Diaz said.

Connor nodded. "I'd say you're trying to repopulate the human species all by yourself."

Diaz placed his arm around his wife affectionately. "Pretty soon, you'll catch up to us."

"I very much doubt it," Connor replied.

Victoria ushered them away. "Go on. I know you two have plenty to catch up on. I'll make sure you're left alone."

"Come on, I have something to show you," Diaz said.

He led Connor toward a staircase off to the side, and they climbed it. When they came to a landing, they continued climbing another set of stairs. There was a solitary door at the top. Diaz gave him a wink and opened it to reveal an outdoor terrace with a few lounge chairs and a perfect view of the landscape around Sanctuary. It was a good spot, and Connor said so.

A desk and chair were off to the side. Above it, a wallscreen cycled through a collage of pictures. Connor recognized some of them, since he was in them. A few of the pictures were from the early days of the colony when there hadn't been a CDF. They'd originally been part of Field Ops and Security. There was even a picture of Lenora speaking with Noah, who looked as if he'd just gotten out of the gawky adolescence stage. But as always, Connor's gaze was drawn immediately back to Lenora, and then he saw himself in the background, glancing in Lenora's direction.

"You never could take your eyes off her for very long," Diaz said.

Connor grinned. "Lenora had no shortage of admirers back then."

"What do you mean, back then? I still remember when the young pups all watched the young pretty doctor lady," Diaz said. "Young pretty doctor lady" was Diaz's nickname for Lenora, especially when he was speaking to somebody who had extended her some kind of favor when Field Ops wouldn't give them anywhere near that kind of cooperation.

"Would you look at us," Connor said and leaned in toward one of the pictures. He sighed and looked at Diaz. "We really had no idea what was coming."

"You're doing it again. You're sucking the joy out of the moment," Diaz said and punched him in the arm.

"I see you've adjusted to civilian life quite well. You look good," Connor said.

Diaz nodded. "I *am* good. You could adjust, too, if you wanted to."

Connor tilted his head slightly to the side and shrugged one shoulder.

"I know, I know," Diaz said. He gestured toward a couple of chairs, poured them each a glass of bourbon, and handed one to Connor.

"I see Nathan and Savannah have made customers of you too," Connor said.

"Oh yeah, this is good stuff."

Connor sipped his bourbon and then drained it. It blazed a path of warmth down his chest and into his stomach. Diaz poured him another. A few minutes later, a young man brought them a couple of sandwiches and then left them alone.

They ate and talked about little things. Diaz asked when Connor and Lenora were going to have more children. Connor had no idea. That sort of talk had a way of never coming up when he and Lenora were alone.

"I'm sure it'll happen one day. I just don't know when," Connor replied.

"Fair enough," Diaz said and took the last bite of his sandwich. "So, when are the Krake coming here?"

Connor's eyebrows raised. The question had come out of nowhere, but he had to admit that it'd been on his mind. He missed Diaz.

"That's the big question. That's what everyone wants to know."

"Well, I hope the real answer is never."

"Me too. The Security Council is pressuring Nathan and me on that very question. They want us to put a timeframe around it. They could be here now, or it could be a few years. The only way for us to find out is to keep going out there," Connor said, gesturing toward the view.

Diaz knew what he meant. He'd been through the gateway a few times as well.

"That's not even the tough question," Diaz said and poured them each some more bourbon.

Connor took the proffered glass and just held it. "They want us to revise our strategy on what we'll do after we find the Krake home universe."

Diaz snorted. "Well that's easy. We bomb them out of existence. Take them by surprise so they'll never see it coming."

"I don't know if the Security Council is quite on the same page as you."

"Well, they better get there because there's no other way for this to end. Just ask any of the Ovarrow," Diaz said.

Everything Connor had seen reaffirmed that the Krake had done truly despicable things to other intelligent species in a show of ruthless pragmatism at its worst.

"We're doing all we can to find them," he said. "We tell the Security Council that our strategy is to take away the Krake's ability to fight, but I don't know if this is good enough. The contacts we've made want revenge."

"They're entitled to it, if you ask me."

"You know the Krake have a fifth column, a group of rebels that are trying to change things."

"I don't know how much good that will do. Would you really trust the Krake to do anything but serve their own purpose?" Diaz asked.

Diaz hated the Krake, with good reason, but Connor didn't care about the Krake all that much. They were an enemy, and they needed to be stopped, but he didn't have the same hatred of them. Connor had seen it in other soldiers, both human and Ovarrow alike. It was the kind of hatred that gave rise to rogue groups doing morally gray things. His thoughts flickered to Lars Mallory. Lars had tortured Ovarrow to get information about the Krake. Connor didn't have to hate an enemy in order to defeat them, but it did raise the question of when a society is responsible for those who are in power.

"God, I can see the wheels are turning in that skull of yours," Diaz said.

"Is it that obvious?" Connor asked in mock surprise.

"I know you. You'll torture yourself about making the tough choices. But if it comes down to the Krake or us, it's going to be the Krake. You know it, and I know it. So do a lot of other people, including everyone in that Security Council."

"We just have to find them."

"How's that going?"

"We've actually made a lot of progress. We even have Ovarrow contacts in other universes that are looking for the Krake home world as well. But the real risk is that the more we bring into the fold—"

"The more it shines a light on our happy little planet here. I get it," Diaz said. "So, I guess the question is, What are you gonna do now?"

Connor feigned ignorance. "You mean after I go home?"

Diaz shook his head. "You know what I mean."

"It's the new me," Connor said. "We have multiple teams out all the time. We're going to find the Krake; it's just a matter of when. But, if you mean what am I going to do tomorrow, well, that's easy. Lenora asked me to take a short trip with her."

Diaz arched a thick eyebrow and regarded him for a few moments. "Are you two planning a weekend getaway in the middle of the week?"

Connor chuckled and shook his head. "No, it's nothing like that. She found something she wants to check out. I need some downtime, so I decided to go with her."

"Good for you, Connor. Try not to think about what the Krake are doing to find us."

"Do you have a few ideas you'd like to toss out there?"

Diaz shook his head. "I was never really the idea guy. You got Noah for that, and . . ." He paused, and his eyes widened. "What's Sean doing these days?"

"Sean is involved in building up our fleets. He and the people of Trident Battle Group have the most knowledge of Krake warship tactics. They're redesigning some of our ships with the Krake in mind. Plus they're working on a few new toys to use against them."

"That kid is pretty smart. That was a helluva thing he had to deal with."

"It was. Not everyone understands though. They think they do, but they really don't . . . never mind. He's doing fine," Connor said.

"That's good."

They both stood up.

"I'm glad we did this," Connor said.

"Anytime, Connor," Diaz said. "I mean that."

Connor breathed in and sighed. "I know you do."

7

Noah engaged the autopilot mode on the civilian aerial transport vehicle—C-cat for short—that flew over thick clouds of a pretty substantial storm currently en route to Sierra. It was always serene above storm clouds, which occasionally flashed with random bolts of lightning.

He leaned back in the pilot's seat. He still got the odd severe headache from his injury, and sometimes he had trouble finding the words to convey what he was thinking. It didn't happen anywhere near as often as it had a year ago, and while Noah thought it was frequent, everyone else assured him it wasn't. He'd been convinced they were biased because they wanted him to keep a positive frame of mind. It wasn't until Kara had shown him the data from his biochip, which tracked his overall well-being, including those symptoms and behaviors related to his injury, that he believed them. His wife knew how to get him to listen. It was hard for him to argue with the data, which showed a steady decline in those symptoms. He was healing.

Years after he'd taken a swan dive off a cliff and nearly died, he'd finally recovered enough to feel almost like his old self, but not quite. Despite rapid advancements in healing the body, there were limits to what medicine could do for the mind. The human brain had a particular way of doing things, and all their medical innovation could assist with that, but they could do only so much. The damaged parts of his brain simply had to learn new pathways to reach the old information, or he had to relearn some of those things. It had been a long and frustrating journey. But he was alive, and he was thankful for it every day.

A comlink chimed, and Noah answered it. The face of Oriana Evans appeared on the holoscreen. There was a Lunar Base icon in the upper right corner, showing where the comlink had come from.

"Oriana, it's so good to hear from you. How are things on base?" Noah asked.

She had long, dark hair and almost delicate cheekbones. She was just Sean's type.

"Hi, Noah. Are you traveling alone?"

"Yes, I am. Kara will be sorry she missed your call."

"Things are great here. Lots of new discoveries being made, which is why I'm contacting you. I have an invitation I'd like to extend to both you and Kara."

"Oh, is it, uh . . ." Noah began and stopped. He'd almost asked if it was a wedding invitation, but he didn't want to add any more fuel to that particular fire. "For what?" he added hastily.

"Smooth, Noah, very smooth," Oriana said and smiled. "I want to know if you're interested in coming to the lunar base for a few months. We're doing a lot of theoretical research here, and to be honest, I could really use your help."

He had thrown himself into everything he'd missed while he'd been in a coma. He'd reviewed all the mission reports and the overviews of the R&D publications resulting from those missions. He was no stranger to Oriana's work on space gates, subspace communications, and reverse engineering the Casimir reactor.

"A few months," Noah said and leveled a look at her.

Oriana tilted her head to the side. "Okay, six months at the very least."

Noah's eyebrows raced up his forehead. He hadn't spent that kind of time at the lunar base since the Vemus War. He looked away from the holoscreen for a moment. "I'm not sure. Six months is a long time." He paused for a few moments and then looked back at Oriana. "Have you figured out how to teleport anyone yet?"

Oriana chuckled. "No. Have you?" she asked.

This had been a bit of an ongoing joke between them.

Noah shook his head. "I don't think it's true teleportation. But I keep banging my head against the wall when it comes to how the Ovarrow stumbled onto something like that. We don't even know where the other half of the town is where they conducted their original experiments. I doubt we'll ever find it."

He had other ideas, but there just hadn't been time to pursue them. He knew that if he and Kara went to the lunar base, they'd probably be up there for a lot longer than six months.

"You don't need to decide anything right now. I just wanted to ask the question."

"I'd need to talk about it with Kara."

"Of course," Oriana said. "There's been a lot of R&D in CDF warship redesign going on up here. I know a lot of that stuff is right up your alley. I've read all the work you did to prepare for the Vemus War."

Noah knew Oriana meant well. There were a lot of people, mostly scientists, who had expressed appreciation for some of the breakthroughs he'd been involved in. What none of them knew was that there were a lot of sleepless nights involved in those breakthroughs, and most of them had occurred right at the end when the Vemus had almost killed them all. He wasn't in any rush to regain that former glory. He liked where he was. He liked having a home at Sanctuary and maintaining offices in Sierra and New Haven.

"I'll give it some serious thought. I promise," Noah said.

"That's all I can ask. Will you be returning to Sanctuary soon?"

Noah was about to answer, but he stopped himself. "I'm taking a short trip to Delphi."

Oriana caught the hesitation in his tone, and her eyes tightened. Then her expression smoothed back to normal. "Oh, I see."

He had no doubt that she understood. Lars was being held in Delphi, and he had killed Oriana's brother. No amount of facts could ever outweigh the loss of family.

"I shouldn't keep you any longer then. I hope you and Kara do decide to come. I really do. We could use your help here, Noah," Oriana said.

He nodded a little. "Thanks for the invite. I'll be in touch in a few days."

"Okay. Until next time."

"Oh, and tell Sean I said not to work so hard."

"I don't think that's possible, but I'll tell him."

Noah smiled, and the comlink closed. It was more than a little tempting to relocate to the lunar base for a time, but he couldn't leave now. He had his own work to do. Besides, he could help them more from down here with access to all his resources. He'd still discuss it with Kara, but leaving New Earth right now didn't seem like the best choice for him. Over the years he'd learned to trust his instincts, and they were advising him to stay put.

8

NOAH LANDED his C-cat on the outskirts of Delphi. The incarceration center was a secure facility, established to house the colonists involved in the rogue group activities led by Meredith Cain. At one point, there had been several hundred colonists detained here as they awaited their trials. Case by case, their actions had been reviewed and justice had been served, but there were still over a hundred detainees left. And there was one person in particular he was determined to see.

He had witnessed a few of those trials and had been called upon to give a statement. He'd been there when Meredith Cain and Kurt Johnson were sentenced to exile, along with many of the other ringleaders. They'd been given survival equipment and were then flown to an isolated island surrounded by a vast ocean where they were being monitored. Once their exile was served, they'd be allowed to leave the island and return to the continent. However, this didn't guarantee them access back into any of the colonial cities.

He recalled the day Meredith Cain had been sentenced to exile. She'd glared at everyone in the courtroom, and her contemptuous gaze froze on him with searing anger. "You!" she growled. "Everyone would have been better off if you had died on those cliffs, Noah Barker. You think you've—"

Whatever else she'd been about to say had been cut off when the security agents immobilized her with stun batons.

In the days following, Noah wondered if that nutcase had set some nefarious event in motion to exact her revenge on him, but nothing ever happened. He'd taken precautions just the same.

Noah walked through the civilian entrance and told the person behind the desk whom he was there to see. About thirty minutes later, he was in one of the private visitation rooms that contained two chairs and a rectangular table. The room was located along the outer wall of the building and had a small window where sunlight shone through. The door on the opposite side of the room opened, and Lars Mallory was escorted inside. He wore a dark gray jumpsuit. Lars was a tall man like his father and could easily look eye to eye with Connor. He'd lost his outdoorsman tan, but he hadn't let his physical conditioning slip. If fact, he appeared solid, as if he had more muscle to him than was readily apparent beneath his jumpsuit.

The guard removed Lars's restraints and gave Noah a friendly nod before leaving the room.

"Hello, Noah. I figured you'd be otherwise occupied," Lars said.

"I wanted to see how you were doing."

They sat down in chairs across from each other, and Lars

folded his hands in front of him, resting them on the table. He just looked at Noah for a few moments.

"I heard your trial was coming up soon," said Noah.

"It is."

"Are you worried?"

Lars leaned back in his chair and sighed. "They don't know what to do with me. I gave them all the intel I could to end it, and it all panned out for them."

"And yet you didn't try to negotiate for a lighter sentence," Noah added.

Lars frowned and shook his head. "I got what I wanted. I negotiated for the safety of my people. And in return, I gave them everything. I wasn't going to ask for leniency after we'd already made a deal."

Noah shook his head. "Aren't you worried you'll be exiled?"

Lars's gaze flicked to the window, and he breathed deeply before turning back to Noah. "I'm guilty of all their charges. I don't see how I wouldn't be exiled, to be completely honest with you."

"You were manipulated by Meredith Cain. She recruited you. She brought you into that . . . *group.*"

"She might've recruited me," Lars said, "but I did those things. I tortured the Ovarrow to get information from them. I hid data from Field Ops and Security. I leveraged their assets to give me what I needed, and I put trackers on comlink traffic, both civilian and CDF-encrypted channels. I also recruited people for Meredith."

Noah remembered trying to figure out who had been spying on them. He'd been squaring off against Lars and hadn't even known it at the time. "It's not that simple," he said. "She used your frustration to get you to do those things. That has to count for something."

Lars shook his head. "It doesn't make me innocent, Noah. Believe me, I've had this conversation with my father, my counselor, and my defense attorney. So what if I'm exiled?"

Noah pressed his lips together and looked away briefly. "Hurting the Ovarrow was wrong. If you tell them you regret doing it, they might be more lenient and allow you to stay in the colony."

Lars looked at Noah for a long moment as the seconds ticked by. His gaze became cold, almost brittle, with a hard edge. "I *don't* regret what I did to them. Don't you understand? It was necessary. You might not approve of the methods, but they did yield results. We're better prepared for the Krake because of them."

Noah clenched his teeth together. "I know you think you believe it, and you sound like you've rehearsed that little speech in your head a lot. Perhaps you even said the same thing to your father, but you're wrong. Cain got into your head."

"I do believe it. I don't regret what I did to the Ovarrow. We can't trust them."

"You're wrong."

Lars raised his chin and his lips flattened. Then he stood up. "I think maybe I should leave," he said, then walked over to the door and banged on it a few times.

Noah stood up and accessed his wrist computer. The guard appeared at the door but was unable to open it.

"You don't get to leave that easily," Noah said and opened a comlink to the guard. "We'll need a few more minutes. It's fine."

The guard looked at him through the window, and Noah held up his wrist, showing he had the room locked down. Then the guard left, and Noah had no doubt that in a few minutes, they'd cancel his override.

Lars leaned back against the wall and looked up at the ceiling. "What are you doing, Noah?" he asked tiredly.

"You've built this wall around you, Lars. The person I know —the friend I grew up with—wasn't okay with hurting anybody. I know you hurt the Ovarrow. And I know you work hard convincing yourself it was necessary and that you were working to protect all of us. But don't stand there and tell me you don't regret it—that you looked into the eyes of intelligent beings, knowing you were causing them pain, and you have no regrets. It's a shield, Lars. Because if you admitted regret for what you did, that would call into question *all* the things you did, and you'd have to realize that maybe you went too far."

Lars's mouth formed a grim line, and he regarded Noah coldly.

"Exiling you to some island isn't going to help you."

Lars shook his head slightly. "It's not about helping me. It's about justice."

"What if they don't exile you? What if you're allowed to stay under some kind of probation?"

Lars considered it for a few moments. "It doesn't matter. I'll never have security clearance again."

"You don't need security clearance to help protect the colony. But before any of that, you have to admit the truth to yourself."

Lars looked away from him and glared toward the window.

"Admit it. Just admit it to yourself at least. It's not going to hurt you to admit you regret what you did," Noah said and stepped toward Lars.

"It doesn't matter," Lars said, his voice sounding raspy.

The locking mechanism of the door opened, and the guard came in.

"It *does* matter. It's the only thing that does, Lars."

The guard took Lars into custody and escorted him out of the room, but Noah remained. For a few seconds there he'd thought he was beginning to reach him. Noah wanted to help his friend see reason, but he wasn't sure if he could.

He sighed.

It didn't mean he'd stop trying. He looked down at the chair. Suddenly irritated, he shoved it toward the table and left the room.

9

CONNOR WALKED into the Colonial Research Institute at Sanctuary. The institute had expanded over the years as more specializations were added. It now rivaled other more well-established schools on New Earth and was still a popular choice among new students, despite its unfortunate acronym. Connor had seen more than a few students cry at some point, but he was also sure it had nothing to do with the name "CRI."

The recovery institute Connor had helped establish here at Sanctuary had a close partnership with the CRI. Connor still remembered when he'd proposed the project to Ashley Quinn while she'd been governor of the colony. He'd done it to help veterans of the CDF, which was later expanded to include Field Ops and Security. A few years later, there was another expansion to include civilians who suffered from PTSD. The model for the Sanctuary Recovery Institute had been copied and implemented at other colonial cities. Connor's involvement was minimal these days, especially since he'd rejoined the CDF. Diaz volunteered there on a regular basis and was involved with organizing events for veterans.

Connor walked through the halls of the CRI and heard a heated discussion coming from one of the laboratories. The young researcher who was standing in the doorway turned, and her eyes widened at seeing Connor.

"I'm sorry about that," she said and gestured toward the room.

He waved it off. "No worries."

She walked back into the room, and Connor heard her urge the others to calm down, then suggested they all go get some coffee.

He kept going, and he wasn't sure if it was because he'd heard coffee mentioned that he began to smell it. He rounded the corner and headed to the end of the corridor where Lenora's office was located. Someone was brewing a medium roast blend. It wasn't the dark and bitter Colonial Death Wish he'd taken a liking to, but it could do in a pinch.

A short distance ahead was an open door, and the sweet scent of freshly baked pastries wafted into the hall, making his stomach growl. Ian must have baked this morning and brought his wares in. Ian Malone was a field researcher specializing in seismology. They had teamed up for a few field missions, exploring various regions of the continent. It would be good to catch up with him.

He was almost to Ian's office door when he heard Lenora's voice echoing down the hall.

"What do you mean the transport has been canceled?" Lenora asked with a slight rise in volume and a tone of irritation.

Connor quickened his pace, bypassing Ian's office, and headed straight to Lenora. "That was me," he said. "Don't bite their heads off. I've arranged for our transport."

Lenora gave him a slightly exasperated look. He should've told her, but he'd forgotten. He looked at her, offering a one-sided smile as an apology. She answered it.

"Never mind then," she said and closed the comlink. She arched an eyebrow. "When I invited you to come with me, I figured we'd use a standard Field Ops escort."

Connor nodded. "Yeah, I know that, but I have a squad with me. The Hellcat will get us there faster."

Lenora's full lips lifted, and her gaze narrowed playfully. "So, you'd like this to be a fast trip is what you're telling me?"

Connor grinned and shook his head slowly. "Yeah, sometimes when we're out there for a few days, you get kind of whiny and needy, and I just can't take it anymore."

"Is that so? I guess this is a good time to bring up what the sleeping arrangements will be on this trip. Separate tents," she said as if she was checking a box, turning her back to him to pick up a tablet computer from her desk.

Connor seized the moment to grab her from behind and swing her around. Lenora erupted into a gale of laughter. "I know exactly where I'm going to be sleeping," he said and set her down. She turned around and put her hands on his shoulders, smiling. Her eyes gleamed. When he was with Lenora, he was home.

She stepped away from him and walked around her desk, putting things into her backpack. "Is Nathan still insisting that you travel with a protective detail?"

"What can I say? I'm essential to the CDF. It's one of the perks that come with the job," Connor replied.

Lenora glanced away from him for a moment and powered off her holoscreen. "It's probably a good idea that they come."

"Why is that?"

"You never know what we'll run into out there."

"All right, now you've piqued my interest. What are we looking for?" he asked.

"Since we have better Ovarrow translators, we've been going back through the archives we found here," Lenora said, fastening her backpack. "Well, not just here—every site we've ever cataloged, but nothing really rivals or has the most intact systems as what we've found here at Sanctuary."

There was no one who knew the Ovarrow data archives better than Lenora. She had spent years here, and even though she'd collaborated on other research efforts outside Sanctuary, this was where it had all started.

Something in her tone gave him a mental jolt of excitement. "Wait a minute. Are you saying you found something?"

"Not exactly," she said.

"I thought the data analysts had done an exhaustive search on everything we collected so far after we brought home the new translators we got from the Krake," Connor said.

As they walked out of Lenora's office, he glanced toward Ian's door, but it was closed. He must have left.

"They did," Lenora said. "They've categorized things, and that data is still being analyzed. What did you expect them to find—something in big bold lettering that says 'The key to defeating the Krake is here'?"

He gave her a look and shook his head. Then he pretended to consider it for a moment and shrugged. "I would accept that. It would make things a lot easier. Could you make that happen?"

"Aren't you the one who says that if it's too easy, it probably means we missed something."

"Yeah," Connor said. "We need a breakthrough."

"Don't I know it, but no, we haven't found anything like that yet. In my experience, at least with any archaeological records, the recorded history isn't something that points a big sign at the data we're most interested in. No treasure maps here, but I found clues and some rumors about what the Ovarrow were doing in the final days of their war with the Krake. I can show it to you when we're en route, but it's . . ." Lenora paused for a moment, gathering her thoughts. "You have to understand—and you do better than most—but there was limited communication among the Ovarrow at the end of their war. There was a whole lot of mistrust, so what I have is just clues that the Ovarrow might have been holding Krake prisoners."

Connor did a double take and his eyes widened. "I love how you just casually throw that out there. This could be huge, Lenora."

She bit her lower lip a little and chose her words carefully. "I know it can have a major impact, but it also might be nothing. We might not find anything. I've chased a lot of red herrings over the years."

Connor nodded in understanding. "Why didn't the Ovarrow just send the data here?"

"Communications were spotty, and this place was a secret. The estimated timestamps for the entries were well after the Ice Age had already begun in earnest. I think we're lucky to have any references at all. Most of our searches into the Ovarrow data we've gathered focus on events that led up to the war they fought, but little focus has been on what came after. We know they went into the stasis pods—the ones that could anyway—

and you found a group that didn't, but *they* don't want anything to do with us."

"Brashirker," Connor said and pressed his lips together for a few seconds. "He did tell me that his ancestors had a working arch gateway. They tried to find the Krake home world but failed."

She nodded and tucked her long auburn hair behind her ears. "It was that report that got me thinking about this and looking in other places. The Ovarrow essentially staged a rebellion in the midst of their own catastrophic war. They destroyed gateways while attempting to reverse engineer Krake technology. I don't think it's that far of a stretch to consider that they had taken Krake prisoners and were attempting to glean some intelligence from them."

"Maybe we should bring a few of Senleon's people with us to help with the search," Connor said.

Lenora was quiet for a few moments as they walked. "I thought about it, but I think we shouldn't for right now. Sometimes it's difficult for the Ovarrow to revisit some of the old sites and not have a certain bias about them. The Ovarrow who went into stasis still remember the world they left behind. I'm not saying we should keep it a secret from them, but maybe we should bring them in after we do our own analysis."

"This is your project; I'm just here to help. We'll do this your way," Connor said.

The Ovarrow had soldiers who were working with the CDF for off-world missions. There was even cooperative military training occurring now for joint task forces. The Ovarrow population had nearly doubled in the past year as they built up their city to be able to accommodate those recovered from stasis pods. It was good that they'd managed to bring more Ovarrow out of stasis, but it took time for them to acclimate to an unfamiliar world. It also took time to build trust. Lenora, and especially Dash, had worked with the Ovarrow, but they weren't the only ones. Relationships were being built, and ever since Cerot had returned with Connor from their mission on the Krake world, the Ovarrow's attitude toward the colonists had begun to change for the better. There was more cooperation, and the Ovarrow had come to respect the colonists and the CDF. More and more Ovarrow were starting to believe that their best chance of surviving another war with the Krake was to work with the colonists. Their help had been instrumental to successful off-world missions, such as what they'd done with the Gesora.

"So how many sites are we going to then?" Connor asked.

"At least six to start with, and their locations aren't as far as you might've expected. We don't have to go to the other side of the continent where you encountered Brashirker, although it *is* several thousand kilometers from here."

"A more central region. Vitory told me those places were among the last to hold out. There had been a strong military presence there," Connor said and pursed his lips in thought. "I wonder if we'll find any equipment they could use."

"You never know. They were good at salvaging old equipment and making something new out of it."

They left the Colonial Research Institute's main building and headed across the campus toward the nearest landing platform.

"I haven't heard from Dash in a while," Lenora said.

"He's been assisting the CDF with off-world missions. He's

rather unique in that he has the expertise from all his Ovarrow research and he's also able to keep up with the physical rigors involved with those missions. He's not the only one. There have been others, and I think that's due in large part to him."

Lenora smiled. "So, you've got him recruiting for you."

"I can't do all the work now, can I?"

"I'd hate to see anything happen to him."

"You say that about all your former students."

Lenora grinned a little. "Not all students are the same, but there are a few of the good ones that kinda stick with you. Like how you feel about some of the soldiers you've trained. Do you remember what Sean was like in the beginning?"

"I'll never forget, but try not to worry. I have good people keeping an eye on Dash, and he can take care of himself."

"I know you do. I . . . It's a shame we can open a gateway between universes, and the only thing we seem to do is use it for war. There are, what, hundreds of worlds we intend to explore, but the primary objective is the Krake. And I get how important that is. I just wish it was different. I wish we could . . . I wish we didn't have to worry about the Krake anymore."

"Me too, Lenora."

Over the years he'd been with her, Connor had watched her come to understand some of the dangers that came along with his line of work, but that didn't make worrying about them any easier for her. Sometimes it came to the surface in a conversation, and he felt a slight pang of regret about it. It was an irrational thing, but he felt it anyway. He wanted to make Lenora happy, and he wanted them all to be safe. She wanted *him* to be safe. Connor knew he wasn't the only person to ever want to change things so the woman he loved wouldn't have to worry. She felt the same too. The best thing for him to do was to let her vent her feelings, even if there wasn't anything he could do about it.

He was glad he'd decided to take some time off to travel with her. In the years preceding the Vemus War, Connor had run himself ragged preparing their defenses and essentially creating the CDF. He'd alienated Lenora and his friends during that time, and it had nearly cost him everything. He wouldn't do that again. These precious moments were just as important as all the other efforts he was a part of to help defend the colony. Sometimes when Connor thought about the person he'd been during those times, he became more aware of just how far he'd come. He supposed he took a certain comfort in it. There were too many people who would never get that kind of chance, and now even more people were going to die in this war with the Krake. Maybe it would even cost him his life. If this happened, Connor wouldn't hesitate. If he could trade his life to prevent the Krake from attacking New Earth, he'd do it, but that didn't mean he'd throw his life away; it was just that he was willing to make the sacrifice. He wasn't the only one. Every soldier who put on the CDF uniform was willing to do the same.

The colonists were a lot different from the people he'd known back on Old Earth, and there were now generations of them here. They'd claimed a home on this planet, made their lives here, started families here. Connor had kept himself apart from all that for years, but not anymore. There'd been many reasons for this separation throughout his military career, whether it was duty and honor or necessity. But none of those reasons could hold a candle to the one that eclipsed them all—his family and his friends. New Earth was his home. It was the place where he'd truly started to live. That was why Connor was willing to take time to accompany Lenora on this trip. These were the moments that made all the work worthwhile.

He reached out and took Lenora's hand. Her eyes widened for a moment, and she smiled. She gave his hand a gentle squeeze, and they headed to the landing platform.

10

Over the next few days, they searched for hidden Ovarrow sites within the borders of one of their most powerful nation-states. The sparse landscape hardly indicated that this had all once been densely populated.

"I thought the places we'd be looking for would be easier to find, sir," Sergeant Benjamin Cook said.

Connor glanced at Cookie. He'd first met the young sergeant after the bridge collapsed in the Ovarrow city. Lenora had helped save his life.

"Are they that good at hiding things, sir?" Corporal Dugan asked.

"Sometimes," Connor replied. "Also, this entire landscape has been altered by glaciers."

They were finishing up another day of fruitless searching and had made camp for the evening. He glanced over to where Lenora stood, studying a map on a holoscreen. She was discussing something with Keras. On a secondary screen, they were reviewing the references that Lenora had found in the Ovarrow archives.

They'd just finished eating dinner, and they'd split up into clusters, talking around the two campfires. Connor loved camping, and it was also a popular pastime for colonists. They had recon drones patrolling the area, which were being monitored by the soldiers on watch.

"Yeah, but could the glaciers really change the landscape that much? To the point where we wouldn't be able to tell if we were standing on top of some kind of Ovarrow facility?" Lieutenant Doug Garfield asked. The CDF pilot was tall and lanky, with narrow shoulders.

"It depends," Connor replied. "The way it was explained to me was that it had to do with the geology of the surrounding area. If this place had been mainly bedrock, then when the glaciers traveled, they would've just formed over the top of it, but this area here would be considered soft. The soil underneath is quite deep. That's why the trees in this area are so tall. So, when the glaciers came through here, they literally pushed everything out of their path, and when they retreated, the same thing happened."

"How do you know so much about this, sir?" Cookie asked.

"We needed to learn it, or *I* needed to learn it when we were searching for Ovarrow bunkers. They were hidden and not always easy to find."

They had spent the last few days flying and surveying regions of the continent. They'd also explored select areas on foot but hadn't really found anything all that encouraging. Lenora was attempting to find places that were secret when the Ovarrow built them. They'd been built away from population centers like cities, so she was trying to triangulate the location based on rumors from a few hundred years ago. So much time had passed that most travel routes or anything resembling roads were gone. They had tasked a few satellites in the area to perform another topographical analysis of the region they were searching to help narrow down their search grid.

Lenora powered off the holoscreen and joined them.

"Dr. Bishop, are we there yet?" Cookie asked, drawling out the question with a grin. Several of the other soldiers joined in.

Lenora smiled. "Very funny," she said and sat down across from Connor. "We have a new site to go to tomorrow, and it looks promising."

"I hope so. Right now, we're striking out. We're oh for three," Connor said.

Lenora drank out of her canteen and then glanced at the group of men around the campfire. "I know you guys like a contest. I'll tell you what. If we don't find anything by lunchtime tomorrow, I'll let General Gates here pick the next destination, and you can vote on it."

Cookie and Dugan looked at Connor for a moment and then nodded.

"Ready, willing, and always able," Connor said.

Lenora gave him a knowing smile.

Keras closed her tablet computer and looked at Connor. She seemed to be considering whether or not to ask him a question. He waited her out.

"General Gates," Keras said formally, "with everything we've built here on New Earth, all our defenses that we have in place, if the Krake came here . . . I guess I'm just trying to understand how bad it would be. I know that when the Vemus attacked us, it was . . ." she paused for a moment before continuing. "I understand that they overwhelmed our defenses. So, what I'm trying to ask is that with what you and the rest of the CDF have built up in our defense, do we even need to worry about the Krake?"

The other soldiers around the campfire glanced at Connor and then focused their attention on the flames. Valerie Keras was an Ovarrow technical expert from the research institute.

"You're asking me whether you should be worried about the Krake. The answer is yes. The Krake concern all of us. But you're right. We *have* been building up our defenses, and we're doing everything we can to keep everyone safe," Connor said.

"Some people I know are worried that if the Krake find our world, they could wipe us out. I just don't know what to think about it," she said.

Connor looked at her for a few moments. He knew people were talking about it, as well they should, but he didn't want to scare the young woman. However, he didn't want to lie to her either. "We've been asked to consider contingency plans if things get really bad. You've heard of the new colony that's going to be set up on Alpha-Zeta-Seventy-Four?"

"I've heard of it. There are going to be only five thousand colonists selected to go though."

Connor nodded. "That's right, and part of the parameters are for them to get the colony up and running as quickly as possible but also to prepare for the possibility of more colonists arriving. They'll have years to prepare and advance warning thanks to recent breakthroughs in communication. Would you consider applying to be a colonial candidate for the new colony?"

Keras frowned in thought for a few seconds. "I don't know. I like New Earth, and my family is here."

He glanced around at the others. "Anyone else considering volunteering?"

There was a small chorus of noncommittal "maybes" interspersed among acknowledgments that they hadn't even considered it.

"What about you, sir, and ma'am?" Cookie asked Connor and then looked at Lenora.

Connor glanced at Lenora for a moment, and she gave him a slight shake of her head. She wouldn't leave New Earth. "We're not volunteering to go. Don't get me wrong. I think it's a tremendous opportunity, but I like it here too much."

Corporal Dugan sighed heavily. "I think I speak for most of us here, sir, and ma'am, but that makes us feel a lot better."

"Why is that?" Connor asked.

Dugan looked at him with an unwavering, determined gaze. "We need you, General."

The sentiment was echoed by the other soldiers, and Connor gave them a nod. They were part of the reason he'd returned to the CDF.

Connor stood up. "I think I'll take a short walk," he said and looked at Lenora with an unspoken invitation to join him.

She got to her feet. When they were far enough away from the others, she spoke. "You were never really comfortable with that sort of thing."

Connor raised his eyebrows questioningly.

"People admire you."

"Not all of them."

"Not everyone's perfect, love," Lenora said. "Tomorrow we'll have to get up early because there's a lot of ground to cover. This one is by what used to be a major city in the area."

"Has anyone been there before?"

"They've done preliminary scouting but nothing substantial. We had probes search the area years ago, and it looked like remnant ruins, but back then, we stuck mainly to settlements that were more easily accessible. What we're looking for is military in nature."

"All right, sounds good to me," Connor said and then added, "Did you know Keras was going to ask me those questions?"

"Yes, she asked me if it was all right if she asked a few questions about the CDF. I told her it was fine."

"Diaz said we should start having more kids."

Lenora snorted and gave him a playful sideways look. "Well, since Diaz wants it, that settles it."

Connor chuckled. "We haven't talked about it."

"I figured you had enough on your mind, and I'm pacing you," Lenora said. He arched an eyebrow toward her. "I'm not in any rush, Connor, and neither are you. I'm afraid Diaz is just going to have to wait."

"I'll let him know," he replied with mock severity.

"Do you think he'll be all right with our decision?"

"He'll just need time. He really had his heart set on it."

THE NEXT DAY, a few hours after sunrise, they'd found something. From overhead, the area had looked like a shallow forest, but they were able to see to the ground with relative ease. What they'd discovered was a network of paths that could only be artificial. Straight edges and ninety-degree angles only occurred when people made them that way—or, in this case, the Ovarrow.

They'd found a safe place for Lieutenant Garfield to land

the Hellcat and set off on foot. The winding path angled downward before opening up and becoming straight. The wind whistled through trees. Normally, descending pathways led to a river or stream, but not here. The path led downward because there had once been some kind of Ovarrow facility here. Collapsed rooftops packed tightly from sediment and overgrowth could be seen like the bones of a buried skeleton.

"I never expected it to look like this," Cookie said.

The path was gritty and coarse, as if the dirt was composed of more rock than actual soil. They reached the bottom, and the path leveled off. Deep tree roots were intertwined among the remnant Ovarrow buildings on either side of them. Connor glanced upward, and the gray skies looked to be a long way above them.

"Sanctuary was like this when we first discovered it," Connor replied.

They had six reconnaissance drones mapping the area, and it was proving to be extensive. He looked at Lenora. "I think we're going to need to split into two teams."

"Yeah, we'll be able to cover more ground that way. We may even want to camp down here tonight," Lenora said.

Connor heard a couple of the soldiers ask if she was serious, and they were quickly hushed. Lenora looked over at the soldiers.

"I have allergies, ma'am," Murray said and sniffled.

"So do I," Lenora replied, knowing that Murray was joking.

"Did someone say they have allergies?" Corporal Dugan said, looking at Murray. "I've got the perfect cure for that. Come with me," he said, and the two jogged ahead, scouting the area.

Connor heard Dugan tell Murray about how exercise was a cure for allergies. They eventually reached an area where there were quite a few paths branching off from the one they were walking on.

"All right, everyone, gather around," Connor said. When they did, he continued. "We're going to split up into two groups. Sergeant Cook, I want you to escort Ms. Keras here and take Green, Jones, and Yemshi," he said, bringing up a partial map based on the recon drone feeds. "Looks like there's a central area here where we can meet. Everyone else is with me." He glanced at Lenora. "Lead the way, Dr. Bishop."

Keras came over to Lenora. They exchanged a few words, and then she rejoined the second group.

As they continued, they noticed that many of the buildings they passed had collapsed and were so overgrown with thick, thorny vines that anything inside had long since been destroyed.

"We need to look for access below ground. Anything that's been on the surface here isn't going to be salvageable," Lenora said.

Connor nodded. "It looks like there's a bigger building not far from here. One of the drones tagged it."

She had cross-referenced the location of this site against any of the known Ovarrow cities they'd found in the records, and there wasn't any record of the site on any map they'd found so far.

"The Ovarrow wouldn't have marked military sites," Connor said as they came to a stop in front of a large building. The walls looked like they'd been reinforced with thick plating that could only be used for armor. Whoever built this place had wanted it to be protected.

He watched as Corporal Dugan set thermite charges to burn through the lock on the door. Connor sent one recon drone to patrol the area around them while tasking the remaining two to help them explore inside.

As they went through the door, the corridors beyond reminded him of that first bunker where they'd encountered Syloc such a long time ago. So much had changed since then.

The musky scent of stagnant water mixed with rotting vegetation quickly gave way to stale air. Dark mold covered the walls in a porous buildup over small puddles of water that dripped down from cracks in the roof. They worked their way through the facility, but Connor didn't think they'd actually reached it yet. They were still walking down one of several interconnecting corridors.

"What do we expect to find down here?" Murray asked Lenora.

"I'm hoping we'll find some data repositories for what happened here," she replied.

"And in them, you're looking for a reference to the Krake?" Murray asked.

"I hope so. Don't worry, I'm not going to do the analysis here. We'll take a copy of the data we find, and I'll do the analysis back at Sanctuary."

They were all quiet after that. They found rooms, but they were empty, and no one could begin to guess what they'd been used for. The facility didn't have power in any of the rooms they found, but they'd brought portable power generators with them to open the doors. Lenora had the latest translator software on her PDA and had distributed it to their group. Connor had his on as well, and the translation of the Ovarrow language automatically showed on his internal heads-up display.

"It's this way," Lenora said.

"How can you be sure?" he asked.

"Because I recognize the layout. I think the archives at Sanctuary were modeled after this place."

Connor had one of the drones fly ahead of them to scout the area and then launched another one to scout a different path just in case they found something else. So far, the drones had found various storage rooms filled with Ovarrow weapons that probably wouldn't work anymore. All their power sources were depleted. He began to wonder if any of the Ovarrow had ever planned on coming back to this place.

"General, I'm getting a power reading up ahead," Dugan said.

Connor gave them a nod, and Corporal Dugan gestured for Murray to follow him. Connor glanced at Lenora. He could remember a time when she'd been impatient with efforts to secure the area, but now she knew the value of a little extra precautionary effort. She wore a sonic hand blaster on her belt, but the rest of them were armed with AR-71s, which were standard issue for the CDF.

A little farther on, they found a room with multiple consoles inside. Most of the consoles in the room were dead and beyond repair, but there was a central console that had a small power supply still available to it. The Ovarrow mesh screen had deteriorated and was unusable. Connor squatted down in front of the control panel and used his combat knife to pry it open. Lenora squatted next to him and connected a data relay device.

"I have an active connection. Downloading the data to my PDA," Lenora said.

Dugan and Murray joined them. "How can anything be stored on that console? It looks like it's falling apart," Murray said.

"That's because the data isn't actually stored in the console. It's linked to another area," Connor said.

Lenora monitored the download on her PDA and then glanced up at Connor. "We should look for the data storage archive too. There might be repositories that this console doesn't have access to but that we could bring back with us. If they're too fragile, I can try a few things to get the data we need."

Connor nodded. "Is there any way to tell whether the data is different from what we already have?"

Lenora had begun to reply when two of their drone video feeds suddenly went dark. Both Dugan and Murray turned and faced the door.

"Sir?" Dugan said, looking at Connor.

"The feed is gone, Corporal. Something took out the drones."

"Yes, sir."

The two CDF soldiers went to the door and checked the corridor just outside.

Connor looked down at Lenora. "How much longer?"

"It's almost finished," she replied without looking up. "What happened?"

"We had two recon drones go down at the same time."

"I guess that rules out a malfunction."

Connor nodded. He brought up each of the drones' video feeds before they'd gone off-line but couldn't see anything. He had maintained a comlink connection to the recon drone that was patrolling outside the building, and that one was still working.

"The one outside is still functioning . . ." he began to say and then stopped. "Scratch that. It's down as well. We have to go."

Lenora took her backpack off and pulled out a small comlink. She attached it to the Ovarrow console, checked her PDA, and stood to put her backpack on. "We can go. I've connected the comlink to the PDA to get the rest of the data."

Connor checked his AR-71 and put his MPS into protect mode. Lenora did the same with her suit.

He walked toward the door. "Have you been able to contact the others?"

"Negative, sir," Dugan replied.

"All right, let's get out of here. You two are on point," Connor said.

The two CDF soldiers led the way, and Connor gestured for Lenora to walk ahead of him so he could bring up the rear. They hadn't detected any ryklars in the area or any Ovarrow, for that matter. Ryklars sometimes hunted the recon drones when they weren't in stealth mode, and they hadn't put the drones in stealth mode. But the drones were able to project the ryklar deterrent signal, so that should've taken care of any predators lurking in the area. He didn't think there were ryklars down here. It was too quiet.

"What do you think took out the drones?" Lenora asked.

"I don't know. Maybe this place had some kind of countermeasure set up . . . you know, some kind of defense," Connor said. He didn't like that they weren't able to reach the others. The colonists needed to develop and distribute handheld subspace communicators. Right now, they had them only on ships and vehicles.

They were all quiet as they made their way back to the main corridor. Connor saw Lenora check her PDA a few times, monitoring the progress of the data dump.

11

Something else was in the corridors with them. Connor and the others heard movement through the tunnels—just snippets of sound but something they couldn't ignore. Even with enhanced vision in the dim light, none of them had actually seen whatever it was.

Lenora put her PDA into her pocket and pulled out her sonic hand blaster. They hurried down the corridor, pausing at each intersection. Murray and Dugan cleared the corners and then gestured for the rest of them to follow.

They repeated this four more times, and then Murray came to a halt. "Gah!" he said, peering down one of the adjacent corridors.

Dugan turned toward him and aimed his weapon. "What is it?"

"I don't know. I thought I saw something moving down that way."

Connor joined them and looked down the long, dark

passageway. It was clear. "What did you see?"

Murray looked at him. "That's just it, sir. I saw it for only a second. It was toward the ceiling."

"There's a corridor that runs parallel over there," Lenora said quietly.

Connor brought up the partially finished map from the recon drones' scouting. "Looks like there are multiple corridors all around here."

Dugan glanced at Connor. "Ryklars?"

It was a good guess. Ryklars could mask their body heat from thermal imagers and were known to stalk their prey.

"Stay sharp," Connor said and looked at Murray. "Cover our six."

The CDF private took up a position at the rear, and they continued onward, moving slow and steady. If there really were ryklars here, they could be circling, waiting to ambush.

They approached the next intersection, and Connor slowed down. He glanced at Dugan, who shook his head. Connor didn't hear anything either. They cleared the corners and moved on. Just one more section of intersecting corridors before they reached the long corridor that led to the exit.

"Be ready," he whispered, and Dugan nodded.

He had observed ryklars in the wild for years, and he'd witnessed the hunting tactics that the deadly creatures executed with cunning efficiency. Connor had seen ryklar packs teach young hunters to stalk prey. They preferred to attack when least expected. Just when their unsuspecting quarry thought they were safe, the ryklars would attack with sudden ferocity, blindsiding their prey.

Nearing the corridor that led to the exit, both Connor and Dugan slowed down, then stopped and waited. Murray moved up behind Dugan on the opposite side of the corridor, hugging the wall, while Connor and Lenora were on the other side. Connor glanced back at her. She looked at him and bobbed her head in a small movement.

They crept to the edge of the corridor. Once they were in position, Connor and Dugan spun around the corner, weapons held ready.

Nothing.

The corridor was empty. They didn't linger for more than a few seconds before heading toward the exit. It was a straight shot right to the outside. Connor saw the open doorway up ahead and slowed down. There was no need to rush outside. Whatever had been stalking them hadn't come any closer. They waited there for a few moments.

"I'm not able to establish a link to any of the recon drones," Murray said.

They stepped outside, keeping their weapons ready, and made a quick sweep of the area.

"Clear," Dugan said, and Murray echoed the same.

Connor opened a comlink to the other team, and Sergeant Cook answered.

"What's your status, Sergeant?"

They began walking down the pathway, and Connor looked at Dugan. "Get a lock on their position," he told the corporal.

"General," Sergeant Cook said, "we were exploring the area when some flying creatures attacked our recon drones. They were large enough to take them out. They swarmed them, forcing them to land, and pounded on them until they stopped working. I don't think we should camp here tonight. There's been a group of those things following us, and more are gathering. Have you seen them?"

"Negative. We were inside one of the buildings when our drones were taken out. We didn't get a good look at what did it," Connor replied and scanned the upper levels of the buildings nearby. In the shadows, there was a flutter of movement. "Hold, Corporal," he said and gestured toward where he'd seen the movement.

"I see them, sir."

"We have company too," Connor said to Sergeant Cook on the comlink. "We're trying to get a better look at them."

They were reptilian in appearance, with wedge-shaped heads and large mouths, which probably had rows of razor-sharp teeth. Connor's internal heads-up display showed infrared on one half. Their bodies glowed with the orange glow of their body heat. One of the creatures walked on bent wings, which looked awkward. These creatures didn't spend much time on the ground. Their rib cages expanded deep in their chests, and there was a grouping of flutters from gill-like slits on their necks. They looked to be about a meter from head to hind quarters. Then Connor caught sight of their long tails that more than doubled the creatures' body lengths.

One of the creatures saw them and grunted a warning to the others. The group swung their heads toward Connor and the others. Their forward-facing eyes glared at them, and the grim set of their mouths appeared moments from shrieking.

"There are more behind us," Lenora said.

Connor turned and saw that twelve of the flying creatures had flown out of the building they'd just come from. Their leathery skin displayed a wide range of complex, earth-toned color schemes. They hovered in the air for a moment and then flew toward them, roaring as they came.

Connor and the others scattered to the side.

"Yemshi, get that deterrent signal up now," Sergeant Cook said, his voice coming over the comlink. "General, we have ryklars in the area," he said and paused for a moment. "What do you mean it's not working?"

Connor couldn't hear the other end of the conversation and waited. He mouthed the word "ryklars" to the others. The flying creatures swooped past them and circled around.

"Sir, the ryklars are not responding to the deterrent signal."

"Are they closing in on you?" Connor asked.

"Negative. They don't seem agitated . . . uh, they aren't red-faced. There are eight of them just a hundred meters away."

A few moments later, Sergeant Cook marked the location of the ryklars on the map, and Connor was able to see it. He looked at Dugan. "Check to the west."

Dugan and Murray went a short distance away from them to the nearest adjacent path.

Dugan opened a comlink to Connor. "No contact," he whispered.

Connor highlighted a waypoint on the map for Sergeant Cook. "Can you reach that location?"

"I think so, sir."

"All right, we'll meet you there."

"Sir, what should we do about the ryklars?" Sergeant Cook asked.

Ryklars could cover a hundred meters in a few seconds in an open area.

"If they don't attack, then don't engage them. We don't know how many of them are here," Connor replied.

"Understood, sir," Sergeant Cook said.

The comlink severed. Connor sent their coordinates to Lieutenant Garfield, who had waited with the Hellcat. After

Connor received confirmation from Lieutenant Garfield, they began heading toward the waypoint. They stayed close to the walls of the pathway, and the flying creatures followed overhead. The narrow pathway prevented the creatures from dive-bombing them.

Connor glanced at Lenora. She held her weapon ready and stayed close by. "Never a dull moment, is there?" he said.

"Only if our luck changes," she replied. "Seriously, this stuff only happens to you." Lenora smiled at him.

The pathway ended, and they had to move along a wider thoroughfare. The flying creatures shrieked and dove closer and closer. Their high-pitched screams echoed all around them.

"They sound like damn banshees," Murray shouted.

"Watch out," Lenora said.

Connor spun around and brought his weapon up. There was a trio of the creatures flying right toward them, their claws extended. Connor aimed and fired. Three controlled bursts of hypervelocity darts tore into the creatures, and they crashed, tumbling to the ground. Dugan and Murray fired their weapons. The banshees flailed for a few moments and then became still.

Ahead of them, six ryklars stood in a phalanx formation. The spotted predators squatted down and watched them intently, their chests heaving as they drew breath. They had a set of smaller arms toward the front and much longer arms behind those. Thick, stubby tentacles hung down, making their hideous faces long and menacing. At least the tentacles were a deep gray like the fur of their spotted hides.

They were nearly two hundred meters away from them.

"They don't look agitated," Lenora said.

If their bearded tentacles had been red, the ryklars would have been in a highly agitated state, and they'd attack anything that moved.

"They're agitating me," Dugan said.

"Hold your fire," Connor said. "Someone is controlling them."

He peered at them, and his neural implants enhanced his vision. Connor looked at the ryklars' ears, almost expecting that they would be mutilated like the ones they'd found before under Brashirker's control. But these ryklars weren't mutilated. One of the ryklars cocked its head to the side, and Connor saw a shiny piece of metal.

"They've got a transmitter on the sides of their heads," Connor said.

They backed away and went down a side street. On each adjacent path they passed, they saw more ryklars. They were being herded.

They kept moving and heard sounds of weapons-fire nearby. They started running, and Connor heard someone scream in the distance. They rounded the corner and saw several dead ryklars lying on the path. Sergeant Cook and Keras were lending a hand to Private Yemshi, pulling him back to cover. Connor and the others joined them.

"They attacked us from above," Sergeant Cook said. "They seem to be coordinating with those flying creatures."

"Is anyone else hurt?" Connor asked.

"Negative, sir."

Connor opened a comlink to the Hellcat. "What's your ETA?"

"ETA is eight minutes, sir," Garfield replied.

"Understood. Be advised the area is hot," Connor said.

He looked at the others. "The Hellcat is on its way. We need to hold out here. Dugan, take Green and Murray and hold that position across the street."

They were at a major intersection. The paths had opened pretty wide, and there was more than enough room for the Hellcat to set down when it arrived. Connor told Lenora to stay back while he and Cookie went to the corner.

Without recon drones, he couldn't get a bird's-eye view of the area. Overhead, the flying creatures circled in an ever-expanding group. There were dozens of them now, with more on the way. Two separate groups of ryklars were also on approach, using the buildings for cover and preventing them from getting a clear shot.

"Conserve your ammunition. Controlled bursts only," Connor said.

More ryklars arrived.

"General," Sergeant Cook said, "are those Ovarrow moving with the ryklars?"

Connor looked where Cookie had gestured with the end of his rifle. The Ovarrow had a distinctive profile. They were tall, with long limbs and pointy protrusions on their shoulders and elbows. These were covered in a pale green metallic armor. They carried long rifles, similar to what the Mekaal used.

The Ovarrow soldiers sprinted in the midst of the ryklars, completely at ease among the deadly creatures. They moved with precision and a soldier's discipline, and they had Connor and the others surrounded.

Connor activated the Ovarrow translator and stepped out from cover until he stood in the middle of the intersection.

"We are not your enemy. We didn't realize this was your territory," Connor said.

The Ovarrow soldiers went quiet, and then there was a burst of sound from their ranks.

"My name is Connor Gates. You're not the first Ovarrow we've met. Which one of you is the warlord?"

One of the groups of Ovarrow soldiers spoke quietly among themselves for a few moments. Then one of them came forward. He removed his helmet and his jade, feline-like eyes narrowed. "How do you speak our words?"

"We use a translator interface," Connor replied, staying where he was.

"Where did you get the translator?"

"From the Krake."

The Ovarrow soldier went rigid. "The Krake are here?"

The soldiers began focusing their attention on the skies overhead, attempting to peer through the tangle of trees above them.

"They're not here," Connor said quickly. "They don't know about this world."

The warlord studied him. "They once knew this world. They will be back."

Connor regarded the Ovarrow. "Yes, they will."

"I am called Kasmon, and we are the Konus." He looked from Connor to the others for a few moments. "Why have you come here?"

"We came here looking for information about the Krake."

The Konus soldiers still had their weapons pointed at Connor and the others.

"How did you find this place?" Kasmon asked.

"Tell your soldiers to lower their weapons, and we'll do the same," Connor replied.

Kasmon regarded him with a hard glare. Then he turned

away and gestured for the soldiers to stand down. Connor followed suit. He also sent a message to Lieutenant Garfield, ordering him to stay back. He'd call in the Hellcat if they needed it.

"I've done as you asked," Kasmon said.

Connor first explained how they arrived on the planet almost fifteen years ago, how they'd explored the ruins, found arch gateways, and encountered the Krake. Then, he told the Ovarrow how they'd found references to this place with indications they might have had Krake prisoners during the war.

Kasmon didn't look like he believed Connor, who then showed him the translator interface. The Ovarrow studied it for a few seconds and then gestured for one of his soldiers to come over. They both examined the interface.

"You might have encountered the Krake, but you could also have found their tech," Kasmon said. "We recognize their technological footprint from our own archives. What I'd like to know now is whether or not you are allied with the Krake."

"We're not," Connor replied. "We've fought them. We've used the arch gateway and constructed our own space gates based on what we found. I can share this information with you. We're not here to fight with you. We're trying to find the Krake home universe. We've encountered other Ovarrow who are helping us."

"The gateways were destroyed."

"They weren't. We found one at the bottom of a lake and the remnants of the space gate elsewhere," Connor said and paused for a moment. "Far away from here."

Kasmon seemed to consider this.

"We've been on this planet for over fifteen years. We've never seen you before," Connor said.

"We work to keep our presence a secret, preparing for when the Krake return. You said you've encountered other Ovarrow. That means you must have found our stasis pods."

"Yes, we have. We've helped other Ovarrow come out of stasis."

"You've brought Ovarrow out of stasis? Where are they?"

"They are living in their own settlement. Their own city," Connor replied.

"How many of them are there?" asked Kasmon. Ovarrow had different ways of showing excitement, and having worked closely with them for the past year, Connor could tell Kasmon was keenly interested in this.

"Over sixty thousand have been brought out of stasis. How many Konus are there?"

Several of the Konus soldiers had joined them and were listening to the conversation. Lenora and the others had also joined, standing by Connor. The Konus soldiers gave a startled reaction to the number of Ovarrow Connor had mentioned.

Kasmon turned back to Connor. "There are many of us. We've brought Ovarrow out of stasis as well. The number of Konus is over one million citizens."

Connor's eyes widened. One million Ovarrow. Could Kasmon be lying? Where could they hide that many?

As if sensing his doubt, Kasmon continued. "We live underneath where it's safe. We have entire cities and a network of tunnels throughout this entire region. We are highly interested in meeting the Mekaal. They are a faction of Ovarrow we've heard of. Soldiers. They can help with the fight against the Krake."

Connor used his PDA to create a holographic screen that showed the continent. He then highlighted the region they were in and then the general region of where the colony was located. "This is where we live, and the Ovarrow city is within that region."

Kasmon studied the map.

"Why did you attack us? Why didn't you just try to contact us?" Connor asked.

"We didn't know who you were. We knew you used technology similar to the Krake and could be allied with them. If you are open to this, I would like to show you our city. You said you were seeking allies to fight the Krake."

Connor didn't like the flimsy excuse, but he did want to see their city. They might have just gotten off on the wrong foot. "I'd like that very much," he replied.

Kasmon shared the coordinates of where they were heading, and Connor forwarded that to Garfield. The Hellcat flew overhead, and Kasmon watched it with a bit of awe. There were over a hundred Konus soldiers escorting them. The ryklars and the flying creatures had left the area.

Kasmon told Connor how a group of them had emerged from their stasis pods over forty years ago. The stasis pods suffered some damage, and many Ovarrow had died. Connor knew this had to do with the faulty stasis technology the Ovarrow had used. Kasmon also told him about how some Ovarrow had rapidly aged after coming out of stasis. However, the survivors continued to rebuild. They sought out other bunker sites, and over the years, many Ovarrow had joined them.

Connor glanced at Lenora more than once. She listened to the conversation, as did Keras. The CDF soldiers were quiet and kept watch over the Konus soldiers. Connor was more comfortable being around so many Ovarrow soldiers since he had done so on many off-world missions. He knew Sergeant Cook was an excellent soldier and would keep a level head. Corporal Dugan would keep an eye on the other soldiers as well.

Throughout Connor's encounters with Ovarrow, they had been curious about human technology, but Kasmon was more interested in learning about the Mekaal. The Konus had mainly explored bunkers to the east.

"We've encountered Ovarrow far away on the eastern side of the continent, thousands of kilometers away from here," Connor said. He told Kasmon about Brashirker and the claim that they represented a group of Ovarrow who hadn't gone to stasis. They'd weathered the Ice Age.

"We've always wondered about that. There were rumors of groups of Ovarrow who banded together. We will try to find them as well," Kasmon said.

"We haven't been able to find them since the initial encounter. When they learned that we had encountered the Krake, they didn't want to get involved. I don't know how many of them are alive. They had adapted ryklars to be controlled like you did but using a different method."

"Different? How so?" Kasmon asked.

"We've encountered the ryklars before and are aware of the control signals used to command them. However, this group of Ovarrow didn't use implants like you do," Connor said and explained how the ryklars' heads had been mutilated so they couldn't hear the high frequency sound waves. Instead, they used flashes of different colored lights to control them.

"We began using implants on the ryklars after the great

migration. Old city sites were coming online, and defense protocols were commanding the ryklars to . . ." Kasmon paused for a moment and looked at Connor. "Ryklars were used to help fight our wars."

They continued onward, and Kasmon led them to a plain building that never would've been spotted from above. Inside, a massive opening led to a dark tunnel.

Lieutenant Garfield initiated a comlink, and Connor answered. "General Gates, there has been an emergency call for you to return to Sierra. It's from General Hayes."

Garfield sent the official orders, and Connor viewed them on his internal heads-up display. He had stopped walking, and Kasmon watched him.

"I'm afraid I must apologize. I can't go with you. I've been recalled," Connor said.

Kasmon frowned for a moment. The other Konus soldiers had paused and waited for Kasmon to give them an order.

"Once I tell my government about you," Connor said, "they'll want to send an official diplomatic envoy to meet you. I'm sure they'll get out here as soon as possible. Meanwhile, I can leave you with a way to communicate with us," Connor said.

"I don't understand what can be so important that you need to leave right away, but I do understand that orders are orders. We take them just as seriously as you do. I look forward to our next meeting," Kasmon said.

Connor had Lieutenant Garfield fly the Hellcat nearby and land. He then left a long-range comlink system with a standard Ovarrow interface they'd used with the Mekaal in the past.

"I'll need to discuss it with our own leadership, but in this instance, I'm confident about what they would say," said

Kasmon. "We have a common enemy in the Krake. And since we share this planet, we need to work together to defeat them."

After his experiences with all the Ovarrow he'd met on New Earth, Connor almost didn't know how to react to such a show of cooperation and an acknowledgment that the Krake were not only a threat, but something that could be overcome. Perhaps it was because the Konus had had over forty years to come to grips with their new lives. They had built themselves up in anticipation of continuing a fight with the Krake. It was almost refreshing.

"Until our next meeting," Connor said.

They returned to the Hellcat and walked up the loading ramp. Once they were airborne, he heard Murray talking to some of the other soldiers.

"I'm so glad we made it out of there. I wasn't sure if they were going to let us leave," Murray said.

"Did you see their reaction when General Gates told him we had to go?" Yemshi asked.

Connor glanced at Dugan and Cookie, and they both gave him a nod. "I think they were just as surprised to see us as we were to see them."

"It's probably that, sir," Cookie said.

Connor sat next to Lenora. "Were you able to get all the data off that console?"

"Yes. It must've finished sometime between when those flying creatures showed up and when the ryklars chased us into the Konus ambush," she said.

Connor's eyebrows raised. He knew that tone. Now that the danger had passed, she was allowing herself to digest what had happened. "You noticed that too."

Lenora nodded.

"I know what you mean, but the Ovarrow are aggressive when it comes to securing their territory. I've read reports of it from other world missions, and I've seen it myself."

She swallowed hard and then shook her head. "I'm just glad you were with us."

"Me too," Connor replied.

"I've been to countless Ovarrow ruins. Some of those expeditions had several hundred people, Field Ops included. Then I've been on others where it's just a handful of us. I figured with a CDF squad we'd be relatively safe," Lenora said, venting her frustration and fear.

"I thought we'd only find some abandoned ruins too. I don't know what to say, Lenora. No one can be prepared for everything."

She sighed. "I know, and you're right. I just haven't been in a situation like that since . . . it's been a while. I kept thinking about Lauren. You know."

Connor wrapped his arm around her shoulders in a hug.

"What's wrong with me? When did I become such an emotional mess?"

"You're not a mess. We have a family now. You're a mother. I feel the same way. There's nothing wrong with it, Lenora. It's natural. Hey," he said, "do you understand what I'm saying?"

Lenora nodded and then took a steadying breath. "I'm fine now," she said. "Do you know what the emergency recall was for?"

"It was just a recall. Nathan would have included more information if he needed to. I'm sure it's important but not . . . life-threatening."

"Okay. I'm not going to be able to do much in the way of analyzing this data until I get back to Sanctuary."

"Really? You're not going to dive right in here and now?"

Lenora chuckled. "No, and you can blame Noah for that. I get much better results when I upload the data to our systems back home. Much more processing and computational power. And, honestly, I'm fine with waiting until we get home."

Connor pursed his lips. "Wow, I mean, I never thought I'd see the day where you'd show that kind of patience."

She elbowed him in the side. "Jerk."

He grinned, but after a few moments, he started to think about their encounter with the Konus. He would have liked to have seen where they lived. Over a million Ovarrow here on New Earth! He didn't believe Kasmon was lying. All his encounters with the Ovarrow had allowed him to develop a keen sense of how they conducted themselves. Kasmon wasn't lying about how many Konus there were, but Connor did wonder whether Kasmon would've tried to stop them from leaving if the Hellcat hadn't shown up. There had been a moment where the soldiers had been poised to take action. He hadn't missed it, and neither had the others. But the fact that Kasmon had all but promised an alliance with the colony to unite against the Krake made Connor pause his suspicions.

He wondered how Senleon and Vitory would react when they learned that so many of their people were alive and thriving. What would this mean for them? Would they seek to join the Konus, or would they want to remain independent? Connor really didn't know and couldn't guess. Too many of the Ovarrow that had come out of stasis carried with them the nightmares of a collapsing civilization. It would take them time to move on and rebuild. Perhaps working with the Konus would help the Mekaal adjust to life after the stasis pods.

12

CONNOR MANAGED to snatch a little bit of sleep on the Hellcat as it flew them to the CDF base at Sierra, and after it landed, he and Lenora went to their on-base apartment. He had some time before he had to report to the Security Council meeting—time enough to take a shower and put on a clean uniform. By the time he was out of the shower, he found Lenora asleep in their bed. Connor quietly left their apartment and headed to the roof, where an aircar waited for him.

It was just after nine in the evening by the time he arrived at the capitol, where they were meeting in the main congressional chambers near Governor Wolf's office. He could hear the low buzz of multiple conversations before he even walked into the room.

He saw Bob Mullins speaking quietly with Selena Brown and Rex Coleman, and Connor frowned. The legislative and judicial branches of the colonial government usually didn't attend Security Council meetings. He spotted Nathan and went over to him. He didn't see Governor Wolf at all.

"Sorry I had to cut the holiday short," Nathan said.

"What's going on?" Connor asked.

"All I know right now is that Governor Wolf collapsed yesterday. She's been at the intensive care unit at Sierra Medical Center."

Connor's eyes widened. "Is she all right?"

"I don't know."

Dana Wolf was an older woman, but she was in excellent health. Connor couldn't think of anything that would knock her off her feet for long. She worked hard and was remarkably resilient. She reminded Connor of Tobias Quinn and was a worthy successor.

"Can everyone please quiet down," Mullins said. "We're going to start the emergency session now."

The people in the room found their way to their seats, and those who were in attendance from afar quieted down.

Mullins sat in the centermost chair where Dana Wolf usually sat. "Yesterday, while visiting New Haven, Governor Wolf collapsed from an unknown illness. This morning she was moved to the medical center here at Sierra. Earlier today, I was informed that Governor Wolf has suffered a massive coronary episode her doctors believe was caused by a rare virus found here on New Earth. The virus attacks the heart muscle, causing inflammation that prevents the heart from working properly. I've just been informed that the virus has spread to her other internal organs. At this time, the doctors are doing everything they can to save Dana Wolf's life."

Connor raised his hand.

Mullins looked at Connor. "Yes, General Gates."

"Has her family been informed?"

Mullins nodded. "Her husband, David, was at Phoenix Station and is currently en route back to New Earth. Her daughter is at the medical center, along with Dana's sister Beverly."

Connor had met Kayla Wolf on multiple occasions, but Lenora had had more contact with her after their harrowing experience together on the bridge that had been sabotaged at the Ovarrow city.

"In the interim," Mullins continued, "and in accordance with our laws, I will take over the governor's duties as the deputy governor until such time that Dana Wolf can resume her duties."

Bob Mullins was Dana Wolf's chief of staff and could be named the deputy governor. However, if he received a vote of no confidence by the other colonial leaders, then that office could be rescinded. Despite their differences, Connor knew Mullins could do the job. He had been suspicious of Mullins for years, especially when he was trying to find the rogue group that had implicated Kurt Johnson and Meredith Cain, and he felt a little of that old suspicion return. Sudden illnesses did occur randomly, and he couldn't entirely discount that fact, but he was still suspicious of the timing.

"I realize this comes as a shock and will be difficult," Mullins said. "I'll be releasing a statement to the colony in the morning. I don't want to keep this emergency session any longer than necessary. Anyone who is not on the Security Council will need to leave or disconnect. My office will be in touch with each of you tomorrow."

It took a few minutes for people to file out of the room, leaving a much smaller group. Connor saw a few new faces in the room—Major Natalia Vassar and a civilian named Jerry Sherman, both of whom were the lead candidates to become director of the Colonial Intelligence Bureau.

The meeting resumed.

"I realize that this news has come as a shock to most of you. I learned of it only this afternoon, and to be honest, I'm troubled by the whole thing," Mullins said.

Connor didn't doubt the sincerity in Mullins's voice.

"Our thoughts and prayers will be with Dana, but she would want us to keep the wheels turning," Mullins said and looked at Major Vassar. "As many of you are aware, the director of the Colonial Intelligence Bureau has not been named. Major Natalia Vassar was Governor Wolf's first choice for that position. In fact, if none of this had happened, she would have been offering you the position tomorrow . . . today that is," Mullins said, looking at Natalia. "Major Vassar, before you decide, I want to make sure you're aware that if you accept this position, you'll be resigning your commission to the Colonial Defense Force."

Natalia always sat ramrod straight, and she looked at Mullins with an unwavering gaze. "I understand, Mr. Mullins. I do accept the position as director of the Colonial Intelligence Bureau."

Connor felt a sense of relief knowing that the CIB would be in such good hands. He'd also need to find a replacement for her in the CDF.

"On behalf of all of us," Mullins said, "we thank you for your service in the CDF and look forward to your contributions leading the CIB," he said and looked at the man sitting next to Natalia. "Jerry Sherman, the position of deputy director of the CIB is offered to you if you will accept."

"I do accept," Jerry said.

Connor couldn't help but think that these were the strings attached to Natalia's new position as director of the CIB.

"Thank you," Mullins said. "There will be an investigation into Governor Wolf's illness. I don't think this comes as a surprise to any of you," he said and glanced at Connor. "There has been no indication of foul play, but we cannot afford to take something like this at face value. Dana Wolf was and is our leader, and given some of the current challenges, I don't want to rule out repercussions from the takedown of the rogue group led by Meredith Cain."

"This investigation will be my top priority," Natalia said firmly.

"How could Meredith Cain be involved?" Mayor Larson asked. "She's been banished and is living at a currently undisclosed location along with the other ringleaders of the rogue group."

"Meredith Cain was highly manipulative, and this is something she could have planned for. But this is why I want the investigation done," Mullins said.

The meeting continued for a little while longer, discussing status updates and next steps to allay the concerns that would be raised tomorrow when the rest of the colony learned what had happened to Dana Wolf.

"I realize it's getting late, but I have news that can't wait," Connor said and proceeded to give a high-level debriefing about his encounter with the Konus.

"This is very important news, and I appreciate your sharing it with us even though you haven't had time to put an official report together," Mullins said.

For years, Connor and Mullins had clashed over various

issues concerning the colony, but he was sure Mullins was feeling emotional over what had happened to Governor Wolf. Maybe a little solidarity would go a long way.

The meeting ended, and after a short conversation with Nathan, Connor went to the medical center. He found Dana Wolf's room and stood outside it for a few minutes. He wanted to go inside, but he wasn't sure if it was appropriate.

"General Gates?"

Connor turned and saw Kayla Wolf walking up the corridor. Her face looked a bit strained, and she held a cup of coffee in her hand.

"Hello, Kayla. I came as soon as I could. I just heard about what happened to your mother, and I'm so sorry."

She nodded and smiled sadly. "The doctors are still identifying the virus," she said and looked at the door, her eyebrows pulling together into a frown.

Connor wanted to ask her if she was all right, but he already knew the answer to that, so he just waited.

Kayla glanced at him. "I know I'm supposed to be strong and sit by my mother's side." Her face crumpled slightly and her voice cracked. "It's just that seeing her like this . . . It's just so . . . It's just so hard."

He put his hand on her shoulder. "I know. I really do," he said, and she looked up at him. "You have to believe that your mother is strong. She's one of the strongest people I know."

Kayla nodded and sighed. "She likes you. A lot. I think you're one of her favorite people."

Connor smiled a little, and his throat became thick. "Do you mind if I wait here with you?" he asked and gestured toward the chairs outside the hospital room.

"I'd like that," Kayla replied.

13

CONNOR WALKED with Nathan across the well-manicured courtyard broken up by islands of brightly colored flowers. One side of the wide path displayed hybrid plants brought from Old Earth, none of which Connor knew the names of beyond a few varieties of roses. He was more familiar with the side that had plants from New Earth. The gardens were well kept since some of the New Earth variety of plants would aggressively wreak havoc on the surrounding plants if left unattended for long periods of time.

They climbed up the steps to enter the colonial administration building in Sierra.

"What is it?" Nathan asked.

Connor finished reading the message he'd just received. "Governor Wolf's condition has taken a turn for the worse. They're putting her into stasis so the doctors have more time to research the virus."

"Oh my God, that's awful," Nathan said.

Two days had passed since Bob Mullins had become the deputy governor of the colony. If the doctors had decided to put Dana Wolf into stasis, it meant they were running out of options for treatment. They were scrambling.

"Who sent you the message?" Nathan asked.

"It came from Lenora. She's been in contact with Kayla Wolf."

Nathan frowned and shook his head. "Have there been any other cases of the virus?"

"I asked Ashley about that last night, and she said it was rare. They've seen some of the symptoms before, but none of those other cases took a turn for the worse like this. Dana Wolf is dying."

Nathan was quiet for a moment. "I still can't believe we don't know how she got the virus."

"Natalia is looking into it. If there's foul play, she'll find it, but—" Just then, Connor received another message from Lenora. "There've been five more cases of the virus in New Haven, but they're milder."

There was an audible chime on Nathan's PDA. "Looks like the news net has gotten a hold of this. We're going to need a way to test whether somebody has the virus or not."

They continued on their way, heading up to the governor's office where they found Bob Mullins sitting at Dana's desk. It felt wrong, and Connor wished Dana would be joining them at any moment.

Mullins was reading his holoscreen and waved for them to come in. "They've put Dana into a stasis pod."

"We just heard," Connor said.

If Mullins was surprised by this, he didn't give any

indication. Connor and Nathan sat down in the chairs on the opposite side of the desk.

"I read your updates about the defensive strategy for colonial cities, but I want to better understand what our offensive doctrine is going to be where the Krake are concerned," Mullins said. He paused while he regarded both of them for a few moments. Then he sighed. "I feel awkward sitting at Dana's desk. It's a bit strange given what's happened."

"I can sympathize," Nathan said. "At the end of the Vemus War . . ." he said and glanced at Connor. "Let's just say the circumstances are somewhat familiar to me."

Mullins pressed his lips together and nodded once. "You've stated that the goal would be to remove the Krake's ability to wage war."

"That is correct," Nathan replied. "Once we find the Krake home world, we look for strategic targets and take out the infrastructure the Krake use to build their ships, weapons, and even the gateways."

"What about after that?" Mullins asked.

"What do you mean?" replied Connor.

"Assuming we succeed, how do we make sure the Krake don't simply rebuild and come after us?"

"We'll need to monitor the situation. We don't have the resources to leave an occupying force. That's not something we should even consider," Connor said.

Mullins nodded and then frowned. "This might never end. This conflict with the Krake could just keep going."

"It's difficult to say, really. When we fought the Vemus, we wiped them out. The Krake are spread out, and there are civilians to consider," Connor said.

"Krake civilians." Mullins sounded as if he hadn't

considered the concept before. "And we don't have any evidence that the Krake are any closer to finding New Earth."

"That is also correct," said Nathan.

"But we can't let that lull us into a false sense of confidence," Connor said.

"I understand that. I'm just merely stating a fact."

"In any war, there are calms between storms. But we can't lose faith."

"I agree with you, Connor," Mullins said. "I'm going to propose that we increase the priority of the new colony. We've received continued updates from the probe we sent to the planet. I have agreements from other colonial leaders that five thousand colonists is the number we're going to move forward with. We haven't elected a project leader yet, but we have a few candidates we're considering. The drone data looks favorable. Actually, there might've been a recent extinction event that the ecosystem is recovering from. The best estimate is that it will take ten years for the colony ship to make the journey there. I wanted you both to know we're going to be calling for representatives from Field Ops and the CDF to go with the colony. Approximately ten percent of the candidates will be from those two organizations."

The last thing Connor had heard was a much lower number. Something must have changed. "I think that's a good start," Connor said.

"It was based on your recommendation," Mullins replied.

"The main goal for the colony is what exactly?" asked Nathan.

"Well, the establishment of the colony is their first priority. Their second priority is . . . Well, it will depend on what happens here. We'll send constant updates to their ship and to the probe. But if things get really bad here, I want plans in place to get as many of our people off this world as we possibly can."

Connor glanced at Nathan for a moment. "Are you proposing we build more colony ships?"

Mullins pressed his lips together. "I had seriously considered it, and I still might want to do that. However, I know there are options to convert our existing fleets into transport ships, where we could save as many people as possible."

Connor was becoming increasingly concerned with how alarmed Mullins was behaving. "So, if not building ships specifically, then you're proposing to at least build stasis pods."

Mullins nodded. "Not here on New Earth. I want them built at the lunar base facilities. A stockpile, if you will. However, I don't want it to detract from the ongoing building efforts there."

"I don't see how that's possible. It's a matter of allocating resources. We can't have our cake and eat it too. If we're going to devote resources to building stasis pods, then it's going to affect something else," Connor said.

"I was afraid you'd say that, and you're right. The other thing is that I want the effort to be kept secret."

"You don't want us to tell anyone?" Nathan asked.

"Since this effort will be confidential, it must be contained within the CDF. I'm sure you guys can guess why this needs to be secret."

The colony was already worried about the threat of invasion from the Krake. If it became common knowledge they were building and stockpiling stasis pods in case they had to flee the planet, then it would negatively affect the colony as a whole.

"Bob," Connor said, "Nathan and I can give you numbers and a projection of what we can do over the course of twenty-four months. But you must understand that if the Krake come here with a significant fleet, there'll be a lot of fighting, and there's a good chance no one will get to use the stasis pods."

Mullins considered this for a few moments. "Do you think it's not worth the effort?"

"No, but I think I need to set expectations. We're talking about stockpiling over six hundred thousand stasis pods on the lunar base. And that's just for the colonists. What about the Ovarrow?" Connor said.

"Our first priority has to be the colony. I realize this might sound kind of sudden, but it's been on my mind, especially since what happened to Dana."

Connor regarded Mullins. He was beginning to accept that the job of being governor was tougher than he had probably imagined.

"I just want us to do everything we can to protect everyone," Mullins said. "If the lunar base is too close to home, what about building a secret storage facility somewhere else in the star system?"

"We'll look into it," Nathan said.

Mullins nodded again. "I read your report on the Konus. We'll be sending a diplomatic envoy to them. It looks like you met one of their military leaders."

"His name is Kasmon. They said they've been preparing for another conflict with the Krake since they came out of stasis," Connor said.

"They've had forty years to prepare. It would be great if *we* had forty years to prepare," Mullins said.

Connor exchanged a look with Nathan. He agreed with Mullins's comment, but the deputy governor needed to adjust to his new role quickly.

"All right, what's next?" Mullins asked.

14

So much had changed in the colony that Noah felt he'd never catch up. Ever since he'd awakened from the coma, he'd felt that things had been out of his control, and he was out of step with everything. He sometimes tried to remember what life had been like before he'd gotten hurt, but it was a distant memory that was sometimes fragmented. He had strong inclinations of the person he'd been, but he wasn't quite the same, and he might never get back to being that person. For the past year, he'd thrown himself into his work, believing that if he could catch up on all the new developments, he'd somehow be made whole again. He'd been playing catch-up ever since, and some days it felt like he hadn't made any progress.

He was walking on a hiking trail near Sanctuary. Towering trees of white hardwood that were highly resistant to moisture stood like an army of sentries in the crisp winter air. They were similar to the birch trees of Old Earth, but near the treetops, branches latched onto neighboring trees, forming an intricate canopy. Colonial scientists had observed that this strange behavior didn't occur until the tree reached maturity. Each new connection reinforced its neighbor until the entire region was united. In recent years, some of Sanctuary's younger residents had climbed to the top and raced along the canopy.

The rustling of fallen leaves brought Noah's attention back to the ground. He watched with a smile as a large chocolate Lab zoomed among the trees. Amos sometimes just had to run. He'd pause for a moment, chest down and hindquarters raised in a play stance. Then, he'd let out a high-pitched playful bark and sprint off again. He went on like that for a few more minutes before coming back to Noah and leaning his body against Noah's legs, waiting to be scratched.

"Hey, buddy," Noah said while giving him a vigorous scratching that sent tufts of fur into the air. Amos raised his head and looked back at him. His mouth hung open, and a thick pink tongue hung off to the side in a derpy canine smile.

Amos was among the first litter of puppies ever to be born on New Earth. They had been genetically enhanced for greater size and slightly higher intelligence than the true-blooded Labrador retrievers of Old Earth. The genetic enhancements had been necessary for the dogs to adapt to New Earth.

Noah heard someone else walking up the path, and Amos began wagging his tail vigorously. He charged forward, and Noah heard his wife greet the Lab. He began walking down the path to meet her.

"I thought I might find you out here," Kara said. Her lips curved upward into a smile that exposed an adorable dimple on the side of her cheek. Her shoulder-length chestnut hair curled at the ends, which bounced a little as she walked.

Noah smiled. "I'm glad you did."

"It's almost decision day," Kara said.

Tomorrow Noah needed to let Oriana know whether they'd be going to the lunar base. He'd asked for a few weeks to consider it.

"Do you still want to go?"

Kara was leaning down to give Amos another rubdown. The Lab couldn't get enough of that sort of thing. "I don't know if I can part with my little man here."

If they went to the lunar base, they'd be up there for six months at least. Amos and his sister Maggie would be put into pet stasis. Noah wouldn't want to burden anyone with caring for his dogs for that long, and it wasn't fair to them either. He couldn't take them to the lunar base, and even if he could, it still wouldn't be right. Oriana was one of the lead scientists working to develop and reverse engineer cutting-edge technology in preparation for their war with the Krake. At least, that was what they told everyone, but he knew better. They were already at war. Even though there hadn't been a full-scale battle, it was obvious.

"We don't have to go," Kara said. Noah arched an eyebrow. "We can have the same access to the data and work on it in our own labs here on New Earth."

"But that's not what you want."

"I worry about you, Noah. You try so hard to save everyone. It's one of the things I love about you. But eventually, you need to let go," she said.

He knew she still blamed Lars for what had happened to him. But she had come to respect—if grudgingly so—Noah's desire to help his friend.

"I know," he said. "Sometimes I really want to go to the

lunar base and spend some time away from here, but part of me thinks I'm just running away from something."

"Or you could be running toward something. It's okay to get away for a while."

"I've already missed so much."

"What do you think you'll miss if we go to the lunar base? We'll still be in contact, and we can still come back to the surface if we need to."

Noah smiled a little. "I know. I didn't say it was smart. It's just how I feel. The two aren't mutually exclusive."

Kara circled in front of him and gently grabbed his hands. "You know it'll be fun up there."

She gave him a knowing glance with a slightly arched eyebrow. They had met on a space station on the edges of the star system. It had been one of the happiest times of his life—and one of the most terrifying. That was when the Vemus War had begun.

"Okay, let's do it," Noah said.

Kara's eyes gleamed, and she hugged him tightly. He felt a bit elated at making his wife happy but still felt a pang of guilt for leaving. It didn't make any sense, but the feeling was still there. Maybe she was right that he needed a change of scenery.

A comlink chimed, and Noah checked to see who was calling before he acknowledged it.

"Hi, Noah," Ryan Lynch said.

"One second, Ryan. My wife is here, and I'm going to transfer this to my PDA so she can join us," Noah said.

He put the comlink on hold and transferred it to his PDA, which projected a holographic image of Ryan Lynch's head and shoulders into the air.

Kara looked at him curiously.

"This is Ryan. He's Lars's lawyer," Noah said.

Kara greeted the lawyer, but Noah thought she stiffened a little. Perhaps he was just sensitive to it.

"It's a pleasure to meet you," Ryan said. Then he looked at Noah. "Normally I can't discuss the details about my client's case, but Lars has given me permission to speak to you about it."

Both Noah and Kara sat down at a nearby bench, and Amos lay down at their feet.

"I'm surprised it's taken this long to get Lars's case into the courts," Noah said.

"These things take time, and it's actually to his advantage. The precedent has already been set with the sentencing of people like Meredith Cain, Kurt Johnson, and several others."

"Lars has cooperated. Do you think they'll exile him to that island like they did the others?" Noah asked.

"It's difficult to say. Yes, Lars did cooperate and was instrumental in exposing the extent of the rogue group's activities; however, he didn't bargain for leniency when he cooperated. Therefore, there's no reason for them to be lenient with him."

"I was there," Noah said. "He was concerned with the lives of the people serving under him. He actually saved the lives of the CDF soldiers that day."

Kara reached over to hold his hand.

Ryan gave them an understanding nod. "I'm not judging him, Noah," he said gently. "I know you're his friend, but I'm just stating the facts. The courts have no reason to be lenient when it comes to Lars Mallory. In fact, there will be many people who would protest if they gave Lars leniency because of his family connections. They'd view it as Franklin Mallory trying to save his son."

"That shouldn't matter. I know it does, but it shouldn't."

"You're right. It shouldn't, and it might not, but I'm trying to be as completely transparent as I can with you. I had a similar conversation with Franklin Mallory. The facts of the case are what Lars will be measured by."

Noah looked away from the holoscreen for a moment. "Is there anything I can do? Would it help if I made a statement? You know, come down and testify or something like that."

"I already have your statement, and there's no need for you to come down."

"There has to be something I can do," Noah said.

"You've done enough," Kara said tenderly.

He glanced at her and saw nothing but love and concern in her gaze.

"His case is special," Ryan said, "but he hasn't done the one thing the courts will look for. He needs to express regret for the actions he's taken. Even then, there's no guarantee he'll get leniency and be allowed to stay in the colony. I've done an exhaustive search throughout our data repositories for war crimes. That's essentially what this is, even though we weren't officially at war with the Ovarrow. It's a gray area. I think the best thing Lars can do for his own defense is to express regret for the actions he's taken. I wish I had something more to offer, but that's where we're at right now."

Noah sighed. He licked his lips and then replied. "Thank you. I know you're doing everything you can."

The comlink closed, and Noah and Kara sat there quietly. He wanted to speak to Ryan more, trying to reason with him, but he'd just be making excuses, which would never outweigh the facts.

"I'm sorry this has happened," Kara said. He looked at her but didn't say anything. "Go talk to him one more time. I know it's what you want to do. It's really all you *can* do. His fate is in his own hands."

Noah had already talked to Lars about this, and he really didn't think speaking to him again would change anything. However, believing that wouldn't stop him from trying one more time.

He kissed his wife. "You're the best."

Kara smiled. "You can never say that too much," she said and stroked his hand. "So are you."

They stood up and walked back to their house, where they began planning to go to the lunar base. She would contact Oriana to let her know the good news. Maybe it would be nice to get away from New Earth for a little while.

15

NOAH WALKED down the echoing hallway of the detention center, his shoes squeaking on the smooth floors, and he looked up to see Franklin Mallory walking toward him. Noah still had the urge to call him Mr. Mallory, as was the habit he'd formed when he'd been a lot younger, but Lars's father wouldn't hear of it.

Franklin Mallory was six foot five and broad-shouldered, with a long, thick beard. The older man's eyes widened, and then he smiled, giving Noah a nod as he walked over. Electronic security doors buzzed at the end of the long hallway.

Noah noticed the worry lines that creased the older man's forehead, and his eyes were a bit strained around the edges.

"Noah, it's so good to see you. I just wish we didn't keep bumping into each other here," Franklin said.

There was something about standing in front of the tall man that made Noah stand a bit straighter. It was much like being near Connor. They both commanded respect.

"It's good to see you too, sir."

Franklin eyed him for a moment. "Sir? You're thirty-two years old now and a veteran of the CDF. You've more than earned the right to call me by my first name."

Noah smiled, and remnants of old feelings crept to the surface. "It's a habit. I'll work on it."

They stepped to the side of the corridor to allow other people to walk by them.

"Lars's trial begins tomorrow," Franklin said somberly.

"I know, and it's one of the reasons I'm here to see him."

Franklin put his hand on Noah's shoulder and looked at him sternly. "Noah, Lars is my son, and I love him very much. I feel the same way about you, and not just because of everything you've done. I appreciate that you come here to see Lars, but he can be extremely stubborn. You don't owe him anything."

Noah's throat became thick and his eyes tightened. He had been selected for the original *Ark* mission based on his aptitude test scores, but in many ways, he was an orphan here. Franklin, Connor, Lenora, and others had become his adoptive family. "I know that, but I have to try. He's my friend."

Franklin's gaze softened. "No, you don't. You've done enough. More than enough, to be honest. You should move on with your life."

"I am. Trust me, I am. I just want to . . ." His voice trailed off. He wanted to help Lars, as if the decisions Lars had made could've been prevented somehow.

Franklin breathed in deeply and sighed. "I know you do," he said and looked away for a moment. "I'm very proud of you, Noah. And I want you to know it's okay for you to move on with your life. Lars will be fine."

Noah didn't know what to say. Franklin released his

shoulder and gave a firm nod, then continued down the corridor. Noah watched him go for a few seconds before resuming his own route.

He walked through the corridors almost on autopilot, knowing the way to the visiting rooms without thinking about it. A few of the people he passed greeted him by name, mainly the security personnel who worked at the detention center.

He stood outside the door to the visitor room and paused. Why couldn't he let this go? He'd already said everything he was about to say to Lars before. Why couldn't he just leave it at that? Noah rubbed his forehead and breathed in deeply.

One more time, he thought to himself. Then he placed his palm on the identification pad, and the door buzzed before opening.

Lars sat at the table in the middle of the room. His hands were folded in front of him, and he glanced up. Without saying anything, Noah sat down across from him.

"No snarky greeting?" Noah asked.

Lars frowned and then shook his head. "My trial is tomorrow."

"I know. I won't be there though."

Lars looked at him and then nodded. "I understand. You don't need to be there."

"Kara and I are going to the lunar base for the next six months. We're working on a couple of projects with Sean," Noah said.

"I'm happy for you. Didn't you guys meet on a space station?"

Noah smiled and then nodded. "Titus Space Station."

Lars smiled a little. "You know, at one point I wanted to join the Colonial Defense Force like you and Sean."

"Why didn't you?"

Lars shrugged one shoulder. "I was heavily involved with Field Ops, and I thought the best way to help the colony was to do it from there."

"And now?" Noah asked.

"Now, what?"

Noah met his friend's gaze. "Now what do you want to do?"

Lars shook his head. "This again. I don't know. I guess it depends on what they decide to do with me."

"That's not entirely out of your hands, Lars. But what if they let you go?" Noah said and raised a hand when Lars began to voice a protest. "Just for the sake of argument. You stand your trial, and tomorrow or the next day you become a free man. What would you do?"

Lars looked away, and his gaze swept the room, looking anywhere else but back at Noah. He shifted in his seat and finally glanced back to Noah. "It really depends on what they would let me do."

Noah tilted his head to the side. It wasn't enough, but he was glad Lars hadn't dismissed the notion all together.

"You could work for me," he said. "I realize it's not Field Ops or that kind of stuff, but it's honest, and it does contribute to the colony. You have a technical background with a specialization in security systems."

Lars was quiet as the seconds ticked by. "You'd do that? I know you've offered before, but I just feel like this would put a strain on you and Kara."

"To answer your first question, yes, I would do that. As for the second, that's between me and Kara. You guys wouldn't need to work together. I have a pretty sizable operation, with research labs in all the colonial cities, and they're all working on different things. Some of those R&D projects are backed by the colonial government, and others are things I'm working on. It's an option is all I'm saying. What do you think?"

Lars swallowed hard and avoided his gaze. He then reached out and drank from his cup. When he set it down, he looked at Noah again and shook his head.

"I'm serious, Lars. You don't have to rot in a cell or be banished to an island with just enough supplies to survive."

Lars pressed his lips together and looked like he was actually considering it, which gave Noah some hope.

"I heard there are multiple islands," Lars said. Noah frowned in confusion. "Where they're banishing people. There are three islands, to be exact."

"Oh, I had no idea."

"Anyone living on the island will be monitored, and a review will be conducted at the end of their term on whether they can return to the colony or be allowed to leave the island."

Lars had spent a lifetime in Field Ops. He was no stranger to surviving outside the cities. If he were banished to the island, he would survive just fine, but at the same time, Noah thought it would be a waste.

"It doesn't sound that terrible when you put it like that, but you and I both know there's a real possibility the Krake will find this world. Where do you want to be when they come here?"

"It's not that simple."

"Yes, it is," Noah said. "It's *that* simple. Why don't you see that?"

"But it's not up to me. I have to take responsibility for all of my actions."

"Yes, but taking responsibility doesn't mean you have to sacrifice your future."

Lars considered what Noah said for a few moments.

"I can send my proposal to the courts. It doesn't mean they'll listen to me, but it's an option, and you'd have to make a statement about how you regret your actions," Noah said.

Lars winced and then shook his head. "That's like taking the easy way out. No one would believe me."

"No, it's not. You've had time to reflect on everything that's happened from the start when Meredith Cain recruited you and convinced you those actions were necessary. It's okay to admit you've been manipulated. It doesn't make you any less responsible, but if they take that into account along with your cooperation, it might just convince them that you're worth keeping around. But you have to give them a reason. You have to fight for this."

Lars stood up and walked away from the table. His head was bowed, and his hands were thrust into his pockets.

Noah stood up. "It's not taking the easy way out, Lars. It proves that you're actually willing to take steps to atone for what you've done. You made a mistake. You're human."

Lars turned toward him, his face a mask of concentration. He then extended his hand, and Noah shook it. "Thank you. Thank you for not giving up on me," he said and paused for a second. "I don't know what I'm going to do. I need time to think about it."

Noah had hoped for more, but he supposed it would have to be enough. Lars had been adamant he didn't regret what he'd done to the Ovarrow. Noah didn't believe that was because Lars was without emotion; he believed it was because Lars would have to come to terms with the darkness inside him. He believed his friend could be redeemed, that he was worth fighting for.

"Good luck," Noah said.

Lars shook his hand again, and for a brief moment, he looked like Noah's childhood friend. It was as if a spark had been lit, and he could see it in his eyes. He hoped Lars could fan it into a flame, but that would be up to him. There was nothing else Noah could do. He had to move on, and so did Lars.

16

There was a secret CDF base on New Earth that was well away from any colonial city, located over six thousand feet beneath the surface of the planet. The CDF soldiers who were stationed there were committed to spending six months on base without access to the world above. The base was known among the senior officers of the CDF as Hammerholde, but it had a much more well-known name.

COMCENT.

CDF Command Central had multiple key components that were grouped under the umbrella of COMCENT, consisting of Hammerholde and the lunar base. There were secondary and tertiary installations that could be tasked with the duties of COMCENT, but they were maintained in a semi-permanent state of standby. Those installations would be used under only the direst of circumstances. These efforts were an improvement in the CDF post Vemus War, during which they'd lost strategic command due to the overwhelming forces of the Vemus. And now the Krake had the ability to conduct hostile operations both on New Earth and in its star system. They needed a unified command center that had the ability to fully function even in a fragmented state of operations.

Colonel John Randall was in command of Hammerholde and was on duty in the main headquarters. They had access to every satellite in orbit around New Earth and city defenses. They were even tied into Lunar Base and Phoenix Station. Eventually, all CDF communications routed their way through COMCENT. The CDF base was equipped with state-of-the-art technology that was constantly evolving, and they also had one of the most complex computing cores ever created. Randall had served multiple rotations in command of COMCENT. Standing watch over the colony was a duty he took seriously.

It was the middle of the afternoon, not that anyone could tell when they lived one and a half kilometers beneath the ground. The command center was a vast chamber where CDF operations and defenses were monitored on an ongoing basis.

The filtered air was cool and carried just a kiss of spicy evergreen-like scent to it. Randall had experienced most of the variations of Hammerholde's atmospheric support systems, which had been developed to help alleviate the stress of a long duty rotation underground. They were well stocked with supplies they could stretch to a full year if they needed to. Hydroponic gardens could extend that timeline even further. They weren't lacking room to expand, even with the recreational areas built for the enjoyment of base personnel. As far as CDF assignments went, Randall preferred it to most others.

The command center was host to multiple teams sitting behind long desks with both personal holoscreens used for specific duties and a main holoscreen that showed the prioritized projects. They coordinated with other CDF teams, as well as colonial government agencies, including Field Ops and Security.

Randall noticed one of his tactical officers, Lieutenant Amber Wong, sit up and lean forward, peering at something on her holoscreen. Wong was one of the good ones. She was highly intelligent, able to sift through many different data feeds to get at crucial, if obscure, data points of reference.

Their mission was to monitor New Earth against the threat of invasion, be that an invasion begun on the surface of the planet or utilizing their extensive monitoring network throughout the star system. Their network was almost constantly being improved upon and had been completely overhauled in the past year to include secondary subspace communication systems. Never before had they had near real-time monitoring of almost the entire star system. It was the kind of advancement that led some officers into a false sense of overconfidence. Not Randall though, and he made sure the people under his command didn't become overconfident either.

"Colonel Randall, I have an anomalous activity report I'm sending to you," Lieutenant Wong said. Several satellite images showing a specific region of the continent appeared on Randall's holoscreen. "Sir, this area is within two hundred kilometers of the known location of the Konus city."

Randall peered at the images. West of a nameless river was a region of grasslands near low-lying mountains that snaked along the continent. A buildup of clouds was beginning to cover the area of the Konus city. He looked closely at the open area Lieutenant Wong had highlighted. The image showed globular clusters that, when the image was zoomed, became digitally enhanced, and he saw that it was a long caravan of Ovarrow vehicles. They ranged in various sizes, but some were massive ground transportation vehicles, the likes of which he'd never seen the Ovarrow use before. The only parallel he could draw on from his own experience was similar images when the CDF had conducted training drills with their ground forces, except that the Konus had fielded a much larger army. They must have been hauling equipment as well, but he had no idea what they were carrying.

"How far back in time does the image history go, Lieutenant?" Randall asked.

"Approximately four hours, sir."

"Where are they going if they continue to follow this heading?"

A map of the region of New Earth appeared on the main holoscreen. Hammerholde was home to one of the most robust AI systems on the planet. It plotted multiple routes based on satellite imagery and quickly provided a probability rating for each destination. Lieutenant Wong highlighted her best guess in accordance with what the AI had provided. One destination brought them close to New Haven, but the highest probability rating had the Konus on a direct—or as near direct possible—path for the Ovarrow city that the colony had helped establish for the Mekaal.

"Tactical, reorient our satellite coverage of the area so we have eyes above them at all times," Randall said. "Ops, work on getting some flight plans ready so we can take a closer look at whatever it is they're doing."

"Stealth protocols, sir?" Lieutenant Zima asked.

"Authorized," Randall said. "Comms, I need General Gates immediately."

"Yes, sir. I'll track him down," Sergeant Terrence Brooks said.

Randall studied the satellite images for a few moments longer. He'd read the briefing that had come out a few weeks ago after first contact had been established with the Konus. It had been disconcerting to learn that there were over a million Ovarrow living undetected on New Earth. And given those numbers, they very well could field an army the size he was seeing on the images. They didn't know how many Ovarrow were traveling inside the large ground transport vehicles, and upon closer inspection, there were ground forces traveling outside the vehicles as well. He couldn't tell from the images what they were. They could be small vehicles, or they could be something else. They had a lot of intelligence to gather, and he knew General Gates would have many questions.

"Comms, put us at Condition Two," Randall said.

For the first time since the Vemus War, the CDF ground forces on New Earth had raised their combat readiness status to a severity just below that of an actual attack. His orders had brought about a sobering silence in the command center, but only for a moment. Then his soldiers went to work.

CONNOR HAD BEEN LIVING at the CDF base at Sierra while Nathan was traveling to Phoenix Station with Savannah. Nathan was long overdue for an inspection of Phoenix Station operations. At this stage of his military career, Connor wouldn't have chosen a long deployment away from Lenora like what

Savannah had done for the past two years. Though the work done at Phoenix Station was extremely important, Savannah was due to return to New Earth, and command of the station would be turned over to someone else. Nathan was the pinnacle professional when it came to running the CDF, but Connor knew his friend was excited that his wife was finally returning home.

For the next six weeks, Connor would be spending the bulk of his time at the CDF base at Sierra, becoming the point of contact for the Colonial Security Council. He'd expected his six-week rotation at the CDF base in Sierra to be a quiet affair. He was always busy, be it reviewing the various developments the CDF was involved in from off-world missions, trying to find the Krake, or building up their fleets and combat capabilities. What he couldn't have expected was the Konus fielding what could only be an army, which was even now making its way to the Ovarrow city that was home to the Mekaal.

He stood in his office, looking at the intelligence reports that had come from COMCENT. Colonel Thomas Beckly was at his side.

"They really could go to either New Haven or the Ovarrow city," Beckly said.

"There's no reason for them to go to New Haven. The diplomatic envoy reports from their meetings with the Konus indicate that they had a significant interest in the Ovarrow we brought out of stasis."

"It makes sense they'd be interested in them."

Connor gestured toward the satellite image on the main holoscreen in his office. "That looks like a little more than interest to me."

Before Beckly could reply, a comlink from Deputy Governor

Bob Mullins came to the forefront on the main holoscreen. Connor acknowledged it, and the connection established.

Mullins was in his office, surrounded by his staff and advisors. "General Gates, patching you into a conference call with High Commissioner Senleon and Warlord Vitory."

"Understood," Connor replied. He had been due to meet with the Colonial Security Council in a few hours, but Mullins must have decided to inform the Ovarrow about the Konus.

A few seconds later, the comlink on the holoscreen changed to show Senleon and Vitory from someplace in the Ovarrow city.

Mullins began speaking. "High Commissioner, I invite you and Warlord Vitory to join us here at Sierra so we can discuss the Konus."

"Deputy Governor Mullins, we must respectfully decline the invitation, given this news."

"If Sierra is unacceptable, then we would be willing to meet with you at New Haven or any of the other colonial cities."

Senleon declined again and looked at Connor. "General Gates, in your meeting with the Konus, did they indicate they would send an army to us?"

"No," Connor said. "They were highly interested to learn we'd been bringing Ovarrow out of stasis. They expressed an interest only in learning more about you." He had told Kasmon about the Ovarrow they'd rescued from stasis. Had this been a mistake?

"We don't know what their intentions are," Mullins said. "We haven't initiated contact with them since our initial envoy left several days ago."

"I request that you do not contact them," Senleon said.

"Why not? We could learn what their intentions are if we initiate communication," Mullins replied.

"They don't understand," Vitory said to Senleon.

"Then help us understand," Mullins said.

"Before the Ovarrow went into stasis, there was war," explained Vitory. "This war was fought until the ice and cold made it impossible to survive. Smaller groups were conscripted into the larger groups. Whoever had the dominant army would swallow up everyone else."

"This is why it's important that we establish communication with the Konus. We're making assumptions. They could be sending supplies and a force to help you rebuild," Mullins replied.

The two Ovarrow leaders were quiet for a few moments, and then Senleon spoke. "Throughout our interactions, we have come to appreciate your desire to communicate. This helps to avoid misunderstandings, but in this . . . Given a choice, we will fight for our independence."

"We respect your independence," Mullins said.

"General Gates," said Vitory, "what do you think the Konus intend, given the images you've shown us?"

Mullins turned toward Connor. His gaze was expectant, and the room became quiet. Connor knew Mullins would look for him to defuse the situation, but he couldn't. He'd been heavily exposed to the way the Ovarrow handled things on New Earth and on other planets. The intention was clear to him.

"I think your concerns are right on the mark," Connor said. "The Konus could have requested to communicate with you through our comlink. Instead, they chose to send a sizable force we believe is heading toward your city. In this situation, you'd be better able to estimate what they intend than we would."

"This is why it's important that we open a line of communication to the Konus," Mullins repeated.

"Again, we request that you don't do that," Vitory said.

"Why not?" asked Mullins.

"The Konus are unaware that we know they're heading for us," Vitory said. "If you established communications with them, this would give them an advance warning of our knowledge. They could change their tactics. The speed at which they're moving gives us time to prepare for them; however, if you inform them, they could move much faster. This would impact our preparations in defense of our homes."

Mullins considered this for a few moments and then turned toward Connor. "General Gates, what do you think?"

"I think Vitory is correct that we should be cautious with how to proceed. The Konus are largely unaware of what our capabilities are."

"They must have some idea. They know we're looking for the Krake, and they expressed interest in an alliance with us against them," Mullins said.

Connor shook his head a little. Governor Wolf never would've made such a misstep. "I think we should keep the two issues separate for now."

Mullins frowned and then glanced at someone off-screen. "High Commissioner Senleon and Warlord Vitory, we will not contact the Konus. We need time to consider our options, but I want you to know that we respect your desire for independence."

"Thank you," Senleon replied. "We need time to consider how best to proceed as well."

The conference call ended, and Mullins requested that Connor come to the emergency Security Council meeting.

"Sir," Beckly said after the comlink closed, "do you have any orders for me?"

"Continue to monitor the Konus. We're not authorized to make any other preparations unless they decide to head for one of our cities. For the moment, our hands are tied."

"Understood, General. I'll update you immediately if anything new develops."

17

A CDF TRANSPORT skimmer flew away from the main CDF base in Sierra. The aircraft could carry a number of human passengers, as well as cargo containers. Connor sat in the copilot's seat, and the pilot was quiet. Sometimes pilots liked to fill the time with idle chatting, but Sergeant Miller had taken one look at Connor and remained all business. Connor had flown with Miller a few times before, and he knew that if he initiated a conversation, Miller would be more than happy to oblige. Today wasn't one of those days.

If the army traveling across the continent had been of Krake origin, the CDF response would have been swift. Both Senleon and Vitory were certain of what the Konus intended. Connor had told Kasmon about the Ovarrow they'd rescued from stasis, and he'd shown them the general location of the Ovarrow city. He'd even given Kasmon specific numbers. He'd done it because it seemed like the best way to ingratiate the colony with the Konus. Now, hindsight was giving him the proverbial kick in the ass.

Connor was busy reviewing the day he'd met Kasmon, trying to recall the entire conversation, looking for some indication of what he'd missed—anything that would've indicated the response they were seeing on the satellite images. Mullins had been happy with the results of the diplomatic meeting with the Konus, and Connor was sure Dana Wolf would've had the same reaction. So, where had he gone wrong with his estimate of them? What hadn't he seen? He'd become accustomed to dealing with the Ovarrow in alternate universes, where they had multiple layers of security between them and the colony. Forward operating bases were established on other worlds. Some of them were automated listening posts, but they also had some that were operated by CDF personnel.

He couldn't have known. He brought up the satellite images of the Konus and tried to think of a legitimate reason for them to commit so many of their population to this. Despite all his experience with the Ovarrow, they were still alien in many ways. They had different motivations and could be brutal when dealing with nonconformity among their peers.

The transport skimmer drew in its small wings as it hovered above the landing pad at the capitol, and Miller guided them down for a perfect landing. Connor thanked him, opened the hatch, and climbed out. He walked across the landing pad and through the transparent entryway doors. The building's security systems registered his ID transmitted via his neural implants, and he strode down the glossy floors to a staircase that would let out near the meeting room where the Colonial Security Council was convening.

The halls echoed with the conversations and goings-on of

the people who worked there. Connor walked into the meeting room, one of the last people to arrive, and bit back a grimace. He really hated being late or close to late, but it couldn't be helped sometimes. The doors shut behind him, and he headed for his seat.

Natalia Vassar sat across from him in civilian attire, and it took him a second to reconcile that she was no longer with the CDF. They both shared a knowing look, and Connor gave her a slight nod.

Mullins cleared his throat. "Let's get started," he said. "A reminder to all of you that the discussions at this meeting are considered confidential and should not be disclosed to anyone who doesn't have the necessary security clearance."

Connor arched an eyebrow at Natalia, and his former lead intelligence officer's lips lifted a little.

"First up," Mullins continued, "is whether we should initiate communication with the Konus. I'm aware that this action goes against what High Commissioner Senleon and Warlord Vitory want, but our highest priority is the welfare of the colony. We should seek to defuse the situation."

"This action seems premature," Jean Larson, the mayor of New Haven, said and looked at Connor.

"I agree," Luther Rosenbaum said.

Mullins frowned in thought. He'd probably expected Connor to voice the initial protest, but instead it had come from the mayors of New Haven and Delphi.

Mullins looked at the holo-image of Sanctuary's mayor. "Bernard, do you agree?"

Bernard Shaw had first come to Sanctuary to help establish it as a city when Connor had been mayor. A few years ago, the residents had petitioned for Bernard to serve as mayor when Connor had rejoined the CDF.

"I'm conflicted about it, to be honest," Bernard began. "I think it's a forgone conclusion that we will at some point initiate communication with the Konus. What we need to decide is when and where we do so."

Unable to wait any longer, Mullins turned toward Connor. "General Gates," he said.

"Their actions are highly suspicious. We left the Konus a way to communicate with us, but they haven't done so. From the Konus perspective, they may believe they don't need to contact us. Our estimates put their numbers in excess of over two hundred thousand soldiers," Connor said.

"Has it been confirmed that they're soldiers?" Mullins asked, looking at Natalia and Connor.

"We're still gathering intelligence, and several stealth reconnaissance missions are scheduled. We'll share our findings with the CIB for their review," Connor said.

Mullins nodded.

"There's more we need to think about," Connor said, and Mullins gestured for him to continue. "If their intentions are hostile toward the Mekaal, is the CDF authorized to aid the Mekaal's defenses?"

Mullins frowned, his forehead wrinkling. "I don't know if this is appropriate."

"How is this not appropriate?" Larson asked.

"The CDF conducts off-world missions with the Mekaal, but we've never had a formal alliance with them that specifically states we will come to their defense for circumstances beyond a Krake invasion," Mullins said.

Connor's thoughts raced. Their treaty with the Mekaal

stated they would join forces against the Krake. Mullins was right. There was nothing specifically stating that their alliance applied to what would be considered a domestic conflict.

"Considering our extensive interactions, I can't believe we're going to stand by and let the Konus come in and do whatever they want," Connor said.

"I think General Gates makes an excellent point," Darius Cohen said. "After all the time and resources we've spent on helping the Ovarrow reestablish themselves, and assuming that the Konus intend to harm the Mekaal, are we just going to allow that? On the other hand, while the Konus' actions appear to be hostile to us, this might just be how their society operates."

"Senleon and Vitory will never go along with the Konus," Connor said. "They already stated they would defend their homes."

Darius raised a hand in front of his chest. "I'm not condoning what the Konus are doing. I'm merely speculating that from their point of view, they're doing something they've always done. Granted, this must be on a much larger scale, and there's also the complication that we represent."

"Agreed. This is a complicated situation," Mullins said. "The Ovarrow would be stronger overall if they were united."

"That's easy for us to say," replied Connor. "We're not the ones being forced from our homes. Conscription is a short-term solution that leads to more problems. We wouldn't tolerate it. Why should the Mekaal?"

Mullins pressed his lips together and glanced at the others in the room. "If we send a delegation to find out what the Konus' intentions are, it would mean taking an intermediary role."

"If we did that at the outset, we'd run the risk of sending the Konus mixed messages," Darius said. "We can't be intermediaries and then take a side later. That might guarantee that any conflict would be resolved only through the use of force."

"We want to avoid that," Mullins said and looked at Connor. "We need allies against the Krake. That's one of the prevailing reasons for our off-world missions and for bringing the Ovarrow out of stasis."

Connor's eyebrows pulled together, and heat gathered around his neck. "I think we should inform Senleon and Vitory that we intend to stand with them if the Konus prove to be hostile. To do anything else would be viewed by them as a betrayal, and they'd be right. Then, we either communicate with the Konus ourselves or jointly with Senleon and Vitory."

The room went silent. He'd just taken the moral high ground away from Mullins's objective approach, and irritation was evident in the deputy governor's gaze and rigid posture. The entire discussion had left a bad taste in Connor's mouth.

"We can't let an oversight in our alliance dictate whether or not we take action right now," Connor said.

Mullins regarded him for a moment. "Even if the Konus would make for stronger allies? Tip the balance against the Krake?"

Connor's shoulders stiffened, and his moral-high-ground response stalled in the back of his throat. He wanted to help the Mekaal. "We're not there yet."

Mullins inhaled deeply and sighed. "You're right. We might be getting ahead of ourselves. We need to wait and see how Senleon wants to deal with it."

There was a general murmur of agreement throughout the

room that Connor didn't like. Senleon might base his actions on whether the colony would support him.

"To be clear, diplomatic channels will remain open to the Mekaal," Mullins said, and his gaze came to rest on Connor. "But at this time, there will be no authorization given for any direct action against the Konus. This includes advising and providing intelligence to the Mekaal about the Konus."

Connor clenched his jaw, and his eyes flicked to the table for a second. Now was not the time to become a stick-in-the-mud. "Understood," he said.

Mullins appeared surprised by his response but didn't belabor the point. They had to work together.

"We should give Senleon some time to confer with his own advisors," Darius said, and Mullins agreed.

The meeting ended, and Darius asked to speak with Connor. The head diplomat waited until they were well away from the meeting room before speaking.

"That was difficult," Darius said.

"Which part?" Connor replied. "The part where we considered abandoning the Mekaal, or the part where we decided not to take an active role where the Ovarrow are concerned."

Darius smiled. "That's one of the things I've always liked about you, Connor. You're straight to the point. Not quite black and white, but in this situation, your mind is already made up."

"You're damn right, it is. The Mekaal have come a long way. The more we work together, the stronger we both become. That's what's going to help us against the Krake. The Konus haven't earned that."

"I understand what you're saying, and I agree with you, but even you have to acknowledge that in some respects, this is a numbers game. There are more Konus than there are Mekaal," Darius said and raised his hand again in a placating gesture. "I'm just stating facts. If the Konus intend to bring the Mekaal into the fold—absorb them, if you will—then they'd be stronger for it, and we'd have a sizable group who are already familiar with working with us. I'm just saying that there isn't an entire downside to what the Konus might do. And I stress the word *might*."

"No," Connor said and shook his head. "How would you react if you were taken from your homes and forced to live by someone else's rules? I know what I'd do. It's easy for us to rationalize it so we feel better about making a bad decision."

"It's all bad, then?"

"Yes, it is, because the Konus won't stop, and they haven't proven that they'll back up their offer to help us against the Krake. The Mekaal have already done so, and that has to count for something," Connor said.

Darius scratched his eyebrow for a few seconds and then nodded. "You make a good point, Connor. I think of all the people in that meeting, you're the closest to really understanding the Ovarrow."

"A lot of good it did back there. I didn't see the Konus doing something like this."

"It just takes time. My advice would be to keep making the arguments," Darius said.

"Thanks," Connor said and meant it, but he couldn't help thinking about how much time they actually had. He wanted to help the Mekaal, and he needed to find some way to do that.

18

THE NEXT DAY, Connor was in his office at the CDF base in Sierra. Preferring to stand up while he worked, he faced a grouping of holoscreens. Colonel John Randall, the commanding officer at Hammerholde, was on one of them, while Nathan and Savannah were on the others.

"Thank you, John, for giving us this update," Nathan said.

If there'd been any doubts that the Konus had fielded an army, they had just been debunked. At least now they had evidence to support the claim. Increasing cloud cover was impacting satellite surveillance, which had been taken over by stealth recon drones.

"Continue to keep us updated at the predefined schedule," Nathan said.

"Yes, General," Randall said, and the comlink to Hammerholde went dark.

Nathan was still at Phoenix Station. He looked at Connor. "We'll need to present these findings to the Security Council."

"Do you think it'll sway them one way or the other?" Connor asked.

Nathan had more experience dealing with the Security Council in recent years, and Connor had to acknowledge that Nathan was better at it.

"Mullins isn't entirely wrong in deciding to wait."

"Oh really? Ever since he became deputy governor, he seems to be more . . ." Connor paused, trying to think of the right word. "Erratic."

"I think it's just Mullins coming to terms with the pressures of the office. It's one thing to be at the right hand of our governor as an advisor, but it's quite another to fill her shoes."

Connor couldn't think of an immediate argument that wasn't sarcastic. He had learned to work well with Dana Wolf over the years, but Mullins . . . "Dana wouldn't have let us pressure her into making a decision early, but I can't see her abandoning Senleon. She just wouldn't do it."

"Mullins hasn't abandoned Senleon."

"You know what I mean. Mullins is in the hot seat now, and he seems as likely to make a rash decision as he is to make a logical one."

Nathan glanced at Savannah. "He's right, Nathan," she said.

The door chime for Connor's office sounded, and a small holoscreen appeared, showing that Lenora was standing outside. He authorized the door to open, and she walked in.

"I'm sorry," Lenora said. "Am I interrupting something? Should I come back?"

"Nonsense," Nathan said. "We could use a fresh perspective."

She walked in and stood next to Connor.

"We're trying to find a way to help Senleon and the rest of the Mekaal," Connor said.

She nodded. "Mullins still won't commit to helping them?"

"No—well, not exactly. He's waiting to hear what Senleon wants to do, but I think he's just delaying making a decision," Connor said.

"Well, I can't see Senleon or any of the Mekaal wanting to join the Konus," Lenora said. "At least, not this way, not with an army coming to their city. It seems like the Konus are skipping a few steps in their plans to bring the Mekaal into the fold."

Nathan arched an eyebrow. "You think the Mekaal would be more inclined to accept an invitation to join the Konus if they'd sent a small envoy?"

Lenora considered it for a few moments and then shook her head. "Point taken. I suppose not. We'll never know now. However, the issue is that we have two major, competing Ovarrow factions, and the colonial government is reluctant to come between them because of certain political pressures."

"I think that about sums it up," Connor said.

Lenora looked at some of the other holoscreens showing the Konus army. She'd done her fair share of satellite image analysis to scout out potential archaeological sites worth investigating. Her head was slightly tilted to the side, and Connor could tell she was thinking. Then she turned toward him. "What if we weren't dealing with two Ovarrow factions? What if the Mekaal became colonial citizens? If the Konus were heading toward one of our cities, then dealing with this situation would be a lot more straightforward."

Connor's eyebrows pulled together, and his mouth opened a little. Then he chuckled and looked at Nathan. "You wanted a fresh perspective. I hadn't considered that at all."

Nathan exchanged a glance with Savannah. "I suppose I did. This feels like it's too simple a solution."

"Simple isn't always easy," Connor replied. "I don't know how Senleon would react to that."

"They might not be as closed off about it as you think," Lenora said. "You've been working together on off-world missions. There's more of an alliance with them now than there ever has been before."

"Yeah, but becoming citizens. That's a whole new direction," Nathan said.

Connor pursed his lips in thought, then tilted his head in a small nod as he considered it. "We have received requests for safe harbor from the Ovarrow in other universes. I know this isn't the same thing, but I do wonder how everyone would react to this kind of proposal."

"I don't know if it would work," Nathan said. "Would they be willing to live under colonial law? They'd need representation. Senleon would effectively become a mayor, of sorts. Colonial laws are more individualistic than the Ovarrow's, which are way more militaristic."

"We're not going to figure all this out here," Lenora said. "It's certainly controversial, especially among our own people. Possibly even for the Mekaal as well."

"The Mekaal have a lot of pride. I don't know how . . . They've changed in recent months, but I don't know if they're willing to take a step like this," Connor said.

Lenora gestured toward the holoscreen showing the Konus army. "Given what's heading for them, what choice do they have?"

"If given enough time, perhaps they might've approached us," Savannah said. "However, if they do approach the colonial government with a proposal like this, it would be looked at with bias, as if they were trying to avoid the lesser of two evils."

"To get a better understanding of just whether or not this is an actual option, we should talk about it with both parties," Nathan said.

Connor shook his head. "You want to add this as a line item to a Security Council meeting? Mullins would never go for it that way."

"You're right. He probably wouldn't. But if it's just a discussion in his office, he might be more open to it," Nathan said.

"Subtle," Connor said slowly and smiled. "There's just one problem. We're not authorized to even speak to Senleon about this. If we go through the diplomatic channels, they'll likely take their direction from Mullins, and we'll have the same problem we have right now."

"Not necessarily," Lenora said. All eyes looked at her, and she smiled. "I'm not in the CDF, and I'm not in the colonial government. I'm just a concerned citizen who happens to have regular communications with the Ovarrow. I can talk to them about this, and there isn't anything anyone can do about it."

This time Connor's mouth did hang open.

"Don't look so surprised," Lenora chided him.

"I'm not," he began. He'd almost said he wasn't surprised, but he was. "I don't like the idea of you going out there with everything that's going on."

"Connor is right, Lenora. There's potential for the situation to become dangerous," Nathan said.

"Oh please," Savannah said. "The Konus are still several days away at their current pace. Lenora can be in and out of there in that time."

Connor watched as the two women smiled at each other. "Mullins isn't stupid. He's going to see right through this."

Lenora shrugged. "So what?"

"All right," Connor said. "But we'll give you a ride, at least to New Haven. We have several troop carrier transfers bringing troops there. You can catch a ride on one of those."

Lenora gave him a look indicating he wasn't going to like what she was about to say. "That's not going to work."

"Why not?"

"If I catch a ride on the CDF troop carrier, someone will say you sent me to Senleon, and I don't want to give them any more ammunition to use against you. I need to get there on my own."

"They're going to say whatever they want, regardless."

"It's better this way. We want to rock the boat only a little bit," Lenora said.

She was right, but Connor still didn't like it at all. The Mekaal would be preparing their defenses, which wasn't exactly the safest situation he could send his wife into. But he wasn't sending his wife there. She was going to go whether he wanted her to or not. He'd seen that look in her eyes before, and there would be no talking her out of this.

"Be careful," Connor said.

Lenora smiled at him. "I'll be back before you know it."

He watched as she left his office and then turned back to the holoscreens. Nathan gave Connor an understanding look.

"I married a strong woman too," Nathan said, and Savannah grinned.

"Lenora can take care of herself, but I'm going to let Major Brooks at Camp Alpha know, and she'll send an escort with her anyway. She can come up with some excuse for being there," Connor said.

Nathan grinned.

"All right, I'll head over to Mullins's office tomorrow," Connor said and looked at Nathan, "unless you want to cut your trip to Phoenix Station off sooner."

"The thought did cross my mind, but you can't give Lenora a twenty-four-hour head start. It's better that Mullins hears it coming from you. We'll be waiting for the call."

Connor shut down the holoscreens. It hadn't taken them long to get used to subspace communications. They never could've had a conversation like that before. There would've been a fifteen-minute lag between responses.

A little over half an hour later, Connor was sitting in Bob Mullins's office. Connor looked around and saw that Mullins had kept all the furnishings Dana Wolf had placed in her office, treating it as if he was simply working there for a few days. Connor's opinion of Mullins ticked up a few notches.

"I can't move her things out of this office," Mullins said.

Connor nodded slowly. "Have there been any updates about her condition?"

Mullins shook his head.

"I wanted to talk to you before our next Colonial Security Council meeting. This really couldn't wait. Nathan wants to join us too," Connor said.

"Of course."

Connor opened a subspace comlink to Phoenix Station, and Nathan appeared on the holoscreen.

Connor proceeded to explain their discussion about the possibility of Senleon and the other Ovarrow becoming colonial citizens. Mullins's initial reaction was pretty much what Connor expected—complete and utter shock—but after that, he seemed to really consider the idea.

Mullins stood up and paced back and forth. "Let me get this straight. You're proposing that we give the Mekaal the option to become colonial citizens, and then we commit resources to protecting them?"

"Only if the Konus push our hand."

"Are the Konus a threat to us?" Mullins asked.

"They've been actively preparing for conflict with the Krake," Connor said. "Their weapons are superior to what we've seen come out of storage caches, which means their army must be well-equipped. It really depends on if it comes down to how we wage the battle. They have a lot more troops than we do, but we have superior weaponry and firepower."

Mullins looked out the window and shook his head. "We didn't expect to find a large group of Ovarrow. They outnumber us by more than double our current population. If they are as militaristic as you think they are, then they have more Ovarrow trained to fight. But on the other hand, we have the Mekaal, who we've already been working with—and successfully, I might add. If they became citizens, would we allow them to travel through colonial cities? Would we allow them to live here? When we take those things into account, it becomes a more complicated discussion. I think it's more complicated than anyone realizes, and the impact to the colony would be significant."

"What if the colonists choose to support the Ovarrow of their own volition?" Connor asked.

Mullins frowned and arched an eyebrow. "Are you saying that we should put this up for a vote?"

"It might make it easier, but I don't know if we have enough time. If the issue of whether or not we allow the Ovarrow to become colonial citizens becomes a talking point or debate, then we run the risk of not making any decision at all, at least not in time to help them."

"I'm not going to promise anything," Mullins said. "I think this is worth an open discussion inside the Security Council and in other offices. I think there are actually some policies already drafted in the event we encountered an alien species."

Connor's eyebrows raised. "You mean as part of the *Ark* program?"

Mullins nodded. "I think so. They tried to account for different scenarios and provided articles to help guide us along. But I doubt any of them could've imagined the situation we find ourselves in." He was quiet for a few moments, then looked at Connor. "I know you think we should just help them."

"You're right; I do. I don't think we should stand by while their freedoms are taken away from them. If they choose to join the Konus, that's one thing, but that's not what's going to happen."

Mullins regarded Connor and then glanced at Nathan. "Well, I think we should examine this in more detail sooner rather than later. I'll be in touch with you."

Connor suspected that Mullins wondered whether he would simply command the CDF to defend the Mekaal. Connor had bucked the system once, and he felt that if he did it again, the repercussions would be even more severe. He had no plans to do any such thing. He wouldn't order any CDF soldier into that kind of situation. As much as he wanted to, he understood he had to work within the current system whether he agreed with it or not.

Connor left Mullins's office and headed back up to the landing pad. A comlink registered on his internal heads-up display, and he saw that it was from Dr. Eric Young.

"Dr. Young," Connor said, "what can I do for you?"

"I need your help, Connor," Dr. Young said. "Do you have a few minutes to talk?"

"What's this about?"

"It's about our Krake prisoner."

19

A YEAR AGO, when Trident Battle Group returned to New Earth, they'd brought a Krake prisoner with them. The prisoner had been taken to a secret facility near Sanctuary, and Connor had taken every opportunity to observe and, on occasion, interact with him over the past year. It was a rare opportunity to associate with a Krake who wasn't trying to kill him. Many scientists were fascinated by Krake physiology, and there was sufficient evidence of genetic modification. They had highly advanced brains, with large portions devoted to complex thinking and critical reasoning. Connor had seen the brain scans, and even he could see they were vastly different than the human brain. There were similarities to the Ovarrow brain, however, which supported the theory that the Ovarrow and the Krake shared a common ancestor.

In under forty minutes, the S7 Falcon Fighter had gotten Connor to the remote location where the Krake prisoner was kept. Dr. Eric Young met him on the landing platform.

"Connor, thank you for coming so quickly."

They went through the double doors and passed through a security checkpoint before being allowed into the secure wing where the prisoner was kept.

"You said we were at a crossroads."

Eric nodded. "Yes, we are. We've run all the biological tests we can run, and we've moved on to behavioral modification."

Connor knew that on multiple occasions, the Krake prisoner, known as Eyman, had tried to commit suicide. Eyman asserted he was already dead. Connor had seen the video recordings of when Sean had first interrogated the Krake prisoners aboard the *Vigilant*, and he'd never witnessed behavior that showcased such fanaticism before. The prisoners had maintained their stark belief that their lives were forfeit because they'd been captured. The CDF hadn't been able to capture any Krake from other missions to decide whether Eyman was a member of an outlier group or if he represented what counted as "normal" among them.

"I read the reports, and the latest ones indicated that some progress was being made," Connor said.

"It was, and then it all stopped. Eyman refuses to cooperate or even acknowledge when we try to speak to him."

"And you think he'll interact with me?" Connor asked.

"Yes, I do. I've checked the logs, and each time Eyman was conscious, he seemed most responsive to you," Eric said.

"I guess that makes me the lucky one, but I don't understand why."

"I discussed this with several colleagues, and we think it's because you've interacted with the Krake before. I think he senses a certain command authority with you. That's something he's familiar with. Many of his responses to our questions are conditioned. I'm hoping we'll get more when you speak with him."

Connor glanced at Eric for a moment, then gave him a long look. "This is your area of expertise."

Eric nodded. "And I'm making an educated guess. If I'm wrong, then I'm right back where I started, but if I'm right, then maybe we can get a little more cooperation from him."

Connor had first met Eric years ago when he'd encountered an Ovarrow out of stasis. Since then, they'd kept in touch. Eric had been on the team that helped develop communications with the Ovarrow, a job that had gotten significantly easier with the Krake translators they were now able to use.

"I'll do the best I can, but what is it you want me to do?"

"I'd be happy if he just reacts to you. If you can get him to talk, that would be good as well."

"Talk about what?"

"Anything, as long as he's participating."

They walked into an observation room, and Connor saw a walled-off cell in the center of the room where Eyman was kept. From the control room, they could make all the walls translucent, but currently they resembled the sparse walls of an ordinary habitation unit.

Connor approached the room with Eric right behind him. The metallic gray doors opened to Eyman strapped to a chair in a reclined position. The Krake had pale blue skin. His brow ridges extended on either side of his head, similar to the Ovarrow, but there was a third brow ridge over the center of his forehead that was more pronounced. His eyes were closed.

Connor glanced at the Krake's wrists and could see scarring from his struggles against the restraints.

"We've had him sedated. I'll bring him out of it," Eric said.

Connor walked over to Eyman, and the Krake prisoner began to stir. After only a few minutes, he was fully awake. Multiple straps secured him to the chair. The Krake watched Connor through alien eyes revealing vertical pupils, like those of a feline, and jade-colored irises.

Connor looked over to the side where there was a holoscreen showing a scene of the landscape outside. Fallen trees leaned drunkenly against one another, and animal burrows were hidden beneath the tree roots. Fresh sprouts grew from a dead stump, and a puddle of sunlight warmed a patch of earth nearby. He looked at Eyman, who was only partially watching the holoscreen.

Connor took control of the screen and brought up an image of the ship Eyman had been captured on. The Krake looked at it for a moment and then simply stared at him.

"This was your ship. Did you live there?" Connor asked.

Eyman tried adjusting his position, but the straps kept him firmly in place. He looked away.

"Do you want to go back to your ship?" Connor asked.

Eyman turned back toward Connor. "The ship is destroyed."

Connor heard Eric shift his feet but ignored him. "What if there was another ship?"

"No," Eyman said and looked away again.

Connor circled around the chair and stopped when he was in Eyman's direct line of sight. "What did you do on the ship?"

"I worked. We searched for materials to reuse."

"A salvage ship," Connor said. "You were able to travel through space gates."

Eyman was quiet.

"You think you're already dead. And yet you're not."

"I am."

"If you know you're already dead, then what's the harm in speaking to my friend or me," Connor said and gestured toward Eric, who came to stand at his side.

Eyman looked away and closed his eyes. Connor tried asking him more questions, but the Krake wouldn't respond.

"This is what happened before," Eric explained. "He'll answer a few questions, and then he just shuts down."

"How can you be sure it's not an act? Maybe it's his way of showing defiance," Connor said.

"It's not, because we monitor his vital signs, and they are relaxed. When any test subject is being defiant, their heart rate increases. In men, testosterone is released, along with stress hormones."

Connor walked to the other side of the bed and leaned in toward Eyman. The Krake hardly moved or gave any indication that he knew Connor was mere inches from him. He stood back up and regarded the Krake prisoner for a few moments. Then he accessed the controls for the chair and all the restraints released.

"What are you doing?" Eric asked.

"If you want more interaction from him, we need to give him a little bit of freedom."

"But he'll hurt himself. Have you seen the video logs of the others when they were held captive on the *Vigilant*?" Eric asked.

Eyman opened his eyes and sat up. He flexed his hands and looked at Connor suspiciously. Then he stood up.

"Would you like to go outside?" Connor asked.

Eyman's gaze darted between Connor and Eric.

"I don't think this is a good idea," Eric said.

"You said we're at a crossroads with him. Let's see what he

does," Connor said, walking toward the door and opening it. He stepped through the doorway and looked back at the Krake prisoner. "You can stay in here, or you can follow me. It's your choice," he said and gestured for Eric to leave the cell.

Eric walked out the door, his eyes wide. Connor stepped away from the doorway, and they walked toward the command center. CDF soldiers were heading toward them with stun batons ready.

"Stand down," Connor said.

The soldiers hesitated for a few seconds and then did as Connor ordered.

"Get us a clear path to the outside," he said and glanced behind him at the cell door. Eyman hadn't come out yet.

Connor walked back toward the cell and heard Eyman scramble back to the far side. His gaze was wild and uncertain, his breathing rapid.

"You're not aboard a ship anymore. You're on a planet. I know you said you're already dead, but maybe you could hang on for a little bit longer."

Eyman looked away from Connor, his shoulders slumped. "Why would you do this?"

"I don't want to help you. I don't feel sympathetic to you at all."

Eyman looked at Connor, and then his gaze quickly darted away. "What do you want?"

"You know you're never going back home, and they're never coming to rescue you. And why would they? You're just a salvager," Connor said and stepped into the room. He used his implants to put an image of Mekaal soldiers on the screen.

"The enemy," Eyman hissed.

"Why? Why are they the enemy?"

"They are . . ." Eyman began and stopped.

A comlink opened on Connor's personal heads-up display, and he heard Eric's voice. "Connor, you're a genius. Keep him talking."

"Do you know why they're the enemy, or were you just told they're the enemy? What did they do to you?"

"They are the enemy of all."

"Is that why you salvage from star systems? You search for things to be used against the enemy?"

Eyman turned toward Connor. One of his hands came to rest on the back of the chair, as if he was using it to hold him up.

Connor put another image up that showed Ovarrow soldiers with CDF soldiers. "They're not *our* enemies."

Eyman glared at him.

"We don't have to be enemies. I would prefer not to be enemies."

"What do you want from me? What do you want to take from me?"

Connor leveled his gaze at the Krake prisoner. Eyman was more than a prisoner of this cell. He was a prisoner of his own mind, conditioned by his own species.

"I want you to tell me where the Krake home system is. I want the space gate coordinates that will take me there. I want to know the name of the Krake home world."

Eyman looked as if he was on the verge of speaking a couple times but clamped his mouth shut.

"What do you know about the overseers?"

Eyman flinched, showing more of a reaction at the mention of the overseers than he had to the image of the Ovarrow.

"Since you don't want to tell me about the overseers, how about you tell me where you would take your salvage."

Connor used his implants to put a holographic interface in the center of the room that had the coordinate interface for using a space gate. He did a quick search for the coordinates of the universe where Eyman had been captured and put them on the holo-interface.

"This was where you were when you were captured. Where were you going from here?"

Eyman brought his other hand to the back of the chair and braced himself.

"Careful, Connor," Eric said. "One of the prisoners ended his life by slamming his throat into the back of a chair."

Connor regarded Eyman for a moment. The Krake was rigid, his muscles shaking. "I already told you that I'm not going to stop you if you want to kill yourself. You don't have to cooperate with me. Your life is in your own hands. Has that ever happened to you before?"

The muscles in Eyman's arms became even more rigid, and his grip hardened on the chair backrest. Then, the last of the translation played back for him, and the strength seemed to drain out of the prisoner.

That's it, Connor thought. He knew Eyman wasn't going to kill himself. Perhaps at one time he would have, but not now.

Eyman backed away from the chair and sat on the floor. "Shipyards," he said quietly. "We bring our salvage to shipyards."

Connor blinked several times, unsure he had heard it correctly. "Do you like the shipyards?"

"I like ships," Eyman said. His gaze seemed to take in the room.

"I like ships too," Connor replied.

He considered asking Eyman about the Krake home system again, but he was beginning to think Eyman didn't know where it was, that he was from a different universe than the Krake home star system. How many alternate universes had the Krake spread to?

Eyman lay on his side on the floor and brought his knees up to his chest.

Connor heard somebody walking over to the cell and saw Eric standing in the doorway. "I wouldn't put him back in the restraints. Get him a bed."

"What if he tries to hurt himself?"

Connor looked back at Eyman for a few seconds. "Let him."

"Are you sure?"

"No, I'm not, but I can't think of anything better. I think if we give him some freedom, he might be more cooperative. If he'd wanted to kill himself right now, I would've let him," Connor said as he watched the Krake prisoner on the floor. "He didn't. It might be the first decision he's made in a long time."

They walked out of the cell and closed the door. Eric looked at Connor with a wide-eyed gaze. "I never would've thought to ask him those questions."

"He knows he's a prisoner. Going in there and pretending to be his friend wasn't going to work. He would've seen right through it."

Eric nodded. "That was a hell of a gamble."

"I don't think he knows where the Krake home system is."

"Why do you think that?"

"A couple of reasons, really," Connor replied. "His response to an image of the Ovarrow was conditioned. I don't think he's ever had any interaction with one before."

"The lack of a personalized nature to his assertion that they were the enemy. That's what you mean, isn't it?"

"I think that's fair to say."

"Do you think he'll share anything else with us?"

"I think so," Connor said, after considering it for a few moments.

"I think I'll try your approach from now on, but if he reverts to how he used to be . . ." Eric said, leaving the rest unfinished.

"If he *is* brainwashed, then this moment right now is the first time he's exerted control over his own world. He defied the conditioning that he should end his life," Connor said.

"Yeah, but what will come next? We can't base it on our own psychology."

"You know more about that than I would. I don't think he'll ever really be free."

"But what do we do with him? Just keep him captive for the rest of his life?"

Connor breathed in deeply and sighed. "I don't know, and it's not up to you or me. If we can get usable intelligence out of him that will help us against the Krake, then this will have been worth it."

"I see your point. Do you have any other suggestions for me?"

"Do you want me to do your job for you?" Connor asked him and grinned. Eric laughed. "I would suggest getting rid of that chair and putting a bed in there. Allow Eyman to start caring for himself. Give him a taste of what a little bit of freedom could feel like. I think if he embraces that at all, he might open up more."

"I was thinking along those lines myself. We'll review this session and come up with another plan. I know you're really busy, and I just want you to know I really appreciate you taking the time to come here and help me with this," Eric said.

Connor smiled. "I owed you."

Eric frowned in thought. "Are you talking about Syloc?"

"He was the first, but with all the Ovarrow coming out of stasis, your contribution has had an impact. Keep it up."

Eric said he would, and Connor headed back out to the landing pad.

20

THE CDF TROOP carrier transport was completely full. Connor stood up, rolled his shoulders, and stretched his neck. He looked behind him and saw a few pockets of men from the 7th Ranger Company speaking to one another, but the vast majority of them were taking a nap. He glanced off to the side at the wallscreen that showed the flight status of the other transports carrying a mix of cargo and the rest of the 7th. They would reach the Mekaal city within the next twenty minutes.

Connor needed to stretch his legs and walked toward the front of the aircraft. There was an alcove off to the side, and Samson was sitting there with a holoscreen in front of him. The big man was reading so intently that he hadn't heard Connor walk up to him.

"Who is Saul Ashworth?" Connor asked.

Samson minimized the message on his holoscreen a little too quickly, and then it flicked off. He glanced up at Connor. "No one."

"That's a pretty long message from a person who doesn't exist."

Samson shrugged thick shoulders, and the muscles in his neck rolled. "He's just some scientist or project lead asking about my time away from the colony. I think they're looking to update some of the survival guides."

Connor nodded. Samson had lived apart from the colony on his own for years. He'd actually explored a pretty large portion of the continent, and he'd done it all on foot.

"Are our hands still tied?" Samson asked.

"We have no official role here. This is a training exercise for the 7th Ranger Company. I'm here to meet with Darius Cohen from the diplomatic envoy," Connor replied.

Samson arched a thick, dark eyebrow toward him. "Right," he said, drawing the word out for a few seconds.

"This is a good time for a field survey around the city."

"And?" Samson prodded.

"You're to discuss defense options and potential ambush sites. Maybe a few choke points. And if any of the Mekaal soldiers happen to be around during those discussions, it'll be fine. It's not confidential," Connor said.

Samson looked at him doubtfully. "I follow orders, sir. But you know that anyone who looks at this is going to see through that flimsy excuse."

"I'll worry about that. This comes under the heading of peaceful cooperation for our off-world initiatives."

Samson grinned. "Now you almost sound like Wil."

Connor smiled with one side of his mouth. "Reisman always had a knack for finding his way around certain regulations. It was part of what made him so good at breaking into secure systems."

Samson nodded, and his eyes became distant. They didn't often speak about the Ghost Platoon. "He had a story for every occasion. I wonder how he slept at night," he said, and Connor grinned. "Seriously, sometimes we couldn't get him to shut up. He kept telling that story about the bucket of frogs."

Connor chuckled, and for a few moments, he recalled the day Wil Reisman died aboard a Vemus ship. He'd become trapped in Vemus exoskeletal material while accessing their systems. There was no way to free him, and Reisman knew it, but he'd never lost focus, even when Connor had wanted to give up. Reisman had been a good friend.

Both of the former Ghosts had become uncomfortably silent. Samson had had the most difficulty adjusting to life in the colony. He'd left behind a lot of people he cared about on Old Earth. They didn't speak about it. There was no need.

Connor glanced at Samson and could see a hardened edge to his gaze. Samson blamed him for being shanghaied onto the *Ark*. Samson looked away and shook his head.

"Not today," Samson said quietly. This was something he said from time to time. It was his way of focusing his thoughts away from painful memories.

There was an audible chime above them, and the pilot announced, "We'll be hitting the landing zone in five minutes."

Someone cried out in mock terror that they hoped the pilot would simply land them safely rather than "hit the landing zone." This drew more than a few jeers from the others. Connor looked back at them and smiled. He remembered a much smaller platoon doing something similar. They'd been hidden in a shipping container bound for a civilian space station. These were different men, but they demonstrated the same camaraderie. It had been such a long time since he'd led the

Ghosts, but sometimes when he least expected it, memories of them amplified, reminding him of a past life he no longer wanted but sometimes longed for in a rare moment of nostalgia. He went back to his seat and gathered up his things.

The troop carrier landed, and Connor exited the side hatch, along with a squad of CDF regulars. Once they were off, the aircraft departed and headed toward the next destination.

The main entrance to the Ovarrow city was just under two hundred meters away. Located in the foothills of a vast mountain range that stretched over four thousand kilometers beginning far to the north, the city was nestled just past the midpoint. The rounded architecture combined the bronze metallic alloy that was extremely resistant to oxidation and a polished form of ebony concrete. Ivory accents along the edges of the buildings had faded to a dull ashen color, and the Mekaal hadn't addressed that yet while they made the city livable. Taller buildings near the southern parts of the city had defense towers in place. Only sixty thousand Ovarrow made their home in a city meant to house millions. Most of it remained untouched, and there were remnants of collapsed buildings that Connor suspected were from the previous war the Ovarrow had fought before they'd gone into stasis.

Connor hadn't been to the Ovarrow city in over six months, and the population over the past year had doubled in size, the result of a joint effort between the colony and the Ovarrow to find the remaining stasis pods in the region and give those Ovarrow a chance at life. Many of the bunker sites that contained stasis pods would have remained in stasis until one of the specialized groups brought the Ovarrow out. He had learned that different Ovarrow factions had reconfigured their stasis pods to reanimate after a certain number of years had passed. It was a heck of a gamble because the technology—at least for the Ovarrow—hadn't been proven, and they didn't know if the equipment would function properly for the length of time required to endure the Ice Age. There had been no shortage of casualties for the Ovarrow in stasis pods, ranging from mechanical failure to power depletion. And if they survived all that, there was a chance they would suffer from cellular degeneration after they awakened.

Near the city entrance, the colonial diplomatic envoy waited for him. Darius Cohen waved as they approached, and Connor walked over.

Darius glanced at the people he was with. "Would you please give me and General Gates a few minutes to talk?"

The twelve people in the diplomatic envoy moved away from them, giving them some space.

Darius smiled and looked at Connor. "I guess you're not violating any orders if you're invited to come here. I have to say that Mullins wasn't pleased about Senleon's request for you to come in person."

"He couldn't have been *that* upset because he didn't forbid me from coming," Connor replied.

"Would you have listened?"

"Yes, but if Senleon really wanted to speak to me, there's very little Mullins can do to stop it. He probably decided it wasn't worth the effort of keeping us apart."

"I suppose you're right about that, and regardless, you're here, so let's make the most of it," Darius said.

The Ovarrow were hardly ever idle. They had a strong work ethic, much like most human colonists. There was also never a shortage of important tasks to be done. But as Connor looked around while they walked through the city, he saw that many of the Ovarrow moved with even more of a sense of urgency than was normal. There was general unrest in the air, and more than a few of them looked his way.

They made their way to a pavilion where High Commissioner Senleon and Warlord Vitory were speaking with faction leaders. When they saw Connor, they quickly ended their meeting and invited him up. There was a show of respect and deference given to Connor as the faction leaders dispersed.

"General Gates, thank you for coming here so quickly," Senleon said.

"You're welcome, High Commissioner. I hope you don't mind, but I brought some soldiers to help with a field exercise," Connor said.

"What is the nature of the field exercise?" Senleon asked.

Connor looked at Vitory for a moment. "They are to evaluate the area, looking for defensive positions and other things that might be of relevance to anyone with similar interests."

Senleon looked at Vitory, who said, "I'll inform Cerot that we have a contest."

Darius cleared his throat. "I don't understand. What contest?"

Vitory looked at Darius. "Cerot is leading Mekaal soldiers in performing a similar function. It will be interesting to see how our two militaries develop solutions based on the field exercise."

Vitory walked away from them and opened a comlink to Cerot.

"I told you *they* wouldn't mind," Connor said when Darius glanced at him. He looked at Senleon. "How are your people holding up?"

"There is much uncertainty," Senleon said. "It is our way that stronger factions absorb the weaker ones as a matter of course, especially at the end of the war with the Krake. We knew when we came out of stasis that this practice would resume."

"But this isn't your practice anymore?" Darius asked.

"The Ovarrow here are free to leave if they choose, but it wasn't always this way," Senleon replied.

"What changed?" asked Connor.

"It surprises me you need to ask that," Senleon said.

"Please, High Commissioner," Darius said. "We don't want to make any assumptions where the Ovarrow are concerned."

Vitory rejoined them.

"We changed," Senleon said and looked out into the city. Groups of Ovarrow were working to set up a gun nest on the rooftops of nearby buildings. "*You* do not force your citizens to remain with you, and yet there is loyalty among you. Our soldiers who work with the Colonial Defense Force return with stories. We encourage our soldiers to share their experiences, and this has triggered a departure from what we've done in the past."

Connor and Darius shared a glance. So much had changed over the past year, but it wasn't so long ago that Connor couldn't remember being extremely frustrated with the lack of cooperation.

"Darius has advised us to contact the Konus," Senleon said.

"Yes, it's important to open the lines of communication," Darius said.

Senleon and Vitory looked at Connor expectantly. They wanted his opinion.

"I agree with Darius," Connor said. "I also think it's important that you make your intentions clear."

"What intentions are you referring to?" Senleon asked.

"Do you want to join the Konus?" Connor asked.

"We desire to keep our independence."

Connor looked at Vitory and saw grim-faced determination.

"Are you open to communicating with the Konus?" asked Darius.

"Not if they come here with their army."

"Then you need to define that for them. In essence, you're claiming a territory," Connor said.

"If the Konus were heading to a colonial city, what would be your response?" Senleon asked.

"First, we would attempt to communicate with them to establish their intentions," Darius began.

"Darius is right," Connor said. "We'd try to communicate with them, but the CDF would make preparations in case diplomacy failed. We'd request their intentions, and if they violated our space, we'd put it in no uncertain terms that there would be consequences and retaliation."

Senleon was quiet for a few moments while he considered what Connor had just said. "Do you believe we could defend the city from the Konus if it came to a military confrontation?"

Connor looked away. The pavilion was at a higher elevation, which gave him a view of the city. Then he looked back at the Ovarrow. "It's possible. It would be better if you had help. It would be bad if you were boxed in here."

Again, Senleon was quiet, and Connor waited him out.

"We cannot ask that you fight on our behalf."

Connor frowned. That was exactly what he'd been expecting them to ask.

"Just to be clear," Darius said, "we're not authorized to engage the Konus here."

Connor stepped toward Senleon. "Why wouldn't you ask for our help? You'd have a much better chance with us."

When he'd spoken to Lenora, she had informed him that Senleon and the other faction leaders were open to the idea of joining the colony. He wondered what had changed. Maybe they'd just been open to considering the idea.

"This is not your fight," Vitory said, and Senleon nodded.

"What if we wanted to show our support to you? Would you allow us to facilitate a meeting with the Konus using our comms drones?" Darius asked.

Connor knew it was just a symbolic gesture. Senleon and Vitory would know it, too, but it couldn't hurt to remind the Konus that the Mekaal had allies.

Senleon told them they would need a few minutes to discuss this, so Connor and Darius gave them some space, walking to the edge of the pavilion that overlooked the city.

"Do you really think the city can be defended?" Darius asked.

"It's not that simple," Connor said. "If I were in their shoes, I wouldn't give the Konus an inch without making them pay for it. And by that, I mean I wouldn't wait for the Konus to arrive at the city to start defending it. I think Vitory understands that."

Darius glanced at Senleon and Vitory, who were still speaking quietly. "But Connor, they're so outnumbered."

"I know," Connor said grimly. "How do you think Mullins would react if we relocated sixty thousand Ovarrow to New Haven? Do you think he'd turn them away, or would he authorize the CDF to stop the Konus?"

Darius's eyes widened. This was the first time Connor had

directly voiced one of his ideas about how to help the Ovarrow here. "Is that what you're really considering? Moving them wouldn't be easy, and that's even if they'd want to leave here. Technically or legally speaking, it's not up to Mullins. It's up to Mayor Larson whether she would allow the Ovarrow to take refuge in New Haven, but I see where you're going with this. You could bypass Mullins altogether, but I think there would be long-term consequences if you did that."

Connor nodded. "Me too, and I don't want to do that. I don't want to play politics with the politicians. The Ovarrow are the ones who need our help," he said and gestured toward the cityscape.

Senleon and Vitory walked over to them.

"We accept your offer to use your communications drone to initiate contact with the Konus," Senleon said.

"That's good," Connor said. "We can have a drone intercept the Konus within the next two hours."

Senleon looked surprised, but Vitory did not. He was familiar with how fast the CDF could move when it had to.

"I shall recall the faction leaders, and we will confer until the comms drone is ready for us," Senleon said.

Connor nodded and began opening a few comlinks of his own to get things moving.

21

THE CDF COMMS drone hovered in the air above the pavilion of the Mekaal city. Over seven hundred kilometers away, there was another CDF comms drone near the Konus army. Connor had deployed stealth recon drones along with the comms drone. The stealth drones broke away on approach and were collecting data about the Konus.

The Konus had brought equipment Connor couldn't identify. Large haulers were carrying giant metallic spirals that could have any number of uses, from drilling into the ground, which didn't make sense to him, to some kind of communications tower. He'd have to show the images to Vitory and get his opinion.

The large holoscreen in the pavilion showed Kasmon, along with what Connor assumed were senior officers in the Konus army. Connor and Darius stood off to the side, and the discussion was led by Senleon and Vitory.

"I have already told you," Senleon said. "We are an

independent city. We've been rescuing Ovarrow from stasis pods and administering a cure for the illness caused by stasis."

"There is no such cure," Kasmon said.

"The cure was developed by the humans. They are sincere in their desire to help us," Senleon said.

"That is possible, but they've also made you dependent upon them."

"We needed their help in the beginning but not now."

"And yet I can see them there beside you," Kasmon said, and his gaze slid toward Connor and Darius.

"We are here because they asked us to be here," Darius said.

"This is a matter for the Ovarrow," Kasmon said, and looked at Senleon. "Why do you fear our approach?"

"Because I know what you'll do when you come here," Vitory said.

"Warlord Vitory," Kasmon said, "this is the way the Ovarrow become strong again. You knew there was a chance when and if you came out of stasis that factions would be forced together for the good of the whole."

"We are not a threat to you, and we are open to working with you. However, we cannot allow such a large military force to come to our city," Senleon said.

Kasmon waited for the length of a pregnant pause. Then he looked at Vitory. "Warlord, does the High Commissioner speak for you?"

Connor kept a careful watch on the exchange. Kasmon had changed since he'd first met him. He'd become more aggressive, but that wasn't what worried him. Kasmon was a believer, and he'd spent decades with the belief that the Ovarrow were stronger together. The Konus were a militaristic society. Kasmon knew the answer to the question before he asked it. It was a slight on Vitory because according to whatever plan the Ovarrow had had for when they awakened from stasis, it wasn't to have a democratic society.

Vitory regarded Kasmon for a few moments. "The High Commissioner and I work together to rebuild. The plans of old needed to change. The Ovarrow who made them are gone."

"Needed to change, or were you forced to change because of the humans?" Kasmon asked. There was no mistaking the vehemence in his voice.

Vitory stepped toward the holoscreen. "We are not under their dominion, and we will never be under yours."

"You are puppets for them, and you don't even realize it. If this is what they made you, then they are no better than the Krake," Kasmon said.

"What would it take to convince you that they are not puppets?" Connor asked. It was the first time he'd spoken up, and Kasmon's harsh gaze swooped toward him.

"I acknowledge that you have assisted my people. Now that we are aware of them, they will not need your assistance anymore. I advise you to stay out of Ovarrow affairs," Kasmon said, and he glanced at Darius. "That is, of course, if you wish to remain allies against the Krake."

Connor knew there was no way Kasmon was going to let this go. They were going to come here no matter what they said.

"Then you give us very little choice," Senleon said.

"Please," Darius said, "there must be a peaceful resolution to these issues. What if High Commissioner Senleon and Warlord Vitory allowed you to send a delegation here?"

Connor's gaze darted toward Senleon and Vitory, but their facial expressions gave nothing away. It was difficult to read the mood of any Ovarrow. Oftentimes, their mood was shown through actions rather than facial expressions. This had taken some getting used to for joint CDF missions.

"Peacekeeper," Kasmon said to Darius, "yours is a world that has not experienced what we have. If this is how you would engage the Krake, then you will lose everything. Delegations accomplish nothing except delaying the inevitable."

"That's just it. We're not Krake," Darius replied.

Kasmon didn't reply. Instead, the comlink severed.

Darius watched the holoscreen for a few moments, and Connor thought the diplomat hoped the comlink would reconnect.

"The comms drone is off-line. They destroyed it," Connor said.

"We can send them another comms drone," Darius said and looked at Senleon and Vitory. "We don't have to close the lines of communications. We should keep trying to speak to them. Perhaps there is someone else we can talk to—someone who can get Kasmon under control."

"Darius, why don't we give them a few minutes to talk," Connor said with a small tilt of his head toward the Ovarrow.

Darius looked at Senleon and Vitory. "Of course," he said.

As they walked away, Connor could hear Senleon and Vitory speaking with the faction leaders.

"The Konus aren't going to stop," Connor said to Darius.

"What makes you so sure?"

"Kasmon isn't interested in working with the Ovarrow here. He sees them as a way of building up his own strength."

"But why bring an army that large?"

"Intimidation for both the Ovarrow here and for us."

Darius's brow furrowed, and he blinked rapidly before his

face went slack. "Do you think he'll attack *us—uh*, one of our cities, I mean?"

"I don't think he wants to attack us. The closest city to here is New Haven, and we've been building up CDF forces there. But if we're here when the fighting starts, I don't think he'll hesitate to attack us here."

Darius shook his head. "If Kasmon wants to make the Ovarrow here join the Konus and they refuse, how many soldiers will he have to lose before the cost is too high, even for him?"

"Darius," Connor began.

Darius inhaled explosively and shook his head. "It's such a waste of time and resources. Why do you look like you've been expecting something like this to happen?"

"I know you were hoping for a peaceful resolution."

"I still hope for it," Darius said.

Both men regarded each other for a few moments. "We need to inform the Security Council," Connor said.

Darius looked away and nodded slowly. They both went back to the comms drone and opened a comlink to Sierra. Darius proceeded to give a report on what had occurred. Connor answered a few questions but otherwise let Darius take the lead.

Senleon walked over to them while the faction leaders left the pavilion. Vitory joined after speaking to a few Mekaal soldiers.

"High Commissioner Senleon and Warlord Vitory," Mullins said, "I think I can speak for everyone in this room by saying you have our deepest sympathies for the situation you're in."

Senleon briefly looked over at Connor, who couldn't hazard a guess as to what the Ovarrow was thinking. Then, he turned back to Mullins and the rest of the Security Council on the holoscreen. "We have many difficult decisions to make. We are at"—he paused and again looked at Connor—"a crossroads. Many things are going to change for us, and I suspect these changes might affect you as well."

"I think you're right about that," Mullins replied.

"We've discussed multiple options with the faction leaders," Senleon continued. "The Konus want to absorb us into their population, and they're willing to exert force to achieve this. Warlord Vitory intends to defend us, but I'm not sure it will be enough." He looked at Vitory, who wore a mask of grim determination. "Another option we were asked to consider was to petition you for help. We've been allies for off-world missions, and perhaps we could negotiate support to help us keep our independence from the Konus. You've expressed resistance to this option in the past, and we understand why. Another option has come to my attention and was something we'd considered even before the Konus were encountered. The option I'm talking about is to join your colony and become citizens." Senleon looked directly at Connor. "General Gates seeks to find a way to help us. If we were to become colonial citizens, then we would have the support of the Colonial Defense Force. Right, General Gates?"

The Security Council looked at Connor, and he cleared his throat. "That is correct. I do want to help you, and there are many others who would like to help you as well."

Senleon turned back to the holoscreen. "The timing for this type of request isn't appropriate, even though it could be perceived as necessary. The perception is that we would request to become colonial citizens only in order to get your protection and not because we choose to merge our two societies."

"The situation is very complicated," Mullins said in agreement.

"Is it?" Connor said before he could think better of it.

"Yes, it is, and Senleon understands this," Mullins said. He looked at the High Commissioner. "We need time to consider the best way we can help you. An armed conflict with the Konus will guarantee the loss of life—both for you and for them."

"We have many of our own preparations to make," Senleon said.

"High Commissioner Senleon, we will be in touch with you," Mullins said.

Senleon and Vitory left the pavilion. Connor and Darius stayed behind at Mullins's request.

Heat gathered in Connor's chest, and he felt his blood near boiling. "'We need time'?" he said, glaring at Mullins. "They will never survive without our help. You can see it in their faces."

"I understand your tactical assessment of the situation," Mullins replied with an edge in his voice, "but I cannot simply make them colonial citizens. We could never force this through without it being challenged. I'm afraid the path to colonial citizenship will not be resolved in the next few days."

"Then authorize me to help them," Connor said.

Mullins was quiet for a few moments, and Connor could tell he was trying to control his own frustration. "Connor, ever since we learned about the Krake, you and Nathan have advised that we need as many allies as we can get to fight them. The reality is we need the support of the Konus, especially if the Krake discover New Earth. I'm not trying to be obtuse; I'm just trying to be realistic."

Connor clenched his teeth for a few tight moments, then breathed in deeply and sighed. Mullins was right that they needed all the allies they could get, but this was too much. "I don't trust Kasmon. I trust Vitory and Senleon."

"If the Council decides to commit the CDF against the Konus, they might never help us in the future," Mullins said.

"What if . . ." Darius began to say and paused. "What if we helped evacuate the Ovarrow here?"

"To where?" Mullins asked.

"The closest city that could take them in is New Haven," Darius said.

There was a commotion among the Security Council, and Mullins called for quiet. "Doing so would put colonial citizens in harm's way. We need to defuse the situation without adding fuel to the fire."

Connor could hear Nathan's warning in his head—the warning that said not to buck the system. So, he didn't. "Well then, let's vote on it right now. The Security Council can vote on whether to allow the CDF to help the Mekaal defend their city."

"We would need more information," Mullins said.

"They're gathering ryklars as they come," Connor said. "Kasmon was always coming to fight, regardless of what we said. I have the video feeds to prove it, and I can further confirm it based on the stealth recon data we've gathered."

"General Gates," Mayor Jean Larson said, "I agree with Bob in that we shouldn't evacuate the Ovarrow to New Haven unless there was no other choice, but that's an entirely different conversation. What we would like to know is the potential impact on CDF soldiers."

"I can't guarantee there will be no losses. Nathan and I have worked on certain tactical scenarios since we first learned that the Konus were heading toward the city. These include the use of our ground forces, as well as our orbital defensive installations."

"You would seek to wipe them out, eliminate all of them?" Mullins asked.

"It could come to that, but no, that wouldn't be our first-strike scenario," said Connor. "Senleon and Vitory are sincere that they do not want to fight the Konus. They want to defend their homes. They are willing to fight for that, but I think they want to convince the Konus that it's not worth the fight to come here. We can help them do that. Do you now have enough information to put it to a vote?"

There was a short discussion among the Security Council members. After a few minutes, they quieted down, and Mullins turned to address Connor. "We need to confer with General Hayes about the specifics of these plans you have. Then, we'll put it to a vote. However," Mullins said before Connor could interject, "we recognize that time is of the essence, and you are given clearance to help the Ovarrow prepare defenses and tactics for defending their city and their territory. You are cleared to defend yourself, but I want you to keep one thing in mind, General Gates. If the Security Council decides to withdraw from this conflict, then you will quit the field. Is this understood?"

"I understand," Connor said.

"Very well."

The holoscreen powered off, and Connor turned to Darius.

"Well, it looks like you got what you wanted," Darius said.

"Provisionally, at least," Connor replied. "I need to make every minute count."

"I understand. Is there anything I can do to help?"

"Stick around and help Senleon. We might need an evacuation plan for Ovarrow civilians," Connor said.

Darius nodded. They left the pavilion, and each of them headed off in different directions. There was work to be done and troops to deploy.

Connor opened a comlink to Samson. "I have a job for you, Captain."

"Finally," Samson replied.

"Get a command center up. I'm coming to you."

22

THE CDF mobile command center was designed for quick deployments in the field, containing all the necessary equipment for conducting military operations. Connor stood at a large holotank that showed a three-dimensional image of the region surrounding the Ovarrow city. They were connected to COMCENT, which was the hub for all CDF activities on New Earth.

The mobile command center and equipment shared many of the same functions as the bridge of a warship. Connor had designed their functions this way to streamline how military operations were conducted. The rudimentary functions of the command center formed the foundation for the officers and soldiers who used them. The bedrock was the same, regardless of whether the CDF required the soldiers to serve aboard warships, space stations, lunar bases, or terrestrial bases. They all required specialized training for the purpose-built application, but Connor had designed the CDF to be as agile a military as possible.

Over the past year, the Mekaal had worked closely with the CDF and had been equipped with certain advancements that had been unavailable to them before—things like comlinks and better weapons. Although they still preferred their energy-based weaponry, they'd come to appreciate the CDF armament for use among their infantry.

The Mekaal didn't have neural implants, and Connor didn't believe they would be getting them anytime soon since that would require further study and experimentation. They were, however, equipped with PDAs in the form of wrist computers designed with an Ovarrow interface. Imitating the basic colonial interface for PDAs had been surprisingly easy with the Krake translator. It hadn't been seamless, and there was still a learning curve, but it had become an essential tool for basic communication. The Mekaal had eagerly seized these advantages, which enticed them to want to learn more ways to use the tools on hand.

A comlink appeared at Connor's personal workstation at the holotank. He acknowledged it, and Samson appeared on the video feed. Thunder rumbled overhead, and Connor heard it echoed from Samson's location. The 7th Ranger Company was deployed near the forward position where defensive installations had been established to deter the Konus from going any farther.

Samson proceeded to give Connor an update. "I don't see how the Mekaal can win against the Konus. Sheer numbers were bad enough, but they're gathering ryklars along the way."

"The numbers are growing, but we've increased the range of

the ryklar deterrent signal, which should help with that," Connor said.

"That deterrent signal won't work if they're able to put implants on the newer ryklars. Maybe we should use the ryklar signal to have them attack the Konus."

"I spoke to Vitory about that. What we have is a purge protocol that essentially forces the ryklars to attack anything that moves. We wouldn't be able to tell them not to attack the Mekaal, or you for that matter, and that's not the kind of chaos we want on a battlefield," Connor said.

Lightning flashed behind Samson's head, and he glanced up for a moment. "I've deployed additional reconnaissance drones to help with our field coverage. The Konus haven't deviated from their present course."

"Understood," Connor said.

"We're authorized to engage the Konus, but why aren't we using the orbital defense platforms for a strike before they even reach our area?" Samson asked.

"For one, we're losing visibility, so we'll be more reliant on you to provide a targeting area. The additional recon drones will help with that. For two, they haven't actually engaged us," Connor said.

Samson gave him a calculated look. "I see."

Connor knew that Samson understood. They were authorized to use force on the ground, but until the Konus reached an area and engaged in hostilities against the Mekaal, the CDF wasn't authorized to use the defense platforms.

"We don't want to annihilate them."

Samson arched an eyebrow. "So, we have a few hundred thousand Konus just out and about, looking for trouble."

Connor tilted his head to the side in a small nod. "We need

to convince the Konus that having us as their enemy isn't in their best interest."

"Roger that, sir."

The wind was beginning to gust strongly. "I want you to send Lieutenant Layton to these coordinates to help with the reconnaissance."

Samson nodded. "I'll have him cherry-pick a few targets for you."

"Sounds good," Connor said, and the comlink severed.

Samson had no illusions about the Konus, unlike the Security Council, which seemed to think that after a small display of force, they could be persuaded to see reason. It was a nice sentiment, and Connor hoped it would happen, but he just didn't believe it was going to. He'd looked Kasmon in the eye, and he knew the Konus warlord wouldn't deviate from his chosen path. He meant to absorb the Mekaal into the Konus, and he had committed a massive force to accomplish the task. Connor believed Kasmon had a two-pronged approach to this. The first was teaching the Mekaal that they couldn't maintain their independence, and the second was convincing the colonists they should defer to the Konus in their war against the Krake. Connor, of course, couldn't agree with that.

An official comlink appeared at Connor's workstation, bearing the seal of the Colonial Security Council. Mullins's face appeared.

"I've just spoken with Senleon," Mullins said. "I wanted you to know that we are postponing the proposal for the Mekaal to become colonial citizens."

Connor frowned. Why would Mullins tell them this now when the CDF was essentially committed to helping the Mekaal defend themselves against the Konus?

"We both decided it was best that we table the discussion until after the Konus have been dealt with," Mullins said.

Connor nodded slowly. "For a moment there, I thought you were going to order me to withdraw."

Mullins shook his head. "No, never."

"Good."

"Inviting the Mekaal to become colonial citizens will be an uphill battle. Regardless of how that turns out, I want you to know you have the full support of the Security Council," Mullins said.

For years Connor had butted heads with Mullins over a variety of issues, mainly surrounding the CDF. Something had changed in the past year. They would never be friends, but they shared common goals for the colony, even though they approached solutions to those goals from very different perspectives. For years, Connor had questioned Governor Wolf's decision to keep Mullins on as an advisor. When she'd become ill, some of those old feelings resurfaced—feelings that Mullins would work to thwart Connor's efforts to defend the colony against the Krake. Although Connor could now see this wasn't the case, Mullins was still adjusting to his role of acting governor, and that was causing a few challenges as he became more adept at leading.

"Thank you," Connor said. "I appreciate it."

"We appreciate you, Connor. I know we haven't always seen eye to eye, but I'm actually glad we can work together with or without General Hayes," Mullins said with a hint of a smile lifting the edges of his lips.

"Nathan is on his way back from Phoenix Station, but he won't be here for another twelve hours."

Mullins nodded. "I spoke to Nathan a short while ago. The

subspace communicators are quite an achievement. But in the end, I agreed with Nathan that he should return to New Earth," he said and paused for a moment. "I'll let you get back to it. If there's anything you need, I hope you'll contact me."

Connor regarded him for a few moments. "I will."

The comlink went dark, and Connor went back to reviewing the latest intelligence data from the recon drones.

23

SAMSON HAD NEVER BEEN what anyone would call a people person, and certainly not any of the colonists. The people who'd known him best were long gone, dead for hundreds of years. They'd either become victims of the plague that had almost consumed all of mankind or fought and died in the ensuing wars after the collapse of Old Earth. Like most colonists, he'd left people behind, but unlike most colonists, he'd never had a choice or a chance to say goodbye. As far as those he'd left behind knew, he'd simply disappeared. It was possible he'd been reported as killed in action, which didn't matter because the end result was still the same.

Gone.

Thunder rumbled powerfully overhead, as if the sky itself were clearing its throat to bellow. A sudden gust of wind howled as it shoved against the trees, causing them to sway violently. Brittle branches from winter snapped and plummeted to the ground like flailing missiles. The powerful winds slammed uselessly against the Nexstar combat suit, and Samson paid them no more notice than he would a summer breeze.

This wasn't a time to think about the family he'd left, but sometimes the echoes of the past forced themselves into the forefront of his thoughts, triggered by seemingly nothing. A snippet of some conversation that pulled him into a memory of his sisters, who'd banded together to protect their baby brother; some intonation of a laugh by someone; or a subtle blend of seemingly unrelated, almost random things could suddenly remind him of home. Coming from a family of nine siblings, they'd had to look after one another. He wasn't like Connor. He'd never made peace with the life he'd left behind. Samson ground his teeth at the thought. No, Connor may have moved on with his life, but Samson doubted he'd ever be at peace with what had happened. None of the Ghosts were, and if they said they were, then they were fooling themselves. The former Ghosts had done as they'd always done. Adapted. They gritted their teeth, buried their pain, and picked up the pieces to carve out a life on this planet. Except him.

He sucked a deep breath in through his nose, his lips lifting into a sneer that threatened to blossom on his face. He'd never liked New Earth, and he'd never quite fit in with the colonists. No matter how long he lived, New Earth would never be his home. Living alone for years while he explored only a portion of the vast continent had imparted harsh lessons about this godforsaken planet. New Earth wasn't for the weak. If they ever left their cities, this world would chew them up and be done with them. That was what he'd expected to happen to him when he left the colony all those years ago. Instead, he'd survived. For years he was alone, walking endlessly across a continent among the graveyards of the Ovarrow. He'd braved everything this planet had to offer and survived, but returning to the colony had allowed him to do what he was best at. His blood still boiled, and he'd found that if he didn't focus those instincts, he'd be washed out in a sea of molten fury.

Rejoining the CDF had allowed him to channel that energy into something worthwhile. But what he lived for was to fight, and he only felt truly alive when facing his own mortality. The only other thing that made him feel human was the people under his command. The 7th had become his surrogate—not quite family but pretty damn close. Connor had probably orchestrated that. Stubborn, that one. There were few men Samson had ever known who were as tenacious as one Connor Gates. This commanded his respect, even when he blamed him for what happened to the Ghosts, but that didn't prevent him from making Connor work for it. How he'd wanted to vilify Connor, make him the reason for everything wrong, but Samson was the one who'd been wrong. Connor wasn't any more to blame than the damn howling wind flinging the rain in a liquid assault.

He'd heard a few of his soldiers complain about the weather, but it was half-hearted. Samson was used to it. The Konus thought they could do whatever they wanted, but they'd picked the wrong fight. If he couldn't fight the Krake, then they'd become the next best thing against which he could use his God-given talent for mayhem and destruction.

Samson opened a comlink to Layton. "What's your status, Lieutenant?"

"Almost to the coordinates, Captain. Had a few issues with the terrain, and the Mekaal don't move as fast as we can," Layton replied.

The Mekaal had a basic version of powered armor, but they were simply outclassed by the CDF combat suits. Even with inferior equipment, the Mekaal, for the most part, were able to keep up. He'd challenge any other CDF soldier to do the same. It wasn't easy. They were a tough act to follow.

"Slow is fast," Samson said.

"Yes, sir. They haven't noticed us. We've engaged stealth protocols, and with this weather, we should be able to flank them easily enough."

"Understood. Let me know when you're in position."

"Will do, Captain," Layton said.

Samson closed the comlink. Layton was leading the 3rd Platoon on a scouting mission and also had an equal number of Mekaal lending support. The Mekaal knew the stakes. They were defending their homes. They'd been given a second chance, and they weren't going to let anyone take that away from them.

Cerot, the Warlord's First, walked over to him. All the Mekaal outside the city were under his command, and the off-world missions they'd been on for the past year had made them familiar with each other. Despite the different species and uniforms, there were some things that transcended life-forms that, for lack of similar appearances, were alike in so many other ways. Cerot exhibited a strong sense of honor and was a good leader. His loyalty to Warlord Vitory, who Samson suspected was some kind of relative, was rivaled by Samson's own loyalty to Connor. And that was something else Connor excelled at. Most people either loved him or hated him. There were very few who walked the middle ground with their opinion of him.

"Our soldiers are in position. The Konus will come down these paths," Cerot said and gestured toward the holoscreen.

"Possibly," Samson replied. "That's what they'd like us to think."

"With such a large force, why would they need to deviate?"

"Just because we can't think of a reason doesn't mean they don't have one. We'll need to pay attention and watch out for any surprise tactics. Kasmon seems craftier than the other Konus," Samson said.

Cerot considered this for a few moments and said, "He has the bearing of having been in command for a long time."

Samson nodded in agreement. "And he's used to getting what he wants."

"Precisely."

The holoscreen showed the deployment of the CDF and Mekaal soldiers. Combat suit heavies and armored rovers were deployed among their ranks. Hellcats weren't far off and would be on hand when the fighting began. Samson felt a spike of energy in anticipation. On the off-world missions, they'd had to work with rebel Ovarrow groups to help overthrow the Krake. Most weren't anyone Samson would want as neighbors, but they were necessary for their war with the Krake. He didn't like that the Konus had proven to be nothing more than a domestic bully who believed might would always be right. Well, today they'd be wrong, and Samson couldn't wait to teach them his part of that lesson.

24

Colonel John Randall stood in the command center at Hammerholde. They'd been fully staffed and on high alert since they first detected the Konus army moving across the continent. General Gates was about to begin his operations at the Mekaal city. They'd deployed troops composed of CDF infantry divisions, along with Spec Ops companies. Air support had been withheld for the time being, and they'd covered the area with reconnaissance drones. Satellite feeds were off-line now because of the storm that had quickly developed, blanketing the region. The orbital defense platform was in position above the target, online and waiting for General Gates to command its use.

The sounds of people talking either to each other or on comlinks to the outside world could be heard throughout the command center. The conversations were even in tone with a slightly heightened energy but with none of the desperation Randall could recall from the Vemus War.

A sudden flashing on the main holoscreen at the tactical and operations work area snatched his attention. Alerts appeared, and then a klaxon alarm sounded.

"Colonel," Lieutenant Wong said, "reconnaissance drones over the Konus have all gone off-line."

Randall frowned and checked the feed on the main holoscreen. Then the defense platform status changed to gray. "We just lost our defense platform."

"Yes, Colonel, checking right now." Lieutenant Wong's hands flew through the holo-interface.

"Ops, confirm the most recent commands to the defense platform. Orbital, has anything been detected on our sensors?" Randall asked, needing to know whether a Krake attack force had suddenly emerged through a gateway.

"Colonel, last orders to the defense platform were from General Gates with targeting updates for the mag-cannons. He wanted them fired."

Randall's shoulder went tight. General Gates wouldn't have ordered those cannons to fire if he hadn't been committed to engaging the Konus. "Comms, we need to deploy reconnaissance drones and combat drones to that area. Send out a general alert to the CDF base at New Haven."

Sergeant Brooks confirmed and began opening comlinks to those places.

"No ships have been detected on any scanners in the star system," Lieutenant Mitchell said.

"Colonel, I've deployed a repair drone task force, and they're heading to the defense platform now. ETA is at least forty-five minutes."

Randall ground his teeth in frustration. "Understood. Keep me updated."

CDF and Mekaal forces began engaging the Konus in a ground battle. The CDF had lost their eyes and ears over the Konus. Randall tried to think of something else he could do. The CDF was mobilizing. How had they underestimated the Konus so completely?

"Colonel, repair drones are making their final approach to the defense platform. It's still not responding to any of our commands. It seems to be in a state of unresponsiveness but not fully off-line."

"Put it on screen," Randall said.

A new window appeared on the main holoscreen, showing the video feed from the lead repair drone on its way to the defense platform. The video feed suddenly cut off and went off-line.

"Ops, what the hell happened to our repair drones?"

"We've lost communications with them, sir. They're off-line. Something . . ." Lieutenant Zima said and paused for a moment. "Sir, the defense platform's countermeasures engaged and took out the repair drones."

Active sensors around New Earth still hadn't detected any enemy ships in the area. At least this wasn't an invasion force, but how the hell had the Konus taken out his defense platform? "Ops, can you access the most recent transmission logs to the defense platform? Timeframe to fifteen minutes before it went off-line."

"I'll try and get them, sir. It's going to take me a few moments."

Randall waited, and then Lieutenant Zima spoke again. "Sir, there was a tight-beam transmission that came from the Konus position."

"That's impossible," Randall said. "Even if they could figure out where our defense platform was, that doesn't . . . Find out what they did."

"Sir, they were using a CDF broadcast comlink to the platform. They had credentials, and then they uploaded the data package. After that, the targeting computer began spewing errors in its FOH systems. The onboard computer automatically launched diagnostics and then the system froze in a partial system reset, but the targeting system is having trouble determining friendlies from hostiles."

Randall's stomach attempted to slither out of his mouth. A highly capable defense platform meant to protect New Earth was malfunctioning, and now it was at the mercy of whatever the hell the Konus had done to it.

"Sir, I can send more repair drones, but the countermeasures are going to take them out."

"Understood," Randall said. "I need options. Is it responsive at all? Can we bring it down? I need that platform down. I can't have a rogue targeting computer on a defense platform that's capable of bombarding colonial cities."

"I'm trying to gain control of the system," Lieutenant Zima said.

"Tactical, I want a firing solution on that defense platform right now. If we can't regain control of it, I want it taken down ASAP."

"Understood, sir, creating the firing solution now," Lieutenant Wong said.

"Colonel," Lieutenant Zima said, "I'm able to put the defense platform into standby diagnostic for a time."

"What does that get us?" Randall asked.

"It gives us a window to get somebody out there to reset the computer systems on the platform. I can't do it remotely because it's hardened against communications in the mode it's in right now."

Randall considered this and then looked at Lieutenant Wong. "Tactical, what have you got for me?"

"It's difficult, sir. The defense platform will treat any approaching vessel as hostile, which would include any missiles we send up to it. If we attempt to take it out, it may unleash its arsenal against us. I advise sending a team up there to fix it."

Randall shook his head. He should have anticipated this. The defense platforms had been designed to engage an enemy from space. In the event it was about to be taken out, it would unleash everything it had, essentially going out in a blaze of glory while attempting mutually assured destruction. Only this time, the receiving end of all that armament was the region of New Earth where the colonists were.

"Understood," Randall said, his voice sounding strained. "Do we have any ships in the area? Who's closest? Get me somebody who can help."

"Scanning now, sir," Lieutenant Wong said.

Randall cursed inwardly. A standard op, even one with combat, shouldn't have gone to shit so fast, but he'd be damned if he'd worsen the situation by making rash decisions. There had to be somebody who could help.

NOAH LOOKED out the floor-to-ceiling windows at the back of his house. They had an elevated view of the natural landscape away from Sanctuary's interior. To his left was the forest, filled with the towering trees Kara informed him had been likened to

Old Earth sequoias. The view was both serene and peaceful, and despite it, Noah still felt a building of anticipation. They were leaving. They'd had to secure the house because they wouldn't be back for over six months. During all his time here, he hadn't spent much of it enjoying the view from his house. To his right, he could see a few other residences before the small city that was Sanctuary began in earnest. It probably wouldn't be long before the borders of the city expanded beyond where he was.

Noah had built an impressive laboratory beneath his house. He wasn't sure where he fit with the saying that one lived to work or one worked to live. Was it really work if he loved what he was doing? Both he and Kara had their own pet projects they liked to tinker with, and they collaborated on some of them.

The front door opened, and Noah turned to the sound of Maggie and Amos running toward him. The clickety-clack of their paws on the smooth floor echoed as they raced over, their tails windmilling excitedly. Noah squatted down and gave them a quick, vigorous scratch along their backs, which they loved.

He looked up at Kara. "I guess it's about that time."

She smiled and then nodded once. She walked over to him and bent over to pat Maggie's haunches. "I wish we could take them with us," she said.

"Me too. Can you imagine them running on the lunar surface? Even if we had a spacesuit for them, they'd probably love it."

"They'd probably build up so much momentum they'd launch clear off into space."

Noah stood up, and Kara did as well. Over by the wall were two specialized stasis pods that had been designed for Maggie and Amos. He'd already put their beds inside so they would smell familiar. The stasis pods were patched into the power in the house but also had redundancies in place should there be any kind of disruption. In addition, the pods would be monitored by their veterinarian. The dogs' vital signs and all other states of being would be monitored as if they were staying in a medical center. Any deviation would trigger an alarm, and someone would be able to address the problem. The alarm would also send a message to both Noah and Kara. Additionally, he could access a video surveillance system and look in on them at any time. The floor-to-ceiling windows would remain clear so the sunlight could reach the stasis pods. It wasn't a requirement, but Noah knew what it was like to be shut away from the outside world.

His time in a coma had brought forth some strange memories that were difficult to place. He remembered hearing voices and snippets of conversation, but it was almost as if he'd been in a great motionless fog. He also had memories of feeling warmth on his face, and he'd awakened to see windows in his hospital room. Kara had told him that when she would visit him, which had been daily for almost a year, she'd open the windows to allow fresh air in. She read to him and told him about what she was working on. Noah shuddered to think of what that must've been like for her.

They walked over to the stasis pods, and both Amos and Maggie approached warily, but after taking a few tentative sniffs, they walked inside fearlessly. They circled around, pawing at the cushions of their beds, and then settled down. Noah activated the door control, and it slid silently shut. A warm amber light came from the back of the pod, and soon both his dogs stopped moving altogether. He frowned with concentration as he tried to see them breathe. The only confirmation of life was on the holoscreen that showed the vitals of his two dogs.

Noah rubbed the top of the stasis pod where Amos slept. "Sleep well, buddy. We'll be home before you know it."

Kara said her own goodbyes, and she turned toward him misty-eyed. They hugged for a few moments. "It's silly," she said. "We'll be back in six months, but this is so much harder than I thought it was going to be."

"Not to them, it won't be. To them, only a short time will pass," Noah said.

Kara wiped away a tear and nodded. They both took one last glance at their babies and left the house.

They'd just closed the door and put the house on lockdown when a comlink registered on Noah's PDA. It was from Sean.

"Are you all packed up and ready to go?" Sean asked.

"Yes, we are," Noah said. "And I expect the white-glove treatment when we get there."

Sean arched an eyebrow. "Of course. I have you down for a room with a view, and I might even throw in a few sandwiches."

Noah grinned, and Kara looked at him questioningly. "We'd gone on a camping trip and left our food back at the base, so I appropriated a recon drone to retrieve them for us."

"Yep, and Field Ops thought they had a drone that had gone rogue," Sean said. "There's been a change in your travel plans. I sent a shuttle to your location, and it should be arriving there shortly."

Noah's eyebrows raised. "Door-to-door service."

"Nothing but the best. But seriously, thanks for agreeing to come up to the lunar base. I think you're gonna love some of the things we're doing here," Sean said.

"There's no doubt about that," Noah said. He'd spent the

last two days reading the briefings from Oriana. "I'll see you in about twelve hours."

"Looking forward to it," Sean said, and the comlink closed.

Noah glanced at Kara, and she was positively beaming. He might've underestimated her desire to go.

High above, a shuttle flew across the pale gray sky, lining up with an open area a short distance from the house. The engines shrieked in a dopplered wail as it came in low and fast. A loading ramp opened at the rear of the Valkyrie class combat shuttle, and standing just inside was a young pilot with brown hair and a dimple on his chin.

"Hey there, I'm Lieutenant Owen Sykes. I'm here to give you a lift to the lunar base."

Lieutenant Sykes stepped off the ramp and helped them load their belongings. They secured their equipment in the rear storage compartment.

Noah looked at the young man. "So, did you draw the short straw or lose a bet?" Shuttle duty could be tedious for pilots.

Owen smiled and shook his head. "Negative, sir. I just happened to be in the neighborhood."

Kara arched an eyebrow toward him. "Or Colonel Quinn orchestrated events so you'd be nearby."

"I can neither confirm nor deny that, ma'am," Owen said. He had an authenticity about him that Noah liked immediately.

"All right, flyboy. Just get us there in one piece," Kara said.

Owen grinned. "Yes, ma'am."

The loading ramp retracted into the shuttle, and they closed the hatch. Owen headed toward the cockpit, leaving Noah and Kara to sit wherever they wanted. The combat shuttle wasn't especially large, and it was meant for quick transport.

Noah sat and opened a holoscreen. Kara took a seat next to him. "What should we do first?" she asked.

"Oriana sent me some updates regarding the subspace theory. She thinks we're only scratching the surface of what it's capable of. I agree. I think there's a lot more we can do with this," Noah said.

"Well, we have a lot of time. Let's get started," Kara said.

As the combat shuttle rose into the air and flew away, Noah and Kara hardly noticed. They were completely focused, with multiple holoscreens up in front of them. Noah knew they'd go on for hours like this. He'd been very lucky to find someone who was a kindred spirit. There was no better woman for him than Kara.

She paused when she noticed him looking at her. "What?" she asked.

Noah shook his head. "It's nothing. I'm just glad you're here."

She smiled and leaned toward him. Her eyes twinkled affectionately. "Same here."

He leaned back in his chair and thought about Lars. He'd done everything he could, and now it was up to him. He hoped . . . Noah frowned, choosing not to allow his thoughts to run down familiar worries and fears.

He just hoped, and that was all.

25

THE CDF MOBILE COMMAND CENTER, located along the northeast region of the Ovarrow city, had become a hotbed of activity. Connor stood at the holotank and studied the aerial layout as the Konus drew steadily closer. The storm had picked up in earnest, and he couldn't remember if it had even been on the latest weather reports. But it didn't matter because the storm was here, and they had to deal with it.

At the top of the holotank range was the designation for the orbital defense platform DPO-47, but the icon for the defense platform was grayed out. It had been grayed out for over twenty-five minutes. They had to wait several hours to get the defense platform in place above this particular region of the continent. The platform was armed with HADES V missiles, which they wouldn't be using, two heavy mag-cannons capable of dispensing extreme destruction that could turn entire cities into slag, and two medium mag-cannons capable of firing smaller, solid projectiles at a rapid rate.

If Connor had wanted to wipe out the entire Konus army, he could've done it with a single HADES V missile and not even with a max load for the fusion warhead. At this instance, he had chosen to use the medium mag-cannons to pepper the Konus army. They were capable of launching projectiles with incredible accuracy, speed, and power. They could also be used for long-range targets, but that wasn't the case for using the weapons to fire down at the planet. For that, they'd have to adjust the mass drivers to a speed that wouldn't pierce the crust of the planet. They'd been experiencing delays in recalibrating the targeting computer on the defense platform.

Connor looked at Major Alexis Brooks and raised his eyebrows.

"Not yet, General. We're almost there," Brooks said.

They had a firing solution and no shortage of targets. Connor wanted to conduct this operation with a minimal loss of lives. He wanted to teach the Konus a lesson, and that was all. They had air support on standby, with squadrons of Hellcats and Talon-V Stinger class vessels waiting to make runs on the Konus lines if they needed them. They had combat drones in the air, deployed along with the reconnaissance drones, and they had more than enough firepower to drive the point home. Kasmon didn't know what was coming for him. There was no way he could know.

They had waited for the Konus to reach a position where they'd be bottled up across a few kilometers, leaving them vulnerable. They knew exactly where the CDF troops were, and the Konus front lines would be within effective combat range.

The heavy defense platform was meant for engaging a target invading them from outer space. When it had become apparent that the Krake could very well invade them by opening a gateway on New Earth, they'd had to upgrade the cyber warfare suite on the defense platforms so they could target enemies on the surface of New Earth. It wasn't as simple as swinging the defense platform around so its armament faced the planet. These were highly sophisticated war machines that required precision. If the targeting was off even just a little bit, it could be disastrous for them.

Major Brooks looked over at Connor. "It's coming online now, General."

"Understood," Connor said. "Lieutenant Morgan, have your team double check the firing solution."

"Yes, General," Lieutenant Morgan said.

The defense platform icon depicted on, or in, the holotank had become green. The systems were online and in sync with the mobile command center. The work area where the tactical team was assembled showed a wall of holoscreens displaying multiple feeds from the reconnaissance drones and CDF troop deployments.

"General Gates," Lieutenant Morgan said, "the firing solution checks out, but the Konus are starting to split their forces. They've increased their speed and—" The tactical officer stopped speaking. Connor's eyes flicked to the holoscreens that had begun flashing—first one, then a couple, and then more spread across the board. "General, our recon drones are going off-line. They're being taken out."

Connor watched the feed in shock as nearly every one of the reconnaissance drones went off-line, seemingly all at once. He'd never seen such a thing before. They had thousands of drones covering the region.

"Run a diagnostic, Lieutenant," Connor said.

"System checks out, General. They're taking out our drones."

"Order the combat drones to fire on their targets."

There was a flurry of activity at the tactical work area. Connor shifted his feet, a sinking feeling dragging at his core, and he felt like he was the one being ambushed instead of the Konus. His orders should only have needed to be confirmed, and then the combat drones would engage, but Major Brooks began conferring with Lieutenant Abernathy at operations.

Connor walked over to Lieutenant Morgan.

"General, I can't get any confirmation from our combat drones. One moment they were all there, and the next . . ." Morgan said and shook his head.

"If they were being destroyed, at least some of them would have registered the attack," Connor said.

Lieutenant Morgan nodded. "The last activity logged was a strange power surge. It affected them all at once."

Connor gritted his teeth. The Konus must have had some kind of weapon they hadn't encountered that enabled them to destroy all the CDF drones. With the intense storm, they could have hidden the attack.

"Does the defense platform firing solution still check out?" Connor asked.

"Yes, General."

"Fire. Authorization given."

"Confirmed. Sending the clearance code for the firing solution to the defense platform," Lieutenant Morgan said.

Connor turned back to the holotank and waited. What the hell could have taken out the combat drones and the reconnaissance drones? That they hadn't even detected? Their eyes, ears, and first-strike weapons had been snuffed out. His mind reeled with the knowledge that the Konus must've been able to track the CDF drones this entire time. They'd just *let* the CDF watch them. He furrowed his brow in concentration. He'd underestimated Kasmon.

"That can't be right," Lieutenant Morgan said in a harsh tone. He looked over at Connor as if fearing to give him a status update that was the precursor to the shit hitting the fan. "The defense platform is not responding."

Connor blinked his eyes for several moments, and Lieutenant Morgan flinched. "Say that again, Lieutenant."

"I sent the command authorization for the firing solution and received no acknowledgment. The system is not responding," Lieutenant Morgan said.

Connor swung his gaze back to the holotank, and he opened a comlink to Hammerholde. Colonel John Randall appeared on a holoscreen. "Colonel Randall, I have a defense platform I can't communicate with."

"We're seeing the same thing, General. We've deployed repair drones that are en route to the defense platform. ETA is thirty-seven minutes."

Connor clenched his teeth and shook his head. Then he looked back at Randall. "Keep me apprised, Colonel."

He severed the comlink.

"Ops, send an emergency broadcast to all forward forces. They are cleared to engage the enemy. Attack orders Bravo."

"Yes, General. Relaying orders now," Lieutenant Abernathy said.

"Major Brooks, we are going to need air support," Connor said.

"Understood, General. How many, sir?" Brooks asked.

Connor swallowed hard. "All of them."

"I'm on it, sir," Brooks replied.

Connor turned back to the holotank, glaring at the lack of information he had on there now. The Konus were on the move, and with each passing moment, the data he did have on hand became less and less accurate. They'd been blinded. Hell, they'd been knocked back on their asses before the battle had even begun. The operation had gone sideways, and now they were scrambling to catch up.

In the distance, Connor heard the shrieking engines of the Hellcats rising into the air. They flew overhead, speeding toward a battle that was about to begin. Connor balled his hands into fists, wanting to lash out. The plan had just gone out the window, and he needed a new one. And something told him deep in his gut that the Konus weren't finished with their surprises. He looked over at Vitory.

"The Konus are coming, and we need to be on high alert. Make sure the soldiers at the defense installations around the city are ready," Connor said.

Vitory leveled a look at him. "They are ready."

Connor wondered if the Ovarrow had suspected the Konus could do something like this, but there was no way they could've known. If Vitory had suspected such a thing, he would've told Connor. They were both veterans enough to understand that the events of a battlefield changed quickly, and now they needed to adapt. Now, they needed to fight.

26

SAMSON DEPLOYED the 7th along the ridgeline of a string of deep forested valleys. Mekaal infantry units were spread throughout the area for half a kilometer. Sheets of rain pelted down in thick volleys, thwacking the CDF soldiers who lay in wait. The muddy ground had become saturated, and Samson expected that mudslides could occur at any moment.

The CDF soldiers hid, using makeshift cover to blend in with the landscape. The storm blowing through the area made it extraordinarily dark, which wasn't so much an obstacle for CDF soldiers, but a darkness this profound, broken by random lightning in combination with an intense storm and a rapidly approaching enemy army, was a potent hurdle to overcome.

Samson knelt behind the corpse of a massive fallen tree that hadn't quite succumbed to its untimely demise. It lay against its neighbors in a tangle of brush that stubbornly kept it from dropping completely to the ground. The highly dense wood could absorb even the most powerful plasma bolts from

Ovarrow weapons. He could exhaust his entire supply of nanorobotic ammunition to chew through the compact hardwoods, but it would take time. He'd take any additional protection to the battle-steel of his combat suit armor, so this was a good location from which to engage the enemy.

The rangers were quiet as they peered into the gloomy veil of darkness. Enhanced night vision through the Nexstar combat suit was as close as they were going to get to seeing clearly this night. The heads-up display of the combat suit helmet filtered out the things they didn't need to see in order to help them identify the targets they were most interested in. The falling rain appeared as a semitranslucent silhouette of oblong drops splattering as they hit the ground. They had infrared for detecting heat signatures, but everyone knew that ryklars could conceal their body heat. Samson wouldn't allow any of his soldiers to assume anything about the enemy. Whether the Konus soldiers could hide themselves as well as the CDF Rangers remained to be seen. They'd deployed acoustic sensors with which their combat suit computers filtered out sounds they'd already accounted for, so their suit computers focused on the anomalies. CDF training included using these tactics as part of their scout training and also for points of engagement at ambush sites.

The Konus had superior numbers, making them able to field more soldiers. They had more weapons, whose abilities the CDF had yet to really see in action, and then there were the ryklars. Samson had hunted the ryklars before and had been hunted by them during his long years of isolation. High frequency sound waves wouldn't send the ryklars with Konus implants running, which made them all the more dangerous.

Ryklars were powerful and quick, and when in a pack, they'd coordinate their attacks.

The heavily forested region would slow the bulk of Konus ground transportation vehicles, forcing them to circumvent the area entirely. They'd either have to come through on foot with smaller vehicles or slow their progress to a crawl, which made for easier targets. But the loss of the forward reconnaissance drones had plunged their bird's-eye view of the enemy into complete and total darkness. Samson had recalled their platoon-specific drones. No use leaving them out there for the Konus to use for target practice. If they could detect and eliminate stealth recon drones, then they could very well see in the dark. The Konus had been preparing for war for years, and Samson had no illusions they weren't well-practiced in armed conflict.

"Look alive. A scouting force is trying to sneak in here," Sergeant Dixon said on an open broadcast comlink to the 7th. The CDF sniper had set up a perch above their position. Armed with an M-Viper rifle, he was among the deadliest sharpshooters in the entire company. "Painting the targets," he said.

The M-Viper had a highly specialized scope that linked to Dixon's Nexstar combat suit. Once he identified hostile forces, the data was uploaded to Samson and the squad leaders in the area. In the absence of recon drones, it was the next best thing.

"I have them on my scope too," Mason said. His squad's position was on another ridge at the adjacent valley.

Chatter began to pick up as more and more of them detected the Konus.

"Hold your fire," Samson ordered. "This is a scout force. Let them come in farther."

They'd know soon enough if the Konus could detect them. The comms chatter ceased. Sound-dampening tech from the combat suits would prevent the CDF soldiers from being overheard, but the Mekaal didn't have that kind of advantage. They relied on gestures to communicate. They wouldn't break the silence until the first shots were fired.

Samson felt cold anticipation gather inside him that he felt in his gut, and it traveled along his muscled arms to his fingertips as he caught his first glimpse of the Konus soldiers. They moved in small groups, carrying long staff-type energy weapons that Samson had seen in Ovarrow military bunkers. They advanced with efficiency and precision that was almost surgical, as one group moved up about ten meters, checked the area, and gestured for the next group to move forward. They spread into the deep valley, and Samson spotted other groups higher up.

Diversion force, Samson thought. They were the bait. They certainly had enough soldiers to spare. He sent a tactical update to his squad leaders that would be trickled down to the men.

Samson opened a comlink to Matheson. "I've got a special target for you, Sergeant."

Matheson's loadout was a combat suit heavy equipped with a quad-barrel M547 gauss cannon, which could mow down forests. It drew its ammunition from multiple nanorobotic blocks that, when activated, could form a number of specialized ammunitions. It could alternate between generic high-density projectiles, incendiary rounds, and explosive rounds, or a combination of all three. This allowed them to conserve ammunition and make it stretch for longer bursts.

"Yes, Captain, just point me in the direction you want gone," Matheson said.

"Coordinates on the way, and wait for it," Samson said.

"Understood, sir."

The Konus continued to delve deeper into the valley, and Samson spotted more units cresting the ridge across the valley. Something caught his eye, and he peered into the darkened sky. Thunder rumbled, and lightning lit up the area. Then he saw it. Large winged vehicles were flying directly to his position, riding on the wind. Their metallic wings glinted in the flashes of light.

The passing moments built up in a pregnant pause, preceded by a shallow gasp.

"Light them up," Samson bellowed.

Next came the unleashing of CDF weaponry, followed by that of the Mekaal. The deep valley blazed into light, and the basin walls reverberated with the concussive blasts of the CDF armament tearing into the Konus scout force. The sudden chaotic cadence of AR-71s and Ovarrow rifles was drowned out by the CDF heavies firing their quad-barrel M547s. Streaks of red burned into the Konus forces, tearing through their armored soldiers, followed by blasts from explosive rounds.

Pop.

Pop.

Pop.

Boom!

The diversionary force was taken completely by surprise, as well as the main attack force that attempted to flank the defensive positions maintained by the CDF and Mekaal protectors.

More Konus soldiers pressed forward into the valley, but they made it only a short distance. Samson heard Dixon's M-Viper sniper rifle hiss into the storm, and Konus soldiers fell one after another.

"Ruo, plug that valley entrance," Samson said.

Specialist Ruo brought up his missile launcher and launched twin scorpion missiles that blazed a path toward the Konus. The explosion engulfed the Konus in molten flame, and the percussive force shoved the downpour of rain back in vengeful defiance as it consumed its victims.

Samson and the rest of the 7th pushed forward. They had to move. The Konus had been marking the CDF positions and would be calling in heavy ordnance of their own. They had ground assault vehicles and the aerial fighter he'd glimpsed before. Samson needed the Konus to think they were committed to seizing the opportunity of their surprise attack and blindly charging forward.

They moved forward fifty meters. Samson had been right. The scouting force had been detached from the Konus' main fighting force. The soldiers painted targets via an infrared laser, and a few moments later, scorpion missiles destroyed the targets.

Samson called for a halt. This had been the easy part. The 7th Ranger Company and the Mekaal soldiers were no strangers to armed conflict. They'd worked together off-world against the Krake and Ovarrow alike. The fog of war would settle in as they engaged the Konus, and then the grind would begin. There was no way they could halt the army indefinitely. They needed the orbital defense platform strikes. In the absence of that, multiple squadrons of Hellcats would make short work of the Konus front lines.

Samson heard Dixon's sniper rifle take out Konus targets. Each platoon had several snipers. The M-Vipers could be heard among the sounds of the other weaponsfire. Samson and the other CDF soldiers fired their AR-71s in controlled bursts of hypersonic darts.

The combat suit heavies held their fire, waiting for Samson's command. Their weapons could unleash holy hell on a battlefield, but there was always a cost. Heat built up, and those heavy weapons needed strict pacing if they were to stay operational for the duration of the battle.

Konus ground assault vehicles barreled toward them. Bright particle beams fired from the mounted weapons atop. The beams blazed through the forests, sizzling through the dense trees in great bursts.

The Mekaal returned fire from their own particle rifles, which heated the metallic alloyed armor plating of the Konus assault vehicles but didn't burn through it. Samson fired incendiary rounds at the base of a vehicle. The high heat burned through the alloyed mesh that composed the vehicle's tires, and it wobbled. Other CDF soldiers followed his example and focused their fire on the other wheels.

The Konus heavy cannon swung toward them, the interior glowing molten yellow.

"Fall back," Samson bellowed. "Get to cover."

They scrambled back, and a thick, deadly particle beam blazed like the sun, so hot it ignited the damp ground as it raced toward them.

He broadcast the mine activation signals. They'd peppered the Konus-occupied region with Ovarrow defense mines, and the CDF enhancement made it possible to detonate them remotely. They didn't need to wait to be triggered by some unsuspecting enemy. The ground roared up, sending bright, explosive blasts that illuminated the area amid the chaotic lightning splitting the sky overhead.

Samson heard the hearty grinning of the CDF soldiers, and he felt a few moments of grim satisfaction, but he wouldn't allow himself to be distracted. He opened a broadcast channel. "All right, let's fall back to the second position."

The Konus would be cautious as they came forward after regrouping. The CDF and Mekaal special forces had just killed thousands of them, but there were many more. This was where the grind would begin. They'd lure the Konus forward, and just when the army became emboldened, they'd strike. The attacks would seem random to them. Samson would keep the Konus off balance as much as possible, and the storm would impact them as much as it had the CDF.

"Corporal Bradley," Samson said, "let's send up a few of our reserve recon drones. I want a quick survey of the damage."

"On it, Captain," Corporal Bradley said and set about to deploy the recon drones she carried.

Despite the success of the engagement, Samson knew it was only the beginning. Now the Konus were aware of them. They'd adapt their tactics, and the real work would begin. This night would be a long endurance run for both sides.

27

"MAYBE WE NEED to think about this another way," Noah said.

They had a cluster of holoscreens around them now with different reports and engineering specs for the subspace communication transceiver.

Kara rubbed her eyes and gave her forehead a gentle massage. Then she rolled her shoulders and sighed. "You want to go back to the space gates again, don't you?"

Noah nodded enthusiastically. "Yes, because it's tied into subspace communications. I know it's tied into that town."

She pressed her lips together in thought. Twin blonde eyebrows pulled together, and then she nodded once. "You mean the Ovarrow town that somehow arrived on Sagan."

"It wasn't an accident. And it wasn't teleported there," Noah said.

"What makes you so sure?"

"I'd tell you that teleportation is impossible, but in light of the other things we've seen, I'm not entirely sure I could rule it out. But I really don't think that applies here. The Ovarrow were attempting to reverse engineer space gates and stumbled upon subspace communication. Those two things have to be related. So, if the space gates are used for transitioning between universes, then before that actual transition takes place, there must be a way to send the matter to subspace."

"So, you think that somehow the Ovarrow stumbled upon sending part of their research installation with multiple buildings across a massive expanse of space nearly instantaneously, and this isn't teleportation," Kara said.

Noah frowned as he tried to follow her logic. Then his eyes widened, and he shook his head. "No, because in order to teleport, you have to disassemble the object being teleported on a molecular level, and that didn't happen. Also, how would it reassemble on the other side? You can't take that step out of it," he said and tapped the tips of his fingers on his thigh. "What I think the Ovarrow stumbled onto was using the space gate as a receiver of sorts. They were conducting the experiment using an arch gateway. For some reason we haven't figured out yet, the Krake had a space gate by planet Sagan."

Kara shook her head. "You're reaching, Noah."

His gaze went skyward for a moment while he gathered his patience. "Yeah, that's kind of the point of out-of-the-box thinking, love. Okay, let's think this through," Noah said, continuing with his line of reasoning. "They send a group of buildings, and it emerges somehow between an arch gateway and a space gateway. Then it winds up on the planet surface completely unscathed—maybe. At least the reports say it was relatively intact. And that's the problem right there. That's the gotcha. The rub. At least one of them anyway. If it had come out of the space gate and headed down to the planet, it would've disintegrated on impact. There would've been nothing left at all —nothing but an impact crater among all the other impact craters. Sagan doesn't even have an atmosphere to speak of."

He minimized all the holoscreens. "I have to show you," he said and drew two circles separated by a short distance. "We have New Earth here and Sagan over here." He then drew a small circle and labeled it as the space gate. "Now keep in mind that this is pure theory, but what if they didn't know they'd actually done this? When they engaged the arch, it simultaneously was connected to the space gate at Sagan. We don't know how that works, but we know that it did work. Sean found that out the hard way, if you remember." Kara nodded, and Noah continued. "So, if the two gateways were joined, then there's a transitioning over vast distances quickly. And if you want to take it one step further, they could've projected whatever came through down to the surface of Sagan."

She sucked in her bottom lip and let it slide back through the top of her teeth. She peered at Noah's childlike drawings with the rigid intensity of an engineer seeing things conceptually. "Okay, if we put all the assumptions aside, there should be evidence of it besides the town that was no longer there."

He nodded slowly. "I'm not sure what evidence would be there. The arch was at the bottom of a great lake. If water were to suddenly appear on the surface of the planet, then it would have evaporated."

"Yeah, but if it periodically happened over several hundred years, then there should be some kind of . . ." she said and paused for a moment, searching for the right word. "I don't want to say 'residue' because that's not right. It's almost like looking for evidence of impact craters from a meteor shower.

But what we're looking for . . ." she paused again, and this time she smiled. "Almost like a comet hit the planet. It does interact with the surface of the planet, but we'd probably need some help with that."

"We need to speak to an astrophysicist, and we'd need to convince the powers that be that this is worth sending a science vessel to investigate," Noah said.

"Are they still salvaging wreckage from the Vemus War on the planet?"

He shrugged. "I don't know. I don't think so. Why would I know this?"

"So, that's one thing we'll need to find out."

"If we do find evidence, we'll have physical evidence to support my theory."

"Let's not get ahead of ourselves," Kara said. "If it all proves true, what exactly is your theory?"

"Just that the technology for subspace communications has more applications than mere communications. We might possibly be able to use it to travel vast distances, but if we can somehow figure out how to link space gates across multiple—"

"Excuse me," Lieutenant Sykes said, "would both of you join me in the cockpit please."

"We'll be right there," Noah said and killed all the holoscreens. He glanced at the time and realized that they'd been at it for almost six hours. That's how it was when they started working on problems. It was as if they'd entered a time machine, and it flowed by at breakneck speeds.

They walked over to the cockpit and saw that Lieutenant Sykes was speaking to another man on the holoscreen.

Years of training kicked in, and Noah stood up straighter. "Colonel," he said.

"Mr. Barker," the colonel said. He looked at Kara. "Mrs. Barker, I'm John Randall, the CO of COMCENT. I need your help."

Noah shared a glance with his wife, then looked back at Colonel Randall. "Our help? What do you need?"

"Less than an hour ago, one of our defense platforms became nonresponsive. We dispatched repair drones to assess the problem, and the automated defensive measures activated and destroyed the repair drones while on approach to the platform."

Noah frowned. "That shouldn't be possible," he said. He had done extensive work with the defense platforms, particularly those of the missile defense platforms that were deployed throughout the star system. They'd been instrumental in defeating the Vemus fleet.

"Be that as it may, it's what happened."

"Yeah, but that would mean the targeting protocols . . ." Noah's eyes widened.

Colonel Randall nodded. "That was our assessment as well."

Kara looked at him. "I don't understand."

"Are the Krake here? Have any ships been detected?" Noah asked.

"Negative. We have no enemy ships near New Earth or in the star system. We believe that a group of Ovarrow called the Konus used some piece of technology we aren't aware of that impacted the defense platform's ability to target properly," Randall said.

Noah felt his stomach flip, and his mouth hung open a little.

"I see that you understand the ramifications of this

technology," Randall said. "I need to send a team to the defense platform."

Noah breathed in deeply. "We're the closest ones, aren't we?"

Colonel Randall nodded. "I know you're not officially with the Colonial Defense Force anymore, and I have no authority to ask you to do this."

None of that mattered to Noah. There were lives on the line. If these Konus had used some kind of tech to neutralize the CDF defense platform, there was a lot more going on than he'd realized. "You don't have to ask," he said. "Just tell me what you need."

He glanced at Kara, and she nodded once, watching Colonel Randall expectantly.

"We can create a window of time for you to reach the platform by triggering a diagnostic shutdown of the system. But you'll have a limited amount of time to figure out the problem before the automated defenses come back up, and we have no way of knowing whether it will perceive you as hostile."

"So, we have a time crunch. How close can we get to the platform in the shuttle before the automated defenses open fire on us?" Noah asked. If the targeting systems had been completely compromised, the defense platform could open fire, using its vast armament against a whole host of targets—from CDF or civilian ships to colonial cities. Right now, it sounded like the defense platform's targeting systems were only partially compromised. This didn't mean they were in any less danger than they'd been before, but it did mean the systems could become completely compromised at some point, and disaster could strike at any moment.

"I'll send you the information right now," Colonel Randall said. "And thank you. You don't have to do this."

Noah felt the edges of his lips lift into a small smile. "Yes, we do."

He didn't know why, but despite the danger they were heading toward, he felt more alive than he had in months. He looked at Kara and saw the same determination in her eyes. They'd both served in the CDF, and the years of service had instilled in them a no-nonsense attitude toward protecting the colony. It was time for them to step off the sidelines and help.

28

"General Gates, SRD groups are flying over the Konus army now," Lieutenant Morgan said.

The stealth recon drones were grouped together with combat drone escorts in an effort to cover the area where the Konus army was supposed to be.

"Acknowledged," Connor replied.

The Konus wouldn't have been idle since their surprise attack had taken out the SRDs they'd had monitoring them for days. The new SRDs were making high-speed passes overhead, and their data feeds were constantly being fed back to COMCENT.

Connor ground his teeth. He'd become too complacent with the advantages they'd had over the other Ovarrow they'd encountered, not only on New Earth but on other worlds as well.

He peered into the holotank, attempting to glean some more useful information from it, but the data they had was a few hours old now. Multiple infantry divisions were fighting the Konus, along with Spec Ops companies. His gaze drifted toward the casualty count. The small amber font showed a number in the hundreds. Each one of them was a life, and this didn't account for the Mekaal losses.

"Ops, we need better coordination with our air support. There are still too many gaps. Concentrate deployment where the fighting is heaviest," Connor said.

Hellcat squadrons were lending support where they could to relieve the pressure on the ground forces. The Konus were paying a heavy price for every meter of ground they took, but the numbers were in their favor. If this conflict remained purely ground-based, when would the Konus decide that the price of taking the Mekaal city was too much? Use of the orbital defense platform would have made a much more compelling argument for the Konus to rethink their strategy.

Connor flicked his gaze back to the holotank and frowned. He'd been focusing the image where the fighting was occurring, but he decided to push it back out to a higher level where he could take in the entire theater of battle. The Konus wanted to get to the city, and they were prepared to fight for it, but that didn't necessarily mean they simply intended to match their army against the combined forces of the CDF and the Mekaal.

His eyes drifted toward an area thirty kilometers away from the city where the fighting was the worst. The storm was impacting the way this battle was being fought, but Connor couldn't afford to dwell on what he couldn't control. He needed to put the shoe on the other foot, so to speak, and get into Kasmon's head to figure out what he really intended to do. Kasmon had allowed the CDF stealth recon drones to observe him, only to take them out when it really mattered.

That would level the engagement to some degree, but it couldn't be all there was to it. The Konus were on the move. His gaze returned to the far side of the holotank, which showed the city. That was the end goal. That's what they wanted.

If Connor had wanted to take control of the city before the battle really got out of hand . . . His eyes widened, and he knew exactly what he would have done. He zoomed in closer to the Mekaal city. The sixty thousand inhabitants occupied only a small portion because much of the city was uninhabitable.

"Ops," he said, "how many reserve forces do we have in the city?"

Lieutenant Abernathy double-checked her holoscreen. "CDF forces, or do you want numbers from the Mekaal as well?"

"Just CDF."

"We have the 3rd Brigade located in the LZ. Four thousand soldiers. We also have troop transports in the area that are waiting to bring them where they need to go. Do you want to send them somewhere?" she asked.

"Yeah, I want five platoons to make a sweep of the uninhabited parts of the city."

"Understood, General Gates. Deploying now," Lieutenant Abernathy said.

He'd been too reliant on stealth recon drones and wanted actual soldiers sweeping the area. If they found the Konus, they would engage.

"Tactical, I want a general advisement sent out to our forces in the city, including the Mekaal. They are to report in on anything that looks suspicious. The Konus might be trying to sneak into the city," Connor said.

A few moments later, Lieutenant Scott Morgan replied. "The update has been sent out, General."

"Major Brooks, what is the status of the orbital defense platform?"

"They're sending in a team to investigate. The initial repair drone group was destroyed by the defense platform's point defense systems," Major Brooks said.

Connor hoped whomever they had going in could get the defense platforms back up quickly. And he wanted to know how they'd been neutralized. Had the Konus done it? He didn't believe in giving the enemy capabilities they hadn't proven they had, but the evidence was clear. He'd underestimated the Konus, and now they were paying the price.

An information alert appeared on his personal holoscreen. Class III Hellcat squadrons had finally left the base at Sierra. They were armed with heavy ordnance, and Connor nodded grimly. The bombing runs would start.

BEING part of the reserve forces really sucked. Sergeant Hunter Riley had been keen to see some action, and he wasn't the only one. Platoons that had been assigned to the reserve force hated the wait while other soldiers were doing the fighting. They were eager to do their part.

"Finally," Corporal Blackman said, "we get to get off our sorry asses and do something."

They'd just received the call a few moments ago.

"Don't get too excited," Lieutenant Thomas Wade said. "We're doing a patrol run."

"Where to, sir?" Blackman asked.

The rest of the men had gathered around.

"They want us to make a sweep of the unoccupied parts of the city," Wade said.

Hunter pressed his lips together for a moment. "They think the Konus are sneaking in? If that's the case, why don't they send more of us over there?"

Thomas gave him a look, and Hunter realized the answer.

"Understood, sir. That's what we're going to find out," Hunter said.

"All right, let's saddle up. Sergeant Riley, you and your squad are on point," Wade said.

"Yes, sir. Roger that, sir. The tip of the spear," Hunter said, and this drew a few hearty grins.

They left the occupied city and headed out into the dark wasteland of another world from another time. The storm raged above them, but inside their Nexstar combat suits, it had very little impact on them.

Hunter was on point, along with Blackman, Dunning, Morrison, Trevor, Bowden, and Gorman. Gorman was their heavy hitter, so he brought up the rear.

The city still had main thoroughfares that they could use to make a sweep out toward the edge. They took it slow and steady, checking the buildings as they went. The rain was still coming down in buckets, but the wind only howled some of the time.

The farther they got from the base, the more desolate and silent things became, and the more isolated they felt. Lightning flashed overhead, and a few of the men jumped at shadows. There were other platoons patrolling the other side of the city. The plan was for them to meet up in the middle and then make their way back.

The Ovarrow city had been constructed with that bizarre rounded architecture Hunter had never really cared for. Someone had told him it was to help with defenses, particularly against the ryklars—as if they couldn't climb up the walls even with the severe overhang these buildings had. They gave a cursory glance at the buildings they were able to access as they moved through the area.

A comlink registered on Hunter's heads-up display.

"Riley, take your squad in toward the outer thoroughfare," Lieutenant Wade said.

"Understood, sir," Hunter replied, accessing the broadcast channel to his squad. "Change of plans. We're heading toward the outskirts."

They broke away from the others and began their patrol, making their way along the outskirts of the city and stopping to do a scan of the immediate area outside the city. They encountered a station broadcasting the ryklar deterrent signal, which was fully operational. Smaller creatures scurried through the area.

They came to a taller building, and Hunter had no idea what its original use had been, but he knew it would give them the bird's-eye view he wanted. He left Gorman, Trevor, and Morrison on the ground while the rest of them climbed to the top using the climbing configuration in their combat suits.

Hunter scaled the wall, along with Blackman, Dunning, and Bowden. When they reached the top, they began to look around. Lightning flashed overhead, but the onboard computer of their combat suits filtered out the flashes of light so they wouldn't be blinded. Hunter caught sight of something moving in the distance. He was on the outskirts of the city, and he wasn't sure if it was actually a trick of the light due to the storm. Now *he* was jumping at shadows, but they had to check it out.

"Blackman," Hunter said, "do me a favor and look out over there. Do you see anything out of place?"

Corporal Blackman came to his side and peered in the direction Hunter had indicated. He waited a few moments. "I don't see anything, sir."

"Did you see something, Sergeant?" Bowden asked.

"I thought I saw something. We need to check it out. Let's climb back down and head over," Hunter said.

They climbed down to the ground and informed the others. Hunter didn't make a straight line toward the waypoint. He preferred to take a different route that would lead to the same area. The squad settled into a quiet routine, moving slow and steady. The main part of the platoon was now half a kilometer away.

They soon made it to the area, and there was nothing there. Hunter wanted to take a closer look, so they moved in cautiously.

"What do you think you saw?" Blackman asked.

"Movement. Just something moving in the distance. I didn't get a good look." Hunter glanced back the way they'd come and could see the tall building they'd climbed. He was in the right area. When he returned his gaze to the ground, he saw a set of tracks and frowned. A vehicle had been through there. He gestured down, and the others saw it too. They immediately began scanning in all directions, looking for the Konus.

Hunter opened a comlink to Lieutenant Wade. "Sir, I have a set of tracks here that aren't from any of our vehicles. They appear to have come from outside the city, and they're heading around toward the other platoon."

"Understood, Sergeant. Keep tracking them, and we'll make our way to you. Sending rendezvous coordinates to you now," Lieutenant Wade said.

A waypoint appeared on Hunter's internal heads-up display. He marked it and distributed the data to the rest of the squad. This time, they set a quicker pace. They were playing catch-up now, and they had to move faster in order to find and stalk their prey. It must've been some kind of Konus ground transport vehicle, and given the number of tracks, there must've been a lot of them. It looked like they were trying to get through the area as quickly as possible.

Hunter peered ahead of them using all the available spectrums the combat suits had to offer. Nothing appeared on infrared, and the only evidence of the Konus being there was the tracks in the muddy ground. They came to an area where they were the farthest away from the CDF base at the occupied section of the city.

"Sir, you're going to want to see this," Corporal Blackman said. Hunter joined them, and Blackman gestured toward the ground. He saw dozens of clawed footprints that seemed to have sprung up from out of nowhere.

"What the hell is this?" Morrison asked.

Hunter squatted down and took a closer look. Then he quickly stood up. "They're ryklar tracks," he said, continuing to study them. "Looks like they're mixed with Ovarrow tracks as well. The Konus are in the city."

"Hold on. The deterrent signal is on. How can ryklars be in the city?" Blackman asked.

Hunter pressed his lips together in a frown. Blackman was right, but . . . He brought up the latest intelligence about the

Konus. "The Konus have ryklars with implants that make the deterrent signal ineffective."

"Holy shit," Morrison said.

Gorman swung his quad-barrel around, pointing it toward the city, looking for any excuse to unleash hell.

"Stay frosty," Hunter said. He opened a comlink to Lieutenant Wade. The lieutenant answered, and Hunter could hear fighting and weaponsfire in the background. "Let's move. They're under attack."

As the squad began to run, Hunter sent an alert to COMCENT, which would make its way to General Gates. Given the number of tracks he'd seen and the fact that they hadn't found the Konus ground transport, the Konus were probably deploying groups at different points of entrance to the city. They were here, and they were going to attack at any moment. Right now, everyone in the city was completely unaware and would be caught by surprise.

The Nexstar combat suits were capable of moving at high speeds, but they couldn't move as fast as Hunter would have preferred since Gorman was equipped as a heavy. However, they could still move at a pretty good clip. Hopefully, they'd be able to take the Konus by surprise.

29

THE COMBAT SHUTTLE flew toward the heavy defense platform. It had been constructed of fourth generation battle-steel alloy with a silicon-based, artificial bacteria that not only helped maintain the hull but also regenerated lightly damaged sections. The defense platform had a thick cross section in the middle where the large missile tube was located, with two sections on either side that held the two classes of mag-cannons. It was an automated space station that carried a tremendous destructive capability to engage fleets of enemy ships.

Noah watched as Lieutenant Sykes kept the tiny combat shuttle on a straight approach vector to the sleeping leviathan in geostationary orbit around New Earth, noting that Sykes and Kara were both tensed as they watched the main holoscreen. They'd changed into individual life-support suits in case they experienced a sudden loss of atmospheric pressure in the combat shuttle.

Noah cleared his throat. "If the automated defenses decide we're a threat, we won't even see a flash of light before it takes out the shuttle," he said.

Kara glanced at him in exasperation. "Not helping," she said.

"I'm just saying that we wouldn't feel a thing." He couldn't help that a small smile lifted his lips despite the danger.

"He's right, ma'am," Lieutenant Sykes said.

"Not you too," Kara said. "I already know that." She glared at Noah for a moment, then her gaze softened. "*Jerk.*"

He grinned. He'd known his comment would work to defuse the tension. "It's off-line. Look, the orbit is deteriorating. The systems are down and so are the maneuvering thrusters that maintain its orbit."

Lieutenant Sykes nodded. "All right, making the final approach now."

Noah and Kara left the cockpit and went to their own life support, after which Lieutenant Sykes vented the atmosphere in the combat shuttle. A few minutes later, they docked near the maintenance hatch and walked to the rear of the shuttle. Two automatic tethers extended from a port on the wall and connected to the rear of their space suits.

Noah saw Kara lick her lips and sigh. "You know, I can go out there and take care of this myself," he said.

"Don't be silly. I'm not letting you go out there alone," she replied.

"It's just that I know you're not a big fan of space walks."

"Will you stop? It's been just as long for you since we've been on a space walk. Let's go see if we can fix this thing and get out of here," Kara said.

"Yes, ma'am," Noah replied and gave her salute.

They engaged their magboots and opened the rear hatch. Then, they stepped onto the defense platform's outer hull.

"Who designed the system this way?" she asked.

"It's designed to be secure. It's supposed to be tamperproof."

They walked along the outer hull near the base of the enormous mag-cannons that loomed above them. New Earth filled the view below them with an azure glow that was offset by the planetary rings. It'd been years since Noah had left New Earth, and he'd almost forgotten how beautiful it was from up here. But he didn't have time to admire the view. He needed to keep moving, promising himself that he'd make time to take in the view soon.

"Once we're inside the maintenance hatch, we should be fine," he said.

He heard Kara let out a startled gasp and turned to find her slightly off balance. One foot was in the air, and she seemed to be leaning too far to the side. Noah walked back toward her and helped her regain her balance. Her other foot hit the metallic alloy of the defense platform, and she righted herself.

"Are you all right?" he asked.

Kara nodded and let out a huge breath. "I'm fine. It's just . . . It's been a while. I'll be fine. Keep going."

"I know you will be. And if we're not, the tether still works. We're not going anywhere," Noah said and smiled.

"How do you do it? How can you be so calm?"

He hadn't realized it, but he was calm. He just focused on the problem. "Later. Now I'm just fine. Let's get this over with."

There was a countdown timer in the upper right corner of his heads-up display. They had plenty of time to diagnose the problem, but he was most worried about how long the CDF ground forces would be exposed to the massive Konus army they were fighting.

Noah turned around and walked toward the maintenance hatch thirty meters away. Using the space suit's comms system, he was able to authenticate and open it. He carefully moved the hatch away and gestured for Kara to go in first. He wouldn't have been able to lift the armored hatch on New Earth, even with the assistance of an exoskeleton. Zero-G did have its advantages sometimes. He followed Kara inside and closed the hatch.

"Lieutenant Sykes, we're in," Noah said.

"Good," Sykes said. "There should be a console just beyond that access corridor."

They headed away from the maintenance hatch and rounded the corner. "Found it."

The defense platform computer systems were essentially paused at the start-up. No systems had come online; the whole thing was in a holding state, which allowed him to bring the systems up one at a time so he could check that they were working properly.

First, he had it perform a diagnostic of the weapon systems, and they were unaffected. According to the diagnostic, they all worked properly. It was the targeting subsystem that controlled the weapon systems operations that had been impacted.

"This is a mess," Kara said. "Are they sure that a single tight-beam data upload broke the system?"

"I don't know," Noah said. "Lieutenant Sykes, initiating a dump of the defense platform's system. Are you ready for it?"

"Yes, sir," Sykes said.

Noah initiated a dump of the entire system to a special storage matrix on the combat shuttle. They'd use that later to figure out how the Konus had broken the targeting systems, which would presumably enable them to prevent the same thing from happening in the future.

Kara walked over and brought up a secondary holoscreen. "I have the backup system online. Are you ready for me to initiate a restore?"

"Wait a second," he said. He was navigating the interface and checking the logs around the time the event had taken place. "Damn."

She turned to look at him. "What is it?"

"There's a firing solution in here that has Connor's authorization."

"We should be able to port that over and make it part of the restore," Kara replied.

"I know that, but it's old now. They'll need to reconfirm the targets before they can be allowed to open fire. Plus, we don't want to be anywhere near here when this thing starts going off."

"Okay, so we restore the firing solution and put it in standby for confirmation, then alert COMCENT. They can coordinate with Connor and take it from there," Kara said.

Noah considered this for a few moments and then began poring over the firing solution. "I knew there was a reason I kept you around."

Kara smiled at him. "You're not so bad yourself. Let's wrap this up."

He checked the start-up scripts, wanting to make sure everything was set up right. It was worth a second look because he didn't want to have to come back here. He found an alternate subsystem to the communications link that contained remnant code from the update. He deleted the code and then initiated a full system reset.

Noah closed his session on the defense platform's systems. "All right, that should do it."

"Looks good on my end too," Kara said.

He activated the comlink to the shuttle. "Lieutenant Sykes, I'm going to enable the point defense systems on the opposite side of the platform. Can you launch a decoy with a CDF ship signature?"

"Will do," Lieutenant Sykes said. "Launching now."

Noah waited a minute for the decoy to pass in front of the point defense systems and brought them online. He tried not to hold his breath as he watched the onboard computer systems do a quick threat assessment. A few seconds later, the point defense systems stopped tracking the decoy.

"Successful test," Lieutenant Sykes said.

"Good," Noah replied.

They headed back to the hatch and were soon walking to the combat shuttle. Noah turned toward the view of New Earth. The rings around the planet were actually quite far away from the atmosphere, maintained by two small moons, but that wasn't what had his attention.

"What are you looking at?" Kara asked.

"That must be the storm," he said. The massive storm front was stretched out, entirely covering the region of the continent where the battle was being fought.

"You're right. It's a storm. Now let's get the hell out of here," Kara said and ushered him along.

They made it to the combat shuttle and stepped inside. She closed the rear hatch while Noah headed to the cockpit. Once they were aboard, Lieutenant Sykes restored the life-support system inside the combat shuttle, and Noah removed his helmet.

Lieutenant Sykes released the docking clamps, and they flew away from the defense platform.

"Can you take us over there?" Noah said, gesturing northwest of the storm.

The CDF pilot frowned for a moment. "No problem."

Noah brought up a secondary holoscreen and zoomed in on the part of the continent where the storm was concentrated. "It doesn't look right."

"What do you mean?" Lieutenant Sykes asked.

"Something about that storm doesn't look right at all. Can you open a comlink to COMCENT?"

A few moments later, Colonel John Randall appeared on the holoscreen. "My tactical officers just informed me that the defense platform is coming back online. We now have full access. Thank you so much for doing that."

"You're welcome, Colonel," Noah said. "Do you have anyone available who can validate the storm system where General Gates is?"

Colonel Randall frowned. "I can get someone."

"I think you should. There's something about the storm that doesn't seem right. Normally a storm system develops and can be tracked through barometric pressure, but what I see down there looks like the storm has an epicenter stemming from a specific area."

Colonel Randall considered this for several seconds and then gestured toward someone off-screen. "We'll chase this down. Stand by."

The comlink went to standby mode, and Noah glanced at Kara.

"Oh my God," she said. "I would've missed it completely."

"We don't know if it's anything yet."

"I think you're right, sir," Lieutenant Sykes said. "Now that you pointed that out, I can't *not* see it."

Kara shook her head. "We need to pull up the history of this region. If the Konus have some kind of technology that allows them to manipulate the weather like this, then . . ." She let the thought go unfinished.

"It might not be their technology," Noah said, his eyebrows raised.

Kara's mouth hung open. "You think this could be Krake technology?"

"That's what we need to find out, and we need to stop it," Noah said and looked at Sykes. "Are the weapons systems on the shuttle operational?"

Sykes nodded. "Always."

30

CONNOR HEARD the faint sounds of weaponsfire in the distance, even above the unrelenting storm. He rested his hands on the edge of the holotank and then gripped it firmly, squeezing it. He wanted to be out there in the fight, but he also needed to be right where he was, coordinating the defenses.

They'd received an alert from Sergeant Riley about Konus soldiers and ryklars found trying to infiltrate the far end of the city, and he'd dispatched his reserve forces over to that area. Warlord Vitory informed him that they had additional defenders Connor considered Ovarrow militia. They weren't professional soldiers, but all Ovarrow who came out of stasis were qualified in the basic use of their weapons. They were no strangers to fighting, and Connor knew he shouldn't hesitate to use them. He had Vitory put them on defensive lines in different areas of the city to provide a much-needed function without calling upon them to achieve mission objectives. What he didn't like about it was that he now had to worry about friendly fire. Any type of untrained soldier, and even some of the greener recruits, would be likely to shoot first rather than check their fire to make sure there was, in fact, an enemy on the other end.

"We've increased the high frequency sound waves for the ryklar deterrent signal, but it's not having an effect on them," Lieutenant Scott Morgan said. He stood at the tactical workstation near the holotank in the mobile command center.

"That's because the Konus use an implant to ensure they follow orders," Connor replied.

"How does it work? Is it something we can initiate a remote override on?" Major Alexis Brooks asked.

Connor shook his head. "We don't know how it works."

"They have to give them instructions somehow, which means there's gotta be some kind of broadcast," Lieutenant Morgan said.

"Send an SRD over the area to see if it can detect any frequencies we can't account for," said Connor. "It'll take time because the drones don't have that kind of computing power, but you can route the data back to COMCENT, where they can isolate the signal."

"Yes, General," Lieutenant Morgan said.

They still didn't have an accurate count of how many Konus soldiers and ryklars had slipped past their defensive lines to breach the city. There couldn't have been thousands of troops, so Connor felt safe in assuming that there were probably hundreds of them, no more than a thousand.

"How did they slip past our defensive lines and all the sensor nets we had out there?" Major Brooks asked, looking at Connor from across the holotank.

"Given the chaos that's going on, it could be any number of things, all of which we'll have to revisit when we—"

"General, reports across all fronts indicate that the Konus are making a massive push," Lieutenant Abernathy said.

The images on the holotank switched to the front lines. The data was piecemeal as the reconnaissance drones made high-speed passes overhead. A few were taken out by Konus weaponsfire, but at least now they had some eyes in the sky to give them insight into their enemy's movements.

"They need to make it to the city," Connor said.

Major Brooks frowned, and she studied the holotank. Then her eyes widened. "They're trying to overwhelm us."

"If they reach us and break through the lines, it makes fighting this battle that much harder. It would limit our air support and anything from our orbital defense platform," Connor said and gritted his teeth. He glanced at the status of the defense platform, and it was still off-line.

"I'll get another status update," Major Brooks said.

Connor nodded. There was a CDF heavy cruiser on the way from the home fleet, but it was still several hours out.

"General Gates," Morgan said, "I have an idea about the ryklars."

The young man's eyes were wide with anticipation. Connor glanced at the SRD they had tasked to fly over the city, but it hadn't even gotten there yet.

"What have you got?"

THE RYKLARS MOVED SO DAMN FAST that Hunter could hardly keep a good bead on them, even with the help of the combat suit systems. The creatures didn't attack head-on but preferred misdirection and blindsiding their prey. Hunter and his team had tracked dozens of them heading toward the rest of the platoon.

Lieutenant Wade's group had taken cover in one of the buildings and were making their way to the roof. Hunter and the rest of the squad had slowed down so as not to draw the ryklars' attention. They hadn't seen any Konus soldiers, but there were reports that the other platoons were engaging them in the city.

Hunter saw the CDF soldiers fire their weapons, and a group of ryklars went down, quivering bodies of torn flesh and blood staining the streets. He'd never had an up-close-and-personal encounter with ryklars, but they seemed bigger in the flesh, or maybe it was just that they seemed more real now. They weren't just some animal that was given to attacking because of a predatory instinct. There was intelligence and purpose behind their movements.

"What are we gonna do, Sergeant?" Corporal Blackman asked.

"We can circle around and try to get to the rooftops of one of the other buildings nearby. Then we can create a kill zone," Hunter said.

"That'll take the pressure off the others, but what happens when the ryklars regroup, sir?"

"I don't know. Look, they need our help, and we're going to give it to them." None of the soldiers said anything, but Hunter could sense some hesitation. "They'd do the same for any of us. Now let's go."

With the storm raging on around them, it was a lot easier to stay relatively quiet while moving quickly. Even the ryklars had limits, it seemed. They headed down a narrow pathway and climbed about seven meters to the rooftop of the building, a feat easily achieved by a combination of raw power from their combat suits and the brittle outer layer of concrete on the buildings. Once on top, they raced to the edge and leaped across to the next rooftop. It sloped up at an incline, and gushing water sloshed past them, splattering onto the ground below. They halted a few feet from the edge of the roof. The rest of the platoon was seventy meters away, but they didn't have a clear view of them.

"Sergeant, we've got eyes on us," Gorman said.

Several dark shapes skittered onto the roof a few buildings across from their location. Hunter brought up his AR-71 just as the ryklars realized they'd been seen and started charging forward. Hunter and the rest of the CDF squad squeezed off several bursts of fire. The kinetic force of the weaponsfire slammed into the ryklars, causing them to stumble. A few ryklars dropped off the roof, disappearing from view.

Hunter ordered them to the next rooftop, and they continued onward. CDF weaponsfire intensified from the location of the rest of the platoon. The ryklars were making a push toward the taller buildings.

"Gorman, unleash the heavy," Hunter said.

The combat suit heavy stepped toward the edge of the roof, bringing up the quad-barrel M547, dealer of death. The heavy weapon wound up and began firing at the ryklars, sputtering so loudly that the ryklars perked up at the noise, only to be cut down. The rest of the squad joined in, firing their weapons and taking the ryklars by surprise.

Hunter opened a comlink to Lieutenant Wade. "Sir, we're southeast of your position."

"Thanks for the help, Sergeant, but I'm ordering you to head back. There are hundreds of ryklars heading toward us. You can't see them from your position," Wade said.

"I'm not leaving you, Lieutenant," Hunter said.

"I know you're not. See if you can get them to chase you."

Hunter looked around, searching for the best path, but ryklars were converging on their location. Everywhere he looked, he saw movement heading toward them. They were on the adjacent rooftops, and he knew they were down on the ground as well.

"Oh shit! We're surrounded," Morrison yelled.

"Well then, give it all you got, soldier," Corporal Blackman bellowed.

"None of us are getting out of here, Lieutenant," Hunter said over the din of weapons fire.

Between the slight pauses of controlled weaponsfire, the screech of the ryklars could be heard above the rolling thunder overhead. Lightning split the sky in bright, flickering flashes, and all they could see was the threat of a deep, deadly menace that was coming to kill them all.

"Understood," Wade said. "I'll see you after."

The comlink went dark, and the CDF soldiers prepared to make their final stand.

The ten-man squad coordinated their attack so they had a coverage area of both their immediate surroundings and those far away. But the ryklars moved fast, and it took a lot to bring them down. They were most vulnerable in the face and neck, which were difficult to shoot once they were on the move.

A combat drone flew overhead, and Hunter happened to look up to see it approach. As it flew over their area, he saw something drop from it. When the object hit the ground, a deafening blast of energy left all the ryklars in the area stunned. They simply stopped moving. The CDF soldiers kept firing their weapons, seizing the opportunity to bring down more of the predators.

The ryklars stopped trying to reach the soldiers, appearing confused, as if taking in their surroundings. Many were shaking their heads, moving erratically and flailing about.

"What the hell did that drone do?" Corporal Blackman asked.

Hunter shook his head. He had no idea. The ryklars scrambled back, fleeing the area. It was as if some unseen force was compelling them to leave. He opened a comlink to Lieutenant Wade. "They're leaving. I don't believe it. What the hell did that combat drone drop?"

"No idea," Wade said. "We'll hold position here for a few more minutes, and then we'll meet up."

Hunter and the rest of the squad watched as small groups of ryklars fled from the city. Comlinks from other CDF platoons were reporting the same thing. The combat drones had dropped EMP grenades, which interfered with the ryklars' implants. With the implants off-line, the ryklar deterrent signal had begun to do its job.

Hunter had no idea who'd come up with using EMP grenades against the ryklars, but whomever it was, he was going to buy them a round of drinks whenever he saw them, for the rest of his life.

REPORTS HAD BEEN COMING in that the ryklars were fleeing the area, and Connor broadcast a flash report to the CDF soldiers out in the field. EMP grenades weren't part of the standard kit for combat operations, so they'd loaded up combat drones and were sending them out as fast as they could. CDF soldiers were now sweeping the area, taking out Konus infiltrators as they went, and the Konus sneak attack was in disarray.

Connor looked at Lieutenant Scott Morgan. "Good work, Lieutenant. You saved a lot of lives today."

The young lieutenant beamed at this recognition from his superior officer. "Thank you, sir."

Connor glanced at Major Brooks, who was speaking to COMCENT. She looked at him and shook her head. The Konus were still making a heavy push toward the city, and the CDF and Mekaal forces were steadily moving back to the city, trying to stall the Konus and buy all the time they could. Connor needed the defense platform operational, and he needed it now.

31

Orders appeared in the upper right corner of Samson's heads-up display. They'd received an ammo drop not too long before, but they'd been fighting the Konus for hours and were running low again. CDF regulars were slowly retreating, and the Konus pushed toward them in a hail of fire. The Spec Ops platoons and companies were mainly in the forward and flanking positions.

"They're sending a troop carrier transport, Captain," Sergeant Matheson said.

They had climbed up the last ridgeline of the fingers, and there were several kilometers of forest between them and the Ovarrow city.

Samson glanced at Matheson. "Say again?"

"Troop carrier transports are incoming, Captain. We are to hold position and wait for extraction."

They couldn't hold the position. They had to keep moving. The Konus ground assault vehicles carried high-powered particle beam cannons that could melt through even the battlesteel armor of the combat suit in seconds. The Konus assault vehicles had such an impact on the CDF that they'd become high priority targets, but they were protected with uncompromising determination.

"Specialist Ruo, the SRD on our six. What's it seeing?" Samson asked.

Specialist Ruo checked the SRD data feeds. "Konus soldiers. A lot of them. We can try to outrun them and circle back to the city."

"Negative," Samson said. "But we can't stay here."

"But Captain, our orders," Sergeant Matheson said.

"I know what the orders are, Sergeant. If we stay here, we'll be overwhelmed."

He was sure the troop transport would make its way to them eventually, but he'd been in too many situations where there was simply so much going on that it was easy to get overlooked. The fact that the troop transports were even making these high-risk runs to extract them meant the Konus must be making a major push toward the city. This was Connor's response, which meant they still didn't have that damn defense platform ready.

Samson opened a broadcast comlink. "Listen up. We're heading east—"

Several Konus ground assault vehicles drove over the ridge at high speed and headed straight toward them. The CDF soldiers dove for cover and began firing their weapons at the assault vehicles. The particle beam cannons on the vehicles had to be cycled; otherwise, they'd overheat. After they were fired, there was a rise of intensity as power built up, but that couldn't be sustained for long periods of time.

"Hold your position," Samson said. "When they cycle the cannons down, then we can take them out."

They returned fire, and Samson, along with a few others, began circling around, moving to flank the assault vehicles. He ordered a group of soldiers to draw their fire, keeping the Konus' attention where he wanted it while the rest of them closed in.

Several squads of Konus soldiers spotted their approach, so Samson and the CDF soldiers fired explosive rounds that tore through them. They reached the first assault vehicle, and Matheson attached an explosive charge to it. They moved on to the next one and set another charge.

Samson activated the charges, and the Konus assault vehicles blew apart.

There were two more vehicles nearby.

"I'm out of explosives," Matheson said.

"Hold on," Samson said and gestured for Cerot to come up. When the Ovarrow came over, he asked, "Do you think you can get them to open the hatch? I want to take a vehicle intact."

Cerot nodded once and gestured for the other Mekaal soldiers to follow. They weaved their way through the trees, cautiously approaching the assault vehicle, but Samson couldn't hear what they were saying. Loud thunder rumbled overhead, drowning the Ovarrow out. The particle cannon locked onto the Mekaal soldiers.

Samson and the others hastened over, using the trees to cover their approach. Whatever Cerot said had worked. Konus soldiers opened the rear hatch, and the CDF soldiers made quick work of them. They never even fired the particle cannon.

Samson went over to Cerot. "Can you drive these things?"

Cerot looked inside the assault vehicle for a few moments,

exchanging a few quick words with the other Mekaal soldiers. Then he looked at Samson. "We can operate them."

"Good. Go on inside and get someone on that cannon," Samson said.

The Mekaal soldiers climbed inside. After a few moments, the particle cannon swung to the side, and the vehicle lurched forward around a tree. They targeted the other assault vehicle, firing the particle cannon. A thick molten yellow beam burst from the barrel, mowing down Konus soldiers. Cerot concentrated fire on the assault vehicle, destroying its particle cannon.

Konus soldiers fled the vehicle, and the CDF shot them. Samson sent a group of Mekaal to the damaged assault vehicle to see if they could still use it, when a distress beacon broadcast alert appeared on his heads-up display. It had Layton's identification. Layton had taken a platoon and was scouting Konus heavy targets for their Hellcat squadrons to take out.

A few moments later, other distress beacons came from more members of the 3rd Platoon. They were in trouble. Samson gestured for Matheson. "Where's the troop carrier?"

"ETA is fifteen minutes, Captain," Sergeant Matheson said.

Samson glanced at the Konus assault vehicles, an idea forming in his mind. "Send them these updated coordinates," he said.

Matheson glanced at the coordinates. They were well within enemy territory, but he didn't question it. There was no need to. The 7th Ranger Company wouldn't abandon their own men. Matheson moved away and opened a comlink to the troop carrier.

Samson quickly relayed his plan and made sure Cerot and the other Mekaal soldiers understood. They'd be leading the charge in the assault vehicles. Samson was gambling that when the Konus saw their own vehicles heading toward them, they'd hold their fire long enough for the CDF soldiers to wreak havoc.

Matheson rejoined him. "Captain, I've been informed by the troop carriers and their Hellcat escorts that they're going to be making an extraction in a hot zone," he said, tilting his head to the side in a slight nod. "Well, *more* of a hot zone. I'd say it's like a cauldron of fury. You know, like bathing in liquid hot magma."

Samson arched an eyebrow toward him. "You're a poet," he said and looked at the others. "I want my combat suit heavies leading the charge just behind the Konus assault vehicles."

Sergeant Dixon gave the assault vehicle an appraising look and then shook his head. There wasn't enough room for him on the back. The sharpshooter would have to stay on the ground just like the rest of them.

Samson opened a comlink to Cerot. "As fast as you can. Let's move it."

The Mekaal soldiers swung the assault vehicles around and began driving back over the ridge, heading toward the enemy soldiers on the other side. The Konus soldiers hesitated, and Samson thought he heard Cerot speaking. He must be using the Konus comms from within the vehicle, but Samson had no idea what he was saying. It didn't matter. Their hesitation was his advantage, and the mighty 7th Ranger Company punched a hole through the enemy lines. The fighting was intense and quick. They charged forward, cutting through the enemy as fast as they could. As the minutes flew by, the distress beacons began going off-line. They were dying.

The 3rd Platoon wasn't so far into the fold of the Konus that it was impossible to reach. This hadn't been a suicidal charge. As they got closer to the distress beacons, they were able to better pinpoint their locations and saw that they were surrounded by the enemy. The lightning seemed to come less frequently, and they thought that perhaps this damn storm was finally starting to relent. Bright flashes came from the particle beam cannons mounted atop the Konus assault vehicles, and the CDF combat suit heavies fanned out, firing their weapons.

The Konus returned fire in a blazing retaliation of defiance before they were overwhelmed. Samson checked the status of the troop carriers, and they were still minutes out. They made it to where the bulk of the 3rd Platoon soldiers were holding out, and the first person Samson spotted was Private First Class Fletcher.

"Where's Lieutenant Layton?"

"I don't know, Captain. We lost him hours ago," Fletcher said.

Samson frowned and scanned for someone else. "Sergeant Schultz, give me a sitrep."

The rest of the 7th Ranger Company formed a perimeter around the exhausted and battered 3rd Platoon.

"They surprised us, sir. Lieutenant Layton went with Herrera and his squad to check on something, and then the Konus arrived. There aren't many of us left, sir," Schultz said.

"They're making another push, Captain," Sergeant Matheson said.

"We're not out of this yet," said Samson.

Layton was gone, and Samson suspected the worst. He reached the perimeter and saw thousands of Konus troops heading toward them. Ground assault vehicles stretched back as far as his enhanced vision could see. He swallowed hard. The

Konus charged, and Samson ordered his soldiers to fall back. They needed every second.

Matheson yelled and gestured overhead. Samson heard the familiar high-pitched scream of Hellcat engines barreling toward them, and the troop carriers weren't far behind. The Hellcats flew toward the enemy weapons hot and stalled the Konus advance. Samson saw them circle around, giving the troop carrier transports time to land. Particle beam weapons lit up the sky, and one of the Hellcats crashed in a fiery explosion.

The sky had become brighter, and Samson could tell that the rain was definitely slowing down. Amid a torrent of particle beam weapons being fired at the CDF soldiers, there was a powerful sonic boom, louder than anything the storm had given them. Then there was another. Something punched through the clouds, blazing into the Konus army. The ground shook beneath Samson's feet, and there was a bright flash of light that was immediately cleared out by the smart filter of his combat suit's helmet.

"Take cover!" Samson shouted. "Orbital strike inbound. Take cover!"

The skies above opened up as hulking projectiles pierced the atmosphere in a deluge. He had never been near an orbital strike in his entire military career. He'd witnessed them only from afar during practice sessions. The ground assault from the orbital defense platform sent waves of kinetic energy, and it was all they could do to endure. They took cover as best they could, waiting for it to be finished. Then, after an indeterminate amount of time, there was silence. He climbed to his feet and looked at the havoc wreaked by the CDF weapons. The devastation had occurred downrange from them, decimating the Konus in the area.

Samson led a group to where Lieutenant Layton's beacon had last been active. He was dead. The Konus had connected something to his suit that looked like it was part of a comms broadcast. They disconnected it, and Samson ordered his men to bring the entire setup with them on the troop carrier. He looked down at his friend and gritted his teeth. He knelt down, picked up Layton's body, and carried it back to the troop carrier transport. Then they retrieved the bodies of the other fallen 3rd Platoon members. They would be brought back home and buried with the honor of those who'd sacrificed themselves. Sorrow attempted to close Samson's throat, but he refused to let it. Instead, he grabbed his rifle as an urge to keep fighting hit him. He glanced up at the sky, willing the orbital defense platforms to keep firing. He didn't care if every Konus died on this battlefield. If he could've killed them all, he would have without hesitation—the Krake be damned.

32

The Konus had gambled and lost. The orbital strikes had brought their massive army to a halt. In the hours that followed, they began to accept the fact that their army was facing annihilation.

Connor had extracted all CDF and Mekaal soldiers caught behind enemy lines. Next, he allowed the Konus soldiers to return to the bulk of their army in a show of cooperation, but that was about as much cooperation as Connor was willing to give. Lives had been lost on both sides of the conflict, and it had all been a pointless waste.

He had communicated to the Konus that Kasmon must surrender himself to the CDF. This was nonnegotiable. Any delay in response or compliance and the CDF orbital defense platform would annihilate the remaining Konus army. Connor had suspected that the Konus would resist, that their most powerful military leader would never surrender and would need to be taken by force. But that hadn't happened, and Kasmon was on his way there now.

Connor rubbed his eyes and sighed. The sky was clearing, and it was already morning.

Noah cleared his throat, and Connor looked back at the video comlink feed. "Sorry. It's been a hell of a day."

"I was saying that we disabled the device the Konus were using to create that storm. We weren't able to stick around and do a thorough analysis because they started firing at us," Noah said.

Connor looked at his friend. "We'll get it sorted out," he said and regarded him for a second. "I don't know if you realize what you've done."

Noah looked away and scratched the back of his head. "Now don't give me that. We were just the closest ones available."

Connor shook his head. "It doesn't matter. You were the ones who got it done, and you spotted something no one else had anticipated."

Noah lifted his eyebrows, smiling a little. "No one can think of everything, Connor. Not even you. Why would they even have that tech anyway?"

"I don't know. It's probably not their tech, which means we'll have to find out what else they have and where they got it from."

"Did you figure out how they disabled the defense platform?"

Connor nodded. "They captured one of our officers and used his comlink to infiltrate the network."

Noah whistled softly. "One officer and all that happened."

"The officer was on a mission to identify targets for us to hit with the defense platform, and that's why he had the access he did, but I hear you. We might need to reconsider some of those things we take for granted," Connor said.

Noah was quiet for a few moments and then said, "Yeah. I know there've been suggestions of using subspace comms to replace all our comms capabilities, but I don't think we should."

"Why not?"

"We're still learning how it works. We can use it, but that doesn't mean we actually understand everything about it."

"I see what you're saying," Connor said. "I won't keep you any longer, and thank you for everything."

"You don't need to thank me. I'm just glad I could be there for you for a change," Noah said and smiled, reminiscent of the young man Connor had met when he'd first come to the colony. "What I don't understand is why the Konus did this in the first place. They lost a third of their troops at least."

Connor shook his head. "I don't know. We know the Ovarrow are territorial, but this was something else."

"It's crazy, is what it is," Noah said. "You still want them as allies against the Krake?"

"Wanting and needing are two different things, Noah."

"You can't be serious."

"I am, but we'll need to figure out what to do with them," Connor said and couldn't keep the edge from his voice. "I have to go. I've got a million other things to do. Good luck at Lunar Base. Make sure Sean gives you a VIP room."

Noah grinned. "Heck, if he doesn't, I'll start calling him 'cadet bling.'"

Connor chuckled and closed the comlink. *Cadet bling,* he thought, shaking his head in amusement.

He received a notification from Vitory that Kasmon was now in their custody. He headed toward the Mekaal pavilion where High Commissioner Senleon and Vitory were, along with the other faction leaders. Connor brought some of the other senior officers with him, and Darius Cohen was there.

Kasmon glared at Connor, still managing to look smug even in defeat. He knew his gamble had almost worked.

Connor walked over and stood in front of Kasmon.

"You need us," Kasmon said.

"I don't think we do," Connor said. "In fact, I'm inclined to turn you over to the very people you sought to enslave," he said and gestured toward Senleon and the others.

Kasmon looked at them for a moment, and there was a darkly gritty intent in his eyes. "They wouldn't have been enslaved. They would've become part of the Konus, and we would've been stronger for it. They would've been stronger as well."

"Do you expect me to believe your intentions were so ethical? There was more to it than that," Connor said and leveled his gaze at the Konus military commander. "Did we pass *your* test?"

Kasmon regarded him. "A demonstration was required."

Connor's fist flew through the air. The MPS he wore became an armored gauntlet that struck Kasmon in the face. The Konus soldier fell backward and sprawled on the floor. He shook his head to clear it and regained his feet. Blood trickled from one side of his wide mouth.

"Strength isn't something you can communicate through anything but conflict. You will need all of yours if you hope to defeat the Krake," Kasmon said.

"You wasted lives and resources for a damn contest," Connor snarled. "We could've been working together against the Krake."

"You still need our help."

Connor's knuckles burned to strike again, but he didn't. "The remainder of your army will go back to your city. They will know that both day and night, our defense platform will be right above that city. If a large group that looks anything like an armed fighting force gathers outside your territory again, I'll order that platform to strike, and we won't stop until every one of you is gone. I'll raze that entire region," he said and leaned closer. "Now do you have the measure of our resolve?"

Kasmon's flinty glare became cold and hard, and Connor felt a modicum of grim satisfaction in that. "You'll be held by the Mekaal until we decide what to do with you," Connor said.

Kasmon swung his gaze toward Senleon and Vitory and then turned back to Connor. "Your faithful servants."

Connor shook his head. "No, not servants," he said, looking at Senleon and the others. "Allies—and one day, fellow citizens."

Mekaal soldiers took Kasmon away. Connor had already assigned soldiers to interrogate him. It would be a joint effort between the Mekaal and the CDF. They would learn everything there was to know about the Konus, especially the Krake tech they'd adapted for their use. But like it or not, Kasmon might be right. They might need the Konus, and he hated that thought.

Senleon walked over to Connor. "There isn't enough gratitude we can show to you and the Colonial Defense Force."

Connor gave him a long look and then nodded slowly. "We're in this together."

"Yes, we are," Senleon said.

If someone had come up to Connor a year ago and told him what was going to happen, he'd never have believed them—the discovery of the Konus, the Mekaal and the other factions petitioning the colonial government to become citizens, none of it. He had underestimated the Konus. They'd had over forty years to prepare for a war with the Krake. They'd used tactics against an enemy that outmatched them technologically, and those tactics had almost worked against the CDF. The last twenty-four hours had reinforced one thing in Connor's mind. They weren't ready for a war with the Krake. They just weren't. Despite all the preparation, there was still so much to do. While this battle with the Konus had cost colonial lives, a colder, more ruthless part of Connor's brain started to believe that this experience would end up saving more lives in the long run. Time would be the judge of that, but they'd be better prepared. He would have to use everything the colony was capable of giving if they were going to survive.

Vitory walked over to him, looking even more exhausted than Connor felt. The Warlord carried the weight of protecting his people on his shoulders. It was a common burden between them. They shared a look that seemed to confirm what the other was thinking. They needed to adapt quicker. They couldn't afford to slow down their efforts on any front, and they'd even have to increase their off-world missions to find more allies against the Krake. And, above all, they must find the Krake home world. There was no way to survive if they couldn't do that.

33

THE COMBAT SHUTTLE flew toward Lunar Base, and a video feed from the forward cameras showed on the main holoscreen. It'd been years since Noah had been here. He glanced at Kara, whose gaze seemed to drink up the view of the vast metropolis on the lunar surface. There were shipyards in orbit around the moon where massive 3D printers worked.

Noah squinted and could just barely make out the space dock for the CDF fleet. He knew that if they were closer, he'd be awestruck at the sheer size of the heavy cruisers being constructed.

"How long has it been since you've been here?" Lieutenant Sykes asked.

Noah cleared his throat. "It's been a while. A few years. They've expanded a lot."

"Eighteen months for me," Kara said. "This is just the surface stuff. There are extensive installations underground."

Noah looked at the view of the lunar base appreciatively.

They'd put so much into building the initial base, and it had provided a crucial function to their overall defensive readiness.

"There's a significant civilian presence here now, particularly in the R&D sections," Lieutenant Sykes said. "There's also a lot more entertainment than there used to be. Can't be all work and no play."

Noah smiled a little and then shook his head. "I can remember when they were scouting for sites to build the lunar base."

Kara nodded. "That was three years after the *Ark* first arrived here."

Lieutenant Sykes's eyes widened. "That was the year they officially created the Colonial Defense Force."

"That's when it was officially recognized, but Connor had been working toward building a military long before that," Noah said.

Lieutenant Sykes glanced away for a moment, looking somewhat uncomfortable. "He might be Connor to you, but he's General Gates to everyone else up here."

Sometimes Noah forgot that the early risers on the *Ark* had lived and worked together for most of a year in preparation for bringing everyone else out of stasis. Friendships had been forged that were still strong to this day.

He watched as Lieutenant Sykes confirmed the landing pad with Lunar Base Control. There was no shortage of space traffic going to and from the base proper. The combat shuttle flew away from the main base facility, and Lieutenant Sykes told them they'd been directed to a secondary location.

"You must have a higher security clearance than I do. I've never been over here," Lieutenant Sykes said and raised an eyebrow toward them. "Are you sure they're not recommissioning you back into the CDF?"

"No, they're not," Noah said.

"We're consulting," Kara said.

The CDF combat shuttle flew over an immense crater that was nearly three thousand kilometers in diameter and fourteen kilometers deep. The waypoint indicating on their main holoscreen showed that their destination along the walls of the crater was three hundred kilometers away.

Eventually, the waypoint highlighted a cave entrance in the distance. Noah peered at it, and as they came closer, he saw massive metallic gray doors that had begun to separate in the middle. He could almost make out the semitranslucent shield that kept the atmosphere contained. As they got closer, Noah saw that the large doors had a sheen that reminded him of the battle-steel bulkheads used on CDF warships. The thick doors could take a pounding and had been built with defense in mind. There were mag-cannons on either side of the doors, as well as some secreted farther away. He wondered what other defenses had been hidden that could be readily brought online.

A comlink registered on the combat shuttle's systems.

"This is Lieutenant Sykes, and I have Noah Barker and Kara Robertson onboard."

"Confirmed identity of Lieutenant Sykes," the flight officer replied. "Please have your passengers forward their identifications via their neural implants."

Noah and Kara sent their identifiers, a combination of a unique ID and their DNA, through the comlink.

"Identities confirmed. Please proceed to docking bay thirty-three. Your escort will meet you there," the flight officer said.

The comlink severed, and Noah glanced at Lieutenant

Sykes. "I guess they don't want you to disembark beyond the docking bay."

Lieutenant Sykes shrugged a shoulder. "I'll try not to take it personally."

"Where do you go from here?" Kara asked.

Lieutenant Sykes smiled. "Wherever they tell me to."

The combat shuttle flew through the massive doors and landed at the designated docking bay area. Noah and Kara went to the back of the shuttle to collect their belongings, and Lieutenant Sykes opened the rear hatch. The loading ramp extended to the ground.

"Thanks for getting us here safely," Noah said.

"A pleasure," Lieutenant Sykes replied.

They walked down the loading ramp, and Lieutenant Sykes went to speak with the deck officer. A CDF soldier checked his tablet computer and then looked at them as if confirming their identities. "Hello, and welcome to Osiris. I'm Corporal Yelland. I'll have your belongings moved to your quarters. You can just leave them there. I'm to escort you to Colonel Quinn."

Noah shared a glance with Kara and then looked at Yelland. "Lead the way."

Corporal Yelland led them away from the docking bay and took them straight to a security processing center where both Noah and Kara registered with the CDF base. Their clearance levels were confirmed, and their identities were officially imported into the system.

They left the processing center and walked down a few corridors to an elevator, which they took down several levels. The elevator doors opened to a train station that had multiple tracks going to and coming from various dark tunnels. They climbed aboard a maglev train, and it accelerated into the tunnel.

"How far away is our destination?" Noah asked.

Corporal Yelland smiled. "It's not far. Just under a kilometer."

Noah pressed his lips together. "I wonder how long it took them to tunnel all this out."

"This part of the base is actually pretty new. Only about . . ." Corporal Yelland frowned in thought for a moment. "It's under two years. And they didn't have to tunnel all this out. They did a seismic survey and found an open cavern under here, so they utilized the space that had already been created."

The dark tunnel began to brighten, and they emerged onto an elevated platform. There was a vast cavern underneath, and Noah's mouth hung open. There had to be thousands of people working here. The vast open chamber was divvied up into sections, and he had no idea what they were meant for.

"Would you look at that," he said with appreciation.

Kara smiled and nodded. "It's amazing."

The chamber was so big that Noah actually had trouble seeing to the other side, and it didn't look like the CDF had used up all the space. There was a network of maglev train tracks that wasn't only at the upper levels where they were but also at the lower levels they could just now see.

The train came to a stop at a platform, and the doors opened. Noah walked out and breathed deeply through his nose. The air smelled clean, with a hint of pine. He'd expected the air to be cool and humid since they were so far underground, but it wasn't.

Corporal Yelland led them away from the train station through a series of white corridors. There were wallscreens spaced out along it that showed images of New Earth landscapes, along with several deep-space images of the star system.

They eventually came to a series of offices, and Corporal Yelland left them in a waiting area. Noah and Kara didn't have to wait long before Sean came out to greet them.

Sean Quinn was of average size and still retained an athletic physique. The skin around his eyes was tight, and Noah saw a much harder glint to his friend's gaze than what used to be there. They'd all been through a lot, but Sean's smile lit up his whole face.

"I heard about what happened," Sean said. "You two couldn't just come up to the lunar base. You had to repair a defense platform and save a lot of lives in the process."

Noah shrugged a shoulder. "Some of us are just lucky, I guess. Luck and timing, my friend. Luck and timing."

Sean gestured for them to follow him through the doors. "I'm really glad you're here."

"Will Oriana be joining us?" Kara asked.

Sean nodded. "Yeah, she'll be along. I figured I'd show you guys around first," he said and looked at them for a moment, "but you've had a helluva day. If you'd like to rest, we can postpone all this. Maybe get something to eat," he said and shrugged. "You know, have some food?"

Noah shook his head, and Kara did the same. "We just spent almost an entire day on a combat shuttle. I don't want to sit around anymore," she said.

"Well, we did get to stretch our legs on the defense platform," Noah replied.

"That's not my idea of fun," Kara said.

They continued, and Sean began showing them around.

"There's a lot of security here, a lot more than I would've expected," Noah said.

Sean led them to his office, where food had been set out for them. Noah's stomach growled and saliva flooded his mouth in anticipation. He hadn't realized how hungry he was.

"Yeah, it was decided that we needed additional layers of security because of the work we're doing here," Sean said and looked at Noah. "I knew you'd both be hungry, so let's just eat. Oriana will join us in a little bit, and then we'll continue the tour."

They sat down and ate a home-cooked meal that tasted delicious. Oriana joined them before too long, and she and Kara began talking in earnest.

Sean raised his eyebrows in mock frustration. "Pretty soon the three of you will start talking, and I won't be able to understand what you're saying."

"I doubt that," Noah said. He studied Sean for a few moments. "Any chance they'll recall you back to New Earth, given what just happened?"

Sean shook his head. "No, this work is too important, and they've got things in hand there. The report I read stated that it escalated quite quickly, but it's settled down now."

"I'm sure you know more than I do at this point."

Sean's gaze took on a somber expression. "Just when you think you have a handle on a situation, that's when the ground falls out from under you," he said and sighed.

Noah sipped his water and set the cup down. "What do you think will happen with the Konus?"

"I don't know. I guess it's pretty much up to them, but you can bet your ass we're going to be keeping a closer eye on them for sure."

"Yeah, I don't get it. They offer to become our allies against the Krake, and then all this happens. It makes you think you really don't know whom you can trust," Noah said.

Sean arched an eyebrow and a bit of mirth crept into his gaze. "I thought brooding was my thing."

Noah chuckled and grinned. "I guess you're rubbing off on me. Or I'm just a little tired. No, not so much that I . . . You look like you have a big secret you want to show me."

Sean laughed, and this drew Oriana's and Kara's attention, Oriana's expression asking a silent question.

"Noah wants to know our secret."

Oriana looked at Noah. "Then I think it's time we show you."

They stood up and left Sean's office, walking down a short corridor to enter a large conference room. Sean led them over to the far wall. He looked at them for a few moments and then tilted his head toward the wall. It sank down into the floor, and they saw a wide-open cavern that was separate from the one they'd seen earlier.

Noah's eyes widened as he looked at Sean. "I thought you were just refitting the fleet, reverse engineering the Krake tech you found," he said and glanced at Oriana.

Sean nodded slowly. "We're doing that, but we also quickly arrived at one conclusion."

"What's that?" Noah asked.

"We don't have enough ships. You're right; we're building up our fleet, but it won't be enough. So, we had to think up other ways to engage the Krake. This is what we came up with," Sean said and gestured toward the cavernous chamber.

Noah observed the vast assembly line. His mind computed a quick production schedule, but he didn't want to go into full engineering mode yet. He looked at Sean. "What else have you got?"

Sean smiled. "There's a lot more to see. We'll bring you up to speed."

Noah smiled and swallowed hard. There was no way he was going to be here for only six months. He stepped toward the open window to gaze out onto a massive assembly line of equipment. Most were implements of war. The CDF and the colony as a whole had already increased its production of the equipment they thought they needed to fight the Krake.

He breathed in deeply and knew this was exactly where he needed to be. "All right, let's get started."

34

The Colonial Security Council listened as Connor gave his report. The battle with the Konus had been only the week before, and it still seemed like they were putting the pieces back together.

"The Konus army has returned to their city, and as of right now, they are in compliance with our demands that they stay in their own territory," Connor said.

"How long can this go on?" Mullins asked.

"It's difficult to say for sure. They'll want Kasmon released."

The leader of the Konus army was currently being held prisoner by the Mekaal. Connor was in regular discussions with Senleon and Vitory, who had assured him that their treatment of Kasmon would be fair and much better than they would have received if Kasmon's plan had actually worked.

"They can come to us with a request. They still have a comlink available to them," Mullins said.

Nathan cleared his throat. He'd returned from Phoenix

Station shortly after the battle ended. "I don't see how an alliance with the Konus will work, at least for the immediate future."

"I'm inclined to agree with you," Mullins said. He looked around at the others in the room. "Does anyone have an objection to rescinding our offer of an alliance with the Konus?"

Stoic silence was the only reply. Connor hadn't expected anyone to be in favor of an alliance.

"I just don't understand their motivation," Mullins said and looked at Connor.

"According to the Ovarrow, the stronger nations absorbed the weaker ones," Darius Cohen said. The diplomatic leader for the colony normally didn't attend Security Council meetings, but given that he'd been at the Ovarrow city when the battle had taken place, he had valuable insight into what was going on.

"That was part of it," Connor said, and Mullins waited for him to continue. "They wanted to see what we were capable of, and I think they also wanted to know how effective their tactics would be against someone with similar capabilities as the Krake."

Mullins shook his head.

"It doesn't make any sense to me either. I would have preferred to work with them, but Vitory didn't seem surprised."

"That brings us to our next order of business," Mullins said. "High Commissioner Senleon and Warlord Vitory have indicated that they still desire to join the colony in a more official capacity."

"I thought we weren't considering it at this time," Jean Larson said.

"They're not expecting a decision anytime soon. I assured them that our mutual defense pact would still apply whether they joined the colony or not," Mullins replied.

Larson frowned in thought. "I guess I just find it surprising since our alliance with the Mekaal already gives them the protection they need."

"I think it's encouraging," Darius Cohen said, "and I think they're sincere in their desire to become colonial citizens. We've been working together closely, especially with the CDF."

"So, you think we should just welcome them with open arms. Make them colonial citizens and call it a day?" Larson asked.

"No, I wouldn't. This isn't something we would decide on a whim," Darius replied.

"You're right about that," Mullins said. "And I would add that this decision isn't up to just us. We'll need to involve the colony. They should have a say in whether or not we move forward with this. Perhaps we'll be only allies with the Ovarrow."

"There was a project proposal to connect the Ovarrow city via a maglev train. That would enable them to travel to other colonial cities," Darius said.

"That's true," Mullins said. "We would have to make the translator available to all colonial citizens. And again, this is something each of us should discuss with the colonial citizens in our cities."

"Why not let the Ovarrow speak for themselves?" Connor asked.

Mullins paused in thought for a few moments. "I'm afraid I don't understand."

Connor leaned forward. "Let them petition the colonial

government and let everyone see them doing it. Broadcast it. Let Senleon and Vitory and their faction leaders make the case on why this is good for everyone."

He glanced around at the others in the room, and there were a few different reactions. What surprised him was that none of them had seemed to consider this before.

"I think this is a good idea," Darius said. "It would allow the colonial citizens to actually see who the Ovarrow are. Maybe we could organize some events where colonists could ask them questions."

"You're not proposing that we just turn them loose in the colony?" Mullins said.

Darius shook his head. "Of course not. But doing this might alleviate certain prejudices against the Ovarrow."

"I'm curious," Mullins said. "Given what we know right now, how would you vote on extending colonial citizenship to the Ovarrow if they wanted it? And this is hypothetical and noncommittal. Feel free to abstain from it. I'm just curious."

They went around the room, and the discussion continued. There were a few well-thought-out concerns, but at least half of them were in favor of coming up with a plan to allow the Ovarrow to become colonial citizens.

Mullins's gaze rested on Connor. "Yes, we should," Connor said. "I know there will be challenges with this—growing pains, if you will. Regardless of what the colony votes for, CDF soldiers have trusted the Ovarrow with their own lives. The joint off-world missions require it. So, there might be more support than you think there is, at least from members of the CDF."

"This will be a controversial topic. It needs to be handled delicately but honestly," Mullins said.

Connor cleared his throat, and Mullins looked at him. "You didn't say how you would vote."

His comment drew a few chuckles from the others in the room, and Mullins smiled. "I share the same concerns that have already been mentioned, but I think this is something we should consider. I think Dana would have been open to this."

The meeting soon ended, and Connor and Nathan walked together as they headed to the rooftop landing pad.

"Are you heading back to Sanctuary?" Nathan asked.

Connor shook his head. "I'm going to Delphi," he said.

Nathan's eyebrows raised. "Delphi? What for?"

"Lars Mallory's trial is ending, and I promised Franklin I'd be there for him."

Nathan's mouth became a grim line. "What do you think will happen to him?"

"I honestly don't know."

"Are they going to ask you to make a statement?"

"I don't think so. I doubt it would change anything. Lars is guilty."

"So, he'll be banished then," Nathan said.

"There are worse things, but I might have a few ideas about that," Connor said.

Nathan lifted an eyebrow. "I'm sure you do."

Connor smiled. "Doesn't Savannah come back today?"

Nathan smiled. "Very soon. That's where I'm going right now. Her ship reached the space dock, and the shuttles will start coming down to the planet soon."

"Well, tell her I said welcome home."

"I will," Nathan said and headed toward his transport ship.

35

THE COURTHOUSE in Delphi was part of the city's government complex where the mayor worked. Connor didn't often travel there. As he walked into the building, he recalled the last time he'd been there, trying to convince Mayor Edwards to help him with an investigation concerning the Ovarrow.

The government complex was similar in layout to Sierra. Wallscreens lining the corridors displayed various images that were agrarian in nature. Delphi could be considered the colony's breadbasket. The vatteries were located here that produced what Diaz liked to call "the most succulent meats available."

Diaz had sent him a message asking when he was going to return to Sanctuary. He wanted to try a new recipe out on Connor, but mostly it was Diaz's way of checking to see if he was all right.

It was half past one, and the afternoon sessions at the courthouse would begin shortly. The corridors revealed the regular foot traffic of the people who worked there. Connor spotted Franklin Mallory sitting outside one of the courtroom doors. He saw Connor and waved.

Connor walked over to him. "I'm here for Lars."

"I appreciate it," Franklin said, shaking his hand. He glanced at the polished wood doors and then back at Connor. "This isn't going to end well."

"Lars is still alive, Franklin. That's gotta count for something."

Franklin nodded. "Yes, but if he gets banished, I won't have access to him beyond restricted messages and maybe the occasional comlink."

There wasn't much Connor could say. Banishment from the colony also included restricted communications.

There was an audible chime from the speakers in the corridor, indicating that the sessions were about to begin again, and Connor followed Franklin into the courtroom. There was space on the bench behind the defendant's table on the left. The jurors were escorted to two rows of seats in a cordoned-off area to the right. A nearby door opened, and Lars Mallory was brought in. He looked at Connor, and his eyes widened for a moment. Then he gave Connor a grim nod in greeting. Connor returned the nod in kind.

The court resumed its session with the Honorable Vivian Kennedy presiding. Connor didn't know her at all, but her eyes came to rest on him after she sat down.

Lars Mallory's defense attorney stood up. The name Ryan Lynch appeared on Connor's internal heads-up display.

"Your Honor, Lars Mallory would like to address the court before sentencing, if you will allow it?" Ryan asked.

Vivian Kennedy's shrewd gaze flicked to Lars. "I will allow it, Mr. Mallory."

Ryan gestured for Lars to stand up.

"Thank you, Your Honor," Lars said. "I've had a lot of time to think about my actions. I'm guilty of all the charges. I also understand that this is a very difficult decision to make, for this case in particular. I've always wanted to protect the colony," he said and paused for a few seconds. "My friend, Noah, kept coming to see me these past few months. He was trying to help me. I know there are psychological evaluations out there that say I was manipulated by Meredith Cain, and I suppose I was. I allowed her to convince me to join her, but that doesn't excuse my actions. I'm prepared to take full responsibility, but I wanted the court to know that I regret the things I did. I regret hurting the Ovarrow. I wish I could change what I did, but I can't. That's all I wanted to say."

Lars remained standing, and the court officer called for all of them to rise.

"Mr. Mallory," Vivian Kennedy said, "your case *is* challenging because while you yourself weren't guilty of directly injuring or killing a colonial citizen, it was your actions that helped build an organization that *did* do those things. So, some of that responsibility does fall on your shoulders. Your actions directly influenced those events. You have served this colony with distinction in Field Ops and Security for a long time. In essence, you were trusted to perform a particular function in society, and the fact of the matter is that you abused that trust. You abused your power within the colony, and it is for our actions that we are judged. I recognize that your assistance helped root out the corruption among our leaders. However, in response to your actions, I have no choice but to sentence you to twenty years banishment from this colony, after which time you can petition to return. This sentence will be upheld immediately."

Court was dismissed. Lars looked up at the ceiling and then turned to look at his father, but he had trouble lifting his gaze. After a few seconds, he exhaled softly and raised his eyes. The only thing Connor could see in Lars's affect was resignation. Lars had to have expected this. He'd known that this court case could have no other outcome.

Connor took a few steps away so Franklin and Lars could speak quietly for several moments before Lars was taken away. More than once, Lars glanced in Connor's direction. He looked as if he had something to say but decided against it.

Connor wanted to say something to Lars too—some kind of platitude about staying strong—but he couldn't. Connor wished things could have been different. He shook the thought from his head, and Lars gave him a small nod.

Connor made a mental note to tell Noah what had happened here. He wanted Noah to hear what Lars had had to say—that he'd finally come to regret his actions against the Ovarrow. Noah had been successful in reaching his friend and had perhaps saved the parts of him that really mattered.

"I have to go," Lars said to his father.

Franklin's hand was on his son's shoulder. "I know," he said, reluctant to let go.

Lars reached up to grip his father's hand. "I'm sorry," he whispered in a voice that was little more than a rasp. "I'm sorry I put you through this, Dad."

The security agents shifted their feet. It was time for Lars to go.

Franklin's eyes became misty. "It's all right. It'll work out.

You take care of yourself. You hear me? *You* take care of yourself, son."

Connor's throat became thick, and his eyes tightened as they escorted Lars away. The courtroom emptied, and Connor looked away as Franklin wiped the tears from his eyes.

Together they walked out of the courtroom and into the corridors beyond. More than a few people glanced in their direction, but no one said anything. They walked outside. The air was humid, if a little bit cool, but the skies were clear.

Franklin came to a stop and looked at Connor. "Thanks for coming today, Connor."

"Of course."

Franklin glanced back at the courthouse and grimaced. "I wish there was something I could do. I knew this was going to happen, but part of me also can't believe it's happening. Do you know what I mean?"

Connor nodded. He licked his lips and regarded Franklin for a few moments. "I know. I feel the same way. Are you going to be okay?"

"No," Franklin replied. "But I'll live."

Colonial news feeds circulated the outcome of Lars Mallory's trial, and banishment from the colony was met with general approval among the citizens.

There were colonists who still viewed the Ovarrow as something to be feared, while others sympathized with the trials they'd had to endure. Connor had his own biases where the Ovarrow were concerned, though his opinion of them had changed over the years, and he supposed that most colonists would just have to get used to the idea that they were here to stay. They would be part of New Earth's future, whether the colonists wanted it or not.

"Are we going to get into trouble?" Lenora asked.

"Are you scared?"

She snorted. "No . . . well, it has been a while since you've flown. I'd hate for us to have to test the escape system."

"You mean the ejector seat?" Connor asked dryly.

Lenora chuckled. "No, I believe it's called the egress system."

Connor laughed. "Now you're just showing off."

"What's this button do?"

He glanced at her in the seat next to him as she reached for the flight controls that would switch over to her.

"No—" Connor began, and she snatched her hand back into her lap, giggling.

They were in a CDF S7 Falcon Fighter. Designed only for atmospheric flight, the ship had a dark, sleek body with stub wings. They were part of the quick-response teams and provided air support for CDF ground forces.

"You should see the look on your face," Lenora said.

Connor's lips curled upward, and he banked hard to the right and then back to the left, straining the inertia compensators. He then executed an aileron roll maneuver, and the S7 spun. The landscape blurred with the open sky around them as pressure built up, and Lenora grunted. He eased up.

"Is that all you got?" she said.

He chuckled and effected another aerobatic maneuver. Lenora squealed in delight.

They were rapidly approaching Sierra, and Connor leveled

off. They both were laughing, and she sighed. He'd sent his flight plan to the CDF base ahead of time.

Lenora checked their heading and looked at Connor. "What are you doing? The base is over there," she said, gesturing toward the left.

"I know," he replied and kept flying in the opposite direction.

They were flying over the main part of the city, and Connor activated the egress system. The canopy split down the middle, opening up, and the wind came rushing in. Then, the thrusters hidden in their seats activated, and they burst from the S7.

Lenora screamed for a few seconds, and he laughed. The thrusters continued to fire, leveling them off as they began to descend.

She glared at him. "You!" she said. Her eyes were wide as she looked up at the S7, which was flying away.

"Relax. It's on autopilot. It'll reach the LZ probably at the same time we'll be landing," Connor said and arched an eyebrow toward her. "You said you wanted to have some fun."

Lenora elbowed him hard. "Next time, *I'll* fly us to Sierra."

They touched down on one of the landing pads at Sierra Medical Center. Connor stood up and helped Lenora get to her feet. She began getting her windswept hair under control.

"I like the new look," Connor teased.

"Maybe I'll cut it all off and go high and tight like your haircut."

He tried to imagine it. For as long as he'd known her, she'd always had long hair that went down past her shoulders.

"Fine, then I'll grow a beard," he replied.

One of Lenora's pet peeves was that the stubble around his

lips was too rough. Connor had jokingly told her that it was what made him irresistible, and she'd rolled her eyes.

They'd received notification yesterday that Dana Wolf had woken up, and the doctors had made a breakthrough in combating the virus she was afflicted with.

As they were about to enter the medical center, Lenora gestured behind them. The S7 seats were sitting on the landing pad. "Don't you need to do something about that?"

"Already done. There's a delivery drone coming to pick them up," Connor replied.

They entered the medical center and went to the level where Dana Wolf's room was.

Kayla Wolf spotted them and walked over.

"Dr. Bishop, it's so good to see you," Kayla said.

"Please, call me Lenora," she said and gave Kayla a hug.

"How's your mom doing?" Connor asked.

"The doctors think she's through the worst of it, but her recovery is going to be a long one," Kayla said.

Connor was a bit surprised to hear that. He'd thought that since they'd had a breakthrough for the virus, Dana Wolf's recovery would have been relatively quick. It must have been much worse than he'd originally thought.

"She'd love to see you," she said to Connor. Then she looked at Lenora. "Can I speak with you for a minute?"

"Of course," Lenora said. "Why don't we go grab a cup of coffee."

Connor watched them go for a few seconds, then knocked on the door to Dana's room and walked in. The head of the bed was raised, and she was almost in a sitting position. To say that she looked tired would have been an understatement. She looked bone-weary and weak, like she hadn't slept for months.

Dana smiled tiredly when she saw him. “Connor,” she said. “Please, have a seat.” Her eyes flicked toward the seat next to the bed.

He walked over and sat down. “How are you feeling?”

“Like I’ve been trampled by berwolves,” Dana said and gave him a long look. “I suppose this is how you feel after one of those missions of yours.”

Connor grinned. “Sometimes.”

She smiled.

“Do you need anything? Can I get you some water?” he asked, gesturing toward the empty cup on the bedside table.

“No, thank you.”

“Do the doctors have any idea where you contracted the virus?” Connor asked.

Dana blinked slowly and shook her head. “They don’t know. They said it could have been dormant in my system for years.”

He nodded. “I’m surprised Bob’s not here giving you an update on what’s been going on.”

She looked at him, and Connor saw some of the strength she’d once had in her gaze. She was tired and maybe a bit beaten up, but it was still there. She was a strong woman. “Not this time.”

He frowned. “What do you mean?”

“What I mean is that I won’t be able to serve as governor anymore.”

His mouth hung open, and his eyes widened. “What?” he asked, stunned.

Dana smiled a little. “You’re stuck working with Bob Mullins, and I expect you two to behave yourselves.”

Connor felt the edges of his lips curve upward and he

chuckled. "No, it's not that. I just can't believe you're not coming back."

"I'm not dying, Connor. I just won't have the strength to . . . well, you know."

He did know. Being the governor of the colony required a high level of endurance and a great deal of patience. He had plenty of endurance, but it was the patience that ran in short supply sometimes.

"I'm sorry," he said. "I know what it meant to you."

Dana blinked her eyes slowly. She was likely getting tired again. "Thank you for coming to see me. But I need to sleep now."

Connor stood up. "Of course. I'm just a comlink away if you need anything."

"What I need is for you to continue to work with Bob. I know you two don't always see eye to eye, but it's important you get past that. The colony is depending on you both," she said and settled back onto her pillow, closing her eyes.

He walked out of the room, making as little noise as possible. Once he was outside, he inhaled deeply and sighed. The virus had been one of those random things, and he supposed it could have happened to any of them. He didn't think someone had made an attempt on Dana's life. He'd been suspicious at first, but sometimes events were a little too random to be suspicious. As much as he wasn't a fan of Mullins, the man was loyal to her and had been genuinely concerned when she'd become ill. Also, there had been an investigation, which had turned up nothing.

Connor glanced back at the door to Dana's room. Something like that could easily have happened to Lenora, and he was thankful it hadn't.

Lenora and Kayla walked up the corridor toward him.

"She's resting," Connor said. His gaze lingered on Lenora for a moment, his eyes tightening with concern. He didn't know why, but he just felt lucky—fortunate to be alive and lucky that the people he loved were healthy. He supposed that when it came right down to it, that was most important of all.

36

As the months passed, Sadoon had been in regular contact with Aurang and his fifth column network. He'd been doubtful of the promises made by Aurang but was curious enough to meet with him after his failure to secure a project from the overseers. In that time, Sadoon had done some recruiting of his own, particularly from among the soldiers who had encountered the Humans. The soldiers that proved loyal would remain useful, and the ones that leaned toward the status quo had been eliminated. His Ovarrow test subjects seemed to become emboldened whenever they managed to catch a squad of Krake soldiers. It renewed their efforts to try to breach the arch gateway.

Hope among the Ovarrow was an interesting field of study that he had devoted nearly fifty years of his life to. A belief in hope was easy to manipulate. It had taken many years of fine-tuning to draw a belief in hope from even the most conditioned subjects, be they Ovarrow or Krake. Even now, Sadoon could feel it inside his own deepest desires.

Sadoon knew that Aurang was familiar with the use of hope as a primary motivator in getting what he needed. Sadoon had tried to find records about Aurang, but there was nothing—no record at all of his existence. He'd even gotten DNA samples to use as a search in their primary data repositories. Aurang was a ghost. He might have never existed until the moment he'd contacted Sadoon. Then, everything changed.

Evening had settled on this world, and the mock wars he'd orchestrated for testing the Ovarrow were eerily quiet. Sadoon didn't want to be here anymore. In his mind, he had already moved on, and he'd delegated a large portion of his work under the guise of giving other Krake a chance to prove themselves.

He accessed a secure messaging system, looking for a reply from Aurang. The fifth column leader was due to contact him, and Sadoon had been growing anxious.

He stood up from his desk and walked toward the balcony. The doors were open, and an evening breeze blew in, but Sadoon hated the smells of this world. Of all the tactics the Ovarrow employed when fighting their wars, one of the most effective was that when they thought they were defeated, they'd inflict their wrath on the habitable world, making it as unlivable as possible. The Krake also employed such tactics, but Sadoon would need to research whether they had been the first. Were the Ovarrow merely copying what they'd learned from the Krake? Sadoon was almost sure of it. Their behavior was controlled and easy to manipulate—predictable, some Krake would say, and Sadoon had to agree.

He had a clear view of the landscape, but he knew he wasn't alone. "How did you get here?"

Aurang came out of his stealth field, seeming to materialize in front of him. "It's not as difficult as you think it is."

Sadoon considered this for a few moments. "I trust the resources I made available to you have been put to good use?"

"Indeed, they have, and I have news to share with you," Aurang said. "The Humans are moving much quicker than even I thought they would."

Sadoon frowned. "They're an active species, but what do you mean by moving? What have they done?"

"There's been a trend of experiments that are experiencing outlier events."

"Where?"

"Dozens of worlds," Aurang said and paused for a moment. "Well, potentially dozens of worlds. It depends on where we draw the line for qualifying a statistical anomaly."

"Can I see the data?"

"Of course," Aurang said. "I don't want there to be any secrets between us."

Sadoon didn't believe him. A data upload registered on his personal systems, and he opened a holoscreen and began peering through the data. "There are no clusters."

Aurang nodded in agreement. "It almost looks random, doesn't it?"

Sadoon's gaze flicked back toward the holoscreen for a moment. "They're probing."

"They're searching for Quadiri."

The fact that the Humans were searching for the Krake home world made perfect sense to Sadoon.

"But they're doing something else I hadn't anticipated," Aurang said. "They're recruiting allies. Wherever they are, their outlier behaviors have been affecting the predictive models, and we've seen an uptick in rebellious activity—almost as if they were being provided knowledge about us."

Sadoon considered this. "I know you don't want to hear this, but we must inform the overseers. They can't ignore this now."

Aurang looked away from him and took a few steps, seemingly to examine the room. "Not yet. There isn't enough information to garner the support of the overseers."

"Yes, there is. If they continue, they'll gain more allies against us."

Aurang shrugged as if it didn't matter. "The Ovarrow aren't a threat to us. They're tools we can use, and they're tools that the Humans *are* using. The more active the Humans are, the quicker we can identify their home system."

Sadoon began calculating probabilities in his mind. Data models and theorems were what he lived and breathed. But something he kept coming back to distracted him. "The risk—"

"It is necessary," Aurang said, cutting him off. "Remember, stagnation is our biggest enemy. And we've been stagnant long enough. The goal hasn't changed. Allow yourself to imagine, if you can . . ." he said, pausing for a moment, and Sadoon waited, ". . . a world without Prime Overseer Ersevin. Without any overseer, allowing the factions to pursue what they want."

Sadoon shook his head. "You speak of anarchy."

"I speak of freedom."

"Freedom is an idealistic ploy. We need structure. Otherwise, we're no better than the Ovarrow."

Aurang regarded him for a few moments, considering. "Then we're both right, and together we can find a solution that's better than what we have today. The Humans are key to this. Stagnation is the enemy."

Sadoon looked back at the reports on the holoscreen. If the

Humans were instrumental in influencing the outliers they'd observed, then they were a shrewd species. He looked back at Aurang. "We need allies ourselves."

Aurang's feline eyes narrowed contentedly. "Now, you finally understand."

37

When Lars left the courtroom, he'd thought he would immediately be brought to the transport ship to begin his banishment. Instead, he was taken back to his cell. No one had contacted him, and he wasn't allowed to contact anyone. He had more restrictions now than when he'd first arrived. After two days, someone had finally come for him.

"Mr. Mallory," the prison guard said, "your transport has arrived. I need you to turn around and put your hands on the wall."

Lars stood up and did as requested. He felt a device attach itself to his back, and he knew what it was. If he made any sudden movements, it would activate and release a shock, rendering him immobile. It was akin to the shock sticks used to enforce compliance.

"All right, follow me," the guard said.

Lars turned around and followed the guard. This was it. His banishment would begin today, and for the next twenty years, he'd be shut away on some island without the means to escape. He walked by the other cells, and their occupants stared at him as he passed.

Lars had heard the other prisoners talk about banishment and where they were heading. Some of them even thought they could build a craft that would take them away. He had no such illusions. Even if they somehow managed to escape the island and, even more unlikely, return to a colonial city, they'd be caught well before then. Each of them wore a personal tracker that was broadcasting their position at all times. Even if they could escape, there'd be no disabling the tracker. The other prisoners didn't like it when he told them that, but Lars didn't care. It was the truth, and sometimes the truth sucked.

Over the past two days, he'd gone over his court case in his mind, particularly Judge Vivian Kennedy's comments about him. She'd been right, and so had Noah. Lars had been stubborn. Noah had to all but push the truth in front of him, and even then, Lars had refused to acknowledge it for such a long time.

He walked down the long corridor, each step bringing him closer to the new life he sure as hell didn't want but probably deserved. He shook his head. No, he *did* deserve it. Noah and his father had questioned him thoroughly about how Meredith Cain had recruited him. They'd been looking for a way to bolster his defense, but there wasn't any *one* thing Meredith had done or said; it had been lots of little things that just seemed to feed off his own frustration and fear—fear of what the Krake would do when they came here. Lars had risked everything to try to find a way to prevent that from happening.

He had to push those thoughts from his mind. Sometimes it

did no good to dwell on his regrets. That's what he'd been told anyway. He'd have plenty of time to think about them later.

He was brought to a holding area where other prisoners were joining them. He recognized most of them because he'd recruited many of them, but not all. There were more than thirty prisoners in the holding area, and they were instructed to go through an outside door where a Field Ops and Security troop carrier waited for them. They climbed aboard and sat down. There were six security agents in the passenger area, armed with suppressors and shock sticks. The suppressor could release a field of energy that would immobilize anyone who was stupid enough to attack them. Lars glanced around at the others, and all he saw was mostly resignation. None of them looked like they wanted to attack the security agents.

There were several wallscreens that showed a video of the outside, but once they took off, the wallscreens powered down. The pilot accessed the intercom and informed them that they had a six-hour flight ahead of them. That was all the information they were given. Lars knew there had been several sites selected for banishment. They'd be given tools to use for their survival and some supplies. After that, they were expected to provide for themselves—grow their own food and build their own shelters. They'd be monitored from afar. If they wanted to live, they'd do the work. It had been made apparent to the prisoners in no uncertain terms that no type of colonial aid would come for them should they neglect to care for themselves.

Lars leaned back in his chair, closed his eyes, and went to sleep. The slight rocking of the transport carrier settled into a familiar rhythm, and then it was gone altogether while he slumbered.

The hours went by as he dozed somewhere between sleep and awareness of his surroundings. He heard snippets of hushed conversations, but mostly everyone was quiet. Eventually, he felt the troop carrier change its altitude. Wherever they were being taken, they'd be arriving soon.

Lars sat up, rubbing the sleep from his eyes and stretching a little bit. He heard the landing gear deploy, and soon the troop carrier landed. An alarm blared for a moment, and then the rear loading ramp opened.

He peered outside. There was a rolling tundra that was almost blinding in the middle of the day.

"This is your stop. Get up and exit out the back," one of the security agents said.

A few of the other guards repeated the same message, and Lars stood up. He walked to the loading ramp and descended, stepping onto the ground. Over to his right were twenty CDF soldiers.

He heard the dopplered wail of another troop carrier approaching, and it came to a landing nearby. Lars and the others looked over and saw that there were more prisoners being off-loaded.

"Eyes front," the security agent said.

Lars looked over at him and saw a tall man with a few days' worth of stubble on his chin. There was a hardened glint to his gaze—the glint of someone who'd been in the thick of it. He had CDF captain's bars on his shoulders.

The CDF captain gestured toward the other carrier. "Sergeant, bring those prisoners over here."

A group of CDF soldiers went to the other troop carrier and began yelling for the prisoners to come over to them. Less than a minute later, nearly a hundred prisoners were clustered in a group.

"Prisoners, I'm Captain Flint, the CO of the 3rd Ranger Company of the Colonial Defense Force. I've been ordered to see whether any of you are worth redemption," he said, and his steely-eyed gaze settled on Lars momentarily before moving on. He was quiet for several seconds, and Lars heard a few of the other prisoners begin speaking.

"First off," Captain Flint said, and the prisoners became quiet, "any one of you who wants to climb back aboard this troop carrier can do so right here, right now, and you'll be taken to your designated banishment site to serve out your term."

Lars watched some of the prisoners glance at the troop carriers with interest, but most waited for Captain Flint to continue.

"That's right. No one is forcing you to do a damn thing. You can be equally as useless in your banishment. I'm told that many of you joined your misguided group because you thought you could do a better job protecting the colony than the CDF. Better than me," Captain Flint said with bitter amusement. "I recognize some of you who used to be in the CDF. What the hell happened to you?" he asked. Then, holding up one of his hands, he said, "Never mind, I don't care. This isn't about your feelings. What I'm offering you is a chance at redemption—not because I think you deserve it, but because I've been ordered to do so. I'm to evaluate the lot of you. Some of you, maybe most of you, are wondering why you should consider this. You've received your sentencing, and you've been convicted. However, if you make the cut and serve your term of enlistment, the CDF will petition on your behalf for a pardon of your past crimes."

Lars's eyes widened, and he felt his pulse quicken in his chest.

"I personally guarantee that this will not be easy or safe," Captain Flint continued. "Many of you will fail. If you're former CDF, I'm going to be twice as hard on you as everyone else because you should have known better. It's my job to pick the best from you. If you make it through, you'll get to experience the most dangerous missions, the ones with the lowest probability of success. Chances are you won't survive, even if you make the cut." He paused for a moment. "You guys wanted to 'protect the colony.' That was your reason for joining the rogue group. Well, here's your chance to make good on that promise. If you agree to this, just walk right over to the CDF troop carrier behind me, and you'll be taken to a particular training ground that has been established just for this mission."

"Where?" someone asked.

Captain Flint smiled widely, showing a healthy set of pearly white teeth standing in stark contrast to his rugged exterior. "Oh, it's nowhere around here. I guarantee it's not anyplace you've ever seen."

Lars believed him. He exhaled explosively and marched toward the CDF troop carrier. He didn't even look back, and the CDF soldiers he passed along his trek scowled in his direction. He ignored them. He didn't want to waste away banished to some island. He'd always only wanted to protect the colony. He still did, and maybe, just maybe, redemption could be his.

A CDF sergeant waited inside the troop carrier. He eyed Lars, seemingly impassive but calculating just the same. He jerked his chin to the side, and Lars sat down in an open seat. More prisoners climbed aboard, but not all of them. Lars glanced toward the loading ramp, expecting to see more people.

He scanned the others and guessed that about half of the prisoners had decided to come, perhaps fifty of them. He'd expected more, and he gritted his teeth a little. Did the others hate the colony now?

He heard the Field Ops prisoner transport ships engage their engines. That was it. The rest of the prisoners had made their choice. They'd rather rot away on an island, bitter at the fact that they couldn't return to the colony. How did they think they'd feel after the terms of their banishment had been served? Would they choose to return, or would they be so far gone that rejoining the colony would never happen?

"Idiots," a man grumbled next to him and shifted in his seat.

Lars didn't recognize him.

"We're heading to the shit now."

"It beats fishing and gardening on an island," Lars replied.

The man grinned a little. "Maybe," he said.

"If you think that, then why did you come?"

"Because I didn't travel sixty light-years to sit on my ass doing nothing."

"We'll get it shot off instead," said another man sitting across from them. He was younger, but not so young as to not know any better. "Derrik," he said and looked at them expectantly.

"Lars."

"Oh boy," the first man said and shook his head. "I thought I recognized you."

"That's me. I'm famous," Lars said, deadpanning.

The loading ramp retracted into the carrier, and the rear doors closed.

Derrik cleared his throat. "If you don't tell us your name, I'll just make one up for you."

"You could try it, but you wouldn't like it. Orin Toshi."

Lars remembered the name from various reports but had never met him. The CDF troop carrier lifted off.

"Where do you think they're taking us?" Derrik asked.

"Does it really matter?" Orin replied.

Derrik leaned back and shook his head. "I was just wondering is all."

Any reply Orin might have made fell silent as Captain Flint walked toward them.

"You're a chatty bunch," Flint said.

They were silent for a few moments, and Flint stood rooted in place.

"I was just wondering where we were going, sir," Derrik said.

Flint nodded and then turned toward Orin. "Toshi, I'm surprised you didn't scurry off to that island with the rest of the deviants."

Orin clenched his teeth and looked away. Flint waited briefly and grunted. Then he turned toward Lars.

"Mallory," Flint said.

Lars expected the CDF captain to make a snide comment or otherwise assert himself, but he didn't. He didn't need to, just like Lars chose not to present a false sense of bravado. He was here, and that's all there was to it.

An hour later, Lars felt himself lift upward as the CDF troop carrier performed a rapid descent. He looked at Captain Flint, who smirked at them. "Time to find out what you're worth," he said.

Lars felt his cheeks burn. The CDF captain's words bit into his chest and sank heavily to his gut. The words stung, and he hated how he'd let it show. He looked at Captain Flint, but the contest was over. He'd blinked first, and the CDF captain knew it.

The landing gear deployed, and the troop carrier touched down. After the rear doors opened, they were ushered off.

Derrik craned his neck, trying to peer past the others to the outside. Orin growled a few incoherent words and glared at Lars for a moment before walking ahead.

Lars walked down the loading ramp and slowed. Twenty meters away was an arch gateway. The metallic alloy gleamed in the afternoon sunlight, but in the middle of the gateway was a deep, dark, gray nothingness. The prisoners had stopped just a short distance away from the troop carrier.

Lars saw Captain Flint off to the side. He watched them all with a tight mouth while he waited. Lars strode through the throng of prisoners.

"I told you that you've never been where we're taking you," Flint said.

The center of the arch gateway shimmered, and Lars could see a hazy view of the other side. It was like trying to peer through ripples of water streaming over a window. He couldn't be sure what was on the other side of the gateway, and it didn't matter. Lars strode toward it. He was either going to appear the fool, or his next steps would carry him away—away from his past and the things he'd done. He'd never be entirely free of either. That wasn't how it worked. But as he closed in on the threshold of the gateway, he quickened his pace to a run, eager to get on with it, eager to matter. But above all else, he wanted to be away from here.

AUTHOR NOTE

Thank you for reading Insurgent, First Colony Book 10. I sincerely hope you enjoyed it and the rest of the books in the series. Telling Connor's story has been a privilege, along with all the other characters in this series. Do you have a favorite character? I'd love to hear who it is.

What's next for First Colony? Book 11 - INVASION

These days it seems like everyone is asking for a review for anything and everything. I get review requests when I go to stores, visit the doctor's office, and even the dentist. Enter for your chance to win...I bet you can guess what's coming next. I'd like for you to leave a review for Insurgent. I know. Not another one! I get it, but they are essential to help spread the word about the book to other readers. Your reviews also help Amazon decide whether to show my books to other readers. I also read all my reviews. Every single one of them. I don't respond to them, but I definitely read them all. If you've reviewed my other books, please accept my thanks and consider writing another one for Insurgent. If you don't want to leave a review, then don't worry about it. I get it. Telling a friend who might like the book also helps a lot.

Again, thank you for reading one of my books. I'm so grateful that I get to write these stories.

If you're looking for another series to read consider reading the Federation Chronicles. Learn more by visiting:

https://kenlozito.com/federation-chronicles/

I do have a Facebook group called **Ken Lozito's SF readers.** If you're on Facebook and you'd like to stop by, please search for it on Facebook.

Not everyone is on Facebook. I get it, but I also have a blog if you'd like to stop by there. My blog is more of a monthly check-in as to the status of what I'm working on. Please stop by and say hello, I'd love to hear from you.

Visit www.kenlozito.com

Thank you for reading Insurgent - First Colony - Book ten.

If you loved this book, please consider leaving a review. Comments and reviews allow readers to discover authors, so if you want others to enjoy *Insurgent* as you have, please leave a short note.

The series will continue with the 11th book - INVASION - First Colony Book 11

If you're looking for something else to read, consider checking out the Ascension series by visiting:

https://kenlozito.com/ascension-series/

If you would like to be notified when my next book is released please visit kenlozito.com and sign up to get a heads up.

I've created a special **Facebook Group** specifically for readers to come together and share their interests, especially regarding my books. Check it out and join the discussion by searching for **Ken Lozito's SF Worlds.**

To join the group, login to Facebook and search for **Ken Lozito's SF Worlds.** Answer two easy questions and you're in.

ABOUT THE AUTHOR

I've written multiple science fiction and fantasy series. Books have been my way to escape everyday life since I was a teenager to my current ripe old(?) age. What started out as a love of stories has turned into a full-blown passion for writing them.

Overall, I'm just a fan of really good stories regardless of genre. I love the heroic tales, redemption stories, the last stand, or just a good old fashion adventure. Those are the types of stories I like to write. Stories with rich and interesting characters and then I put them into dangerous and sometimes morally gray situations.

My ultimate intent for writing stories is to provide fun escapism for readers. I write stories that I would like to read, and I hope you enjoy them as well.

If you have questions or comments about any of my works I would love to hear from you, even if it's only to drop by to say hello at KenLozito.com

Thanks again for reading ***First Colony - Insurgent***

Don't be shy about emails, I love getting them, and try to respond to everyone.

ALSO BY KEN LOZITO

First Colony Series

Genesis

Nemesis

Legacy

Sanctuary

Discovery

Emergence

Vigilance

Fracture

Harbinger

Insurgent

Ascension Series

Star Shroud

Star Divide

Star Alliance

Infinity's Edge

Rising Force

Ascension

Safanarion Order Series

Road to Shandara

Echoes of a Gloried Past

Amidst the Rising Shadows

Heir of Shandara

Broken Crown Series

Haven of Shadows

If you would like to be notified when my next book is released visit kenlozito.com

Made in the USA
Columbia, SC
11 March 2021

34321715R00193